Decoration Day

and other stories

ALSO BY GERALD DUFF

FICTION
Fire Ants and Other Stories
Coasters
Snake Song
Memphis Ribs
That's All Right, Mama: The Unauthorized Life of Elvis's Twin
Graveyard Working
Indian Giver
Blue Sabine

POETRY
Calling Collect
A Ceremony of Light

NONFICTION
Home Truths: A Deep East Texas Memory
Letters of William Cobbett
William Cobbett and the Politics of Earth

DECORATION DAY

and other stories

GERALD DUFF

STEPHEN F. AUSTIN STATE UNIVERSITY PRESS
2012

DECORATION DAY AND OTHER STORIES

For information, address
Stephen F. Austin State University Press
PO Box 13007, SFA Station,
Nacogcohes TX. 75962.
sfapress@sfasu.edu

Book Design by: Laura McKinney
Cover Design by: Laura Davis

First Edition: May 2012
978-1-936205-56-1

1. Fiction 2. Short Stories

For Adelaide and Cliff
of Probst's Hundred near Good Hope

Contents

"Lord, I was walking round her bedside
These was the last words she had to say
Bring me some flowers – be sure, honey –
on every Decoration Day."

-Howlin' Wolf, *Decoration Day Blues*

THE SOUND OF WATER

She comes into the room the way Richard always would when he thought he might be in danger of surprising or alarming somebody. Making a little noise at the door at first, more than needful to effect an entrance, but not so loud he ruins what he was trying to accomplish by it.

I try to open my eyes to let her know she's successful, but they're the way my fingers used to feel when a little syrup had leaked out of a biscuit on the way to my mouth, not stuck together but tacky to the touch. I like that stickiness, and I move my fingers back and forth, up and down, playing with the feel of it until it's gone. Abigail doesn't like that, and she grabs at my hand when she sees me do that. It's messy, Maudie, she says, you'll get it on your dress and then who'll have to wash it? Me, I tell her, me, I'll wash it. Let me do it. I don't mind.

"Are you dreaming, GrandMaude?" Dicia asks and puts her hand on my forehead as though she's seeing if I've got fever, but I know she's trying to find a way to help me open my eyes. Richard is not with her, I know that, though they come into the room the same way. I won't mention her father to her, though.

"Dicia," I say, "it's the syrup. A little dab squeezed out and got on my fingers." That's not right, I know that as soon as I say it, but those are the words that came out when I spoke. I don't intend to say anything like that, in one part of me, the part of me that decides what I'll let people see and know, the part that parcels out how much I'll allow to show and how much I'll keep to myself.

It's harder to make that part work exactly when I want it to now, though, and I find myself waiting to see what I'm going to say time and time again. I'm my own audience, then, when that happens, and something is opening wider and wider inside me in the place where I am.

That was altogether once in one location, and if it were sketched out on a map you could unfold and display for viewing, I could have pointed to a place name and put the tip of my finger on it and said this is me here, Maude Holt Blackstock Winston, here am I taking up my part of Texas. And here are the roads that lead here, that a person could follow when looking for me. Wherever you came from before, no matter what settlement you left on your journey to Maude, here is where you fetch up when the traveling is done.

But the roads on that map I was able once to snap open so briskly to find that spot I thought I knew so well, those roads are all leading away from that spot now, away from Maude, headed out of town. When the eye lights on Maude, it does not settle solid and fixed any longer. It wants to wander. It finds the ways out of the settlement, ones more attractive to follow, and it is lured to go where they lead. From, not to, now. Where the roads lead.

Maude in Texas on its share of the map has become lighter on the land.

The part of me that let me pick and choose which portion of

myself to reveal to travelers coming my direction is like a store steadily closing down. Almost all the timber that kept people coming to the territory has been cut now, and the lumber company commissary store does less and less trade.

When the last trees are felled and topped and cut and planed into measured board feet, no one will stay around to trade for what the store offers. Another location in Texas that once drew people will go back to volunteer cedar in the fields and fences down and at the heart of the settlement nothing but a mound of coarse wood dust left from the time the big saws did all that cutting.

I never wanted Richard to go into the logging woods, to pick up tools, to listen to the sawmill whistle, to make a living for himself that way with his back and his hands.

I thought of other ways for him, as a mother will, and I looked at his hands, his long delicate fingers and the gestures they made when he talked and the grace in his movements and the way he would look so deeply into the eyes of anyone who spoke to him, the way he listened to stories told him or books read to him, and I knew he was not suited for the shapes that men's lives take here.

And when he was taken by the army and sent to the war in France, I knew he would be killed by some other mother's son able to be hard, to deal death with a bullet or bayonet, to look on what he had done with no sorrow, no satisfaction, no feeling. God, I prayed, let this one not be lost in mud and darkness and blood and ripped flesh. Let him not be taken out of the light and air and open spaces where he has lived such a little time yet.

Let him return whole and unharmed and himself, God, I said, and I will promise you this. And I remember I looked up at the ceiling of the Double Pen Creek chapel, after I had said that, and I waited for something to come to my mind, something that God might want from me, something worth the trade of that thing for the life of my boy, my only son with Valery Blackstock, my true love, and nothing seemed good enough or big enough that I could provide that God could want from me.

Wasps were going in and out of the cells of the nests they were building above me, and the heat of the sun beating on the roof of the church was causing the pieces of tin to groan and strain against the nails holding them down. God, I said again inside my head where no one but me and Him could hear me, because a verse says somewhere in the Bible that it is better and more righteous to pray in a closet than to shout from the rooftop, God, I will promise this.

But again nothing came to me that He could want, and the buzzing of the wasps in the heat above me was loud enough to cause me to look up, and I saw them at their work, insects with no minds nor souls, possessing nothing but one thing, but that in abundance. And that was intent, and that was will.

God, I said, I will promise you in exchange for safe return, for him to be brought home to me, for him to be granted more time on this earth and in this life, a nothing. I will promise you a nothing, God, an absence of something. The things that are in me are not worthy of a gift to You, a trade for a favor so immense in Your keeping. What I can give You is not a provision in my care, but a giving up.

Return Richard, my son, to a further portion of life, and I will kill in myself that desire, and need, and want for something other than what I am and what I have. I will shun and abjure and abdicate and quell and reject and stifle that thing in me that hurts for what I am not. I will turn my eye into myself and live all my days with no longing turned within and look no more over the walls of my fortress to the fields and the trees and the open sky beyond which always call me.

My intent will be to have no intent, my will to be unwilled, my self to be selfless.

And God made that trade with me, took me at my word, and the wasps working their way into the cells of their nest above me in the Double Pen Creek chapel continued with their striving and carried out the sealing of the walls of the compartments from which their young would spring to build their own homes and lodgment, and their's and their's after.

Richard Blackstock, my son, came home from the war in

France with his body intact and unscarred, and to our eyes untouched by all that took the lives of so many in that place.

When he came that day into the house in the Double Pen Creek community where I lived, no one expected him, and I was in bed already, not yet full asleep, drowsing with a book on my chest. I knew that he was coming, but not when, and when he opened the door to the bedroom, I thought it was my husband Ezra back late from Saturday trading in Annette. And I admit to keeping my eyes closed so that my husband would think I was asleep and I wouldn't have to listen to his recounting his day in town and the pricings and the costs and the payments. And I owed my husband the attention, but I did not want to honor that debt just then. Tomorrow, I thought, tomorrow will do.

"Mother," he said in that tone and volume calculated not to disturb should the circumstance not be fitting. "I'm home."

I opened my eyes from what was not a dream, and looked at Richard beside the bed in an army uniform too big for him, and though the tears came in such an amount as to blind me, I saw clearly that trading with God is an exact transaction and that His accounting leaves no grain of sand unnumbered.

My son was in my house, returned to me as bargained for, and he would live further portion of a life with me and the Holts and Fergusons and all our kin, but not even God could bring all of him intact home again as he was when he left.

"I don't care," I said to God out loud, "I don't care," pulling Richard to me so hard that the buttons on his uniform dug into my chest like barbed wire, but the rest I said to Him in private in my mind, picking each word out of those available to me, choosing them one by one, and looking them over in turn the way you will each egg you lift from a hen's nest to mix into a dish for serving those dependent on your cooking – coldly and with care, favoring one over the other only as to its use, not its appeal to you.

I'll keep my bargain, I said to God inside my mind where He lives and where He has set up His long tables for accounting. I'll take this in place of nothing, and I'll give you the nothing I promised in trade. I'll treasure it for what there is of it, and I accept that I couldn't have the all I would have taken if it was offered. Not even You, I said to God, could make that pure transference of what was into what is and have it be still what was.

But I'll not waver, and I'll not want, and I'll turn my eye inside myself to study the nothing at the core of all things in this world, whether the center of an egg or o. the sun or of the earth itself, the point that is not, around which all that is, circles.

I will not want what is not. I will behold what is.

"You don't care?" Richard said, his lips turned into a smile as he pulled back from my arms to look at me, the smile from childhood, except now for his eyes which would never be touched again by whatever it is that leads a face to show pleasure or satisfaction or peace. I knew that spark was gone from him, then, and that it would not be coaxed back into a glow, nor a flame. But I would not ask for it, not desire it to leap up as itself again, and I would keep my bargain with God by strict accounting.

But I had not said I would not mourn the loss, only that I would not let others see it, and that would be mine in place of the nothing I had traded with God for Richard's life. That loss I would keep at the core of where I was located, the point of absence around which all that was Maude Holt revolved.

"Don't pay any mind to what I say," I said to my son back in Texas, wearing an army uniform too big for him, "looking at you here again with me, there's nothing in my head, and my words just tumble out with not a speck of meaning to them."

"What do you mean about syrup, GrandMaude?" Dicia is saying, her hand now leaving my forehead as she sees my eyes open to look at her, and now she's arranging the bedclothes to lie more neatly about me.

"Would you like some syrup and biscuit this morning? I'll bring you some of that good ribbon cane that Mr. Shackleford gave us. It's not heavy at all. It's sweet and light."

"No, little girl," I say to her. "I'm not hungry. But your Papa would have liked that ribbon cane syrup."

"Did he have a sweet tooth?" Dicia says. "I guess that's where I got mine. I'll blame him for it."

She has the covers arranged to suit her now, and she stands back from the bed to get a better view, pursing her lips a little as she's always done when testing the quality of anything she's attempted. Satisfied enough, she says something about my needing to eat a little and leaves the room headed for the kitchen. I hope she doesn't blame Richard for the syrup. She steps lively, as always.

They let me sleep, all of them, as much as I want to pretend to do. People never want to wake or disturb a person who's dying. They seem to know, without having to be told it or having to talk it over with each other, that dying is hard work and requires attention and effort from the one doing it and rest from that while it's fully underway. All of my kinfolks and the ones who aren't, the neighbors who come, take me at my word, if you can call keeping your eyes shut when you're awake a message by word. If it's a word, it's an unspoken one, but of course that's the strongest word there is.

"Here's that good syrup and a warm biscuit," Dicia is saying, her hand on my forehead, "GrandMaude. I know you're not asleep. You can't fool me."

"You're right, sweetheart," I say, "as always. I'm just resting my eyes."

The sound comes most of the time, and I can hear it continually when it's going on, and I'm afraid. It wasn't that way at first, coming almost all of the time, but then when it was interrupted for a space, I would notice it more when it started again. That was worse, when it would stop, and the quiet would come, cool and distant in my ears and putting me at a remove from where I was, worse because I never knew when the sound would come again. Waiting for something you dread is worse always than being in its presence, whatever it is, when it finally is upon you and close enough to seize you in fact and truth.

The pain of being in the throes of something hurtful is lessened because it concentrates the way time feels. When you're in it, everything is now, and nothing is past or to come. It's here, and here is all, and there is a comfort in that, the way it must be to the mind of a moth flown into a candle flame. But a moth can't think, and know what it's lost or hope for change. All is immediate to such a creature, the way it is not to a woman or a man, doomed to be able to imagine what an alternative to suffering might be, and that is why it's better to me when the sound is constant and does not tantalize by granting spells of silence.

The sound is not all, even at its strongest. I can hear them behind it talking to each other, trading stories, making jokes, taking offense, explaining themselves, chuckling, even laughing aloud and full-throated at times. The sound is there always, but it is not all. It is not a blanket that covers me completely, that cuts off evidence of others existing in the world outside me that is not me. It has not settled finally with all the air pushed out from beneath it, the way a sheet over you will do when you lift it and then let it fall until everything touching you is flat and settled and still again. How many times can you bear to lift the cover again, though, knowing in the way the moth burning in the flame cannot that no variation is possible, that all results come to the same?

I do not hear them through the sound, however, my sister and brother and granddaughter, Richard's child, and my grandniece and the others who come, in the manner you hear someone speaking to you in a quiet voice even though a thunderstorm may be raging outside the room you find yourself in. Hearing them speak to each other doesn't come by means of my successful competition with another sound working against that which they make.

I hear them not by piercing through the sound that's come to be always with me now, but by discovering ways around it. I can fool the sound at times, not by any effort to defeat it on its own terms, not by willing my understanding to prevail against it, not by main strength, but by another way altogether, a way of weakness and yielding, a way of appearing to offer up my myself to it with no defense.

That sound between me and all that is not me is a wall, built high and wide and set deep in the earth, too strong and thick and massive to prevail against by main strength. So there is no hope for me in struggle, and if I attempt to move against the sound, it knows that and grows stronger, for its resources are vast, like the one of water steadily freezing in a temperature below zero, set to last.

If I scream, as I once did in my struggle, no one can hear me, only the sound can do that, and it is encouraged and fed by that admission, and it grows.

But if I am soft and quiet and patient and to all appearances yielding, I feel my understanding begin to move, like a small stream of warm water working in runnels through an ice floe, making a passage unnoticed and faint and silent.

Then, though the sound is still there with me, as proud and present as ever, yet so am I, yet me, yet Maude. And I use the power of what the sound represents to remind me of those times when I was what I was.

My husbands knew me, both of them did, I thought at first after I had met each one in turn and had come to know we would marry. We would be man and woman together, joined for all time as the Bible teaches, as people always say in church and even in their lives lived outside the house where God is said to have His habitation. But He is always with us elsewhere, they say, and He listens when we cry out and He knows what we want and what we really need before we do, and He parcels out his gifts to each of us as fitting in due and full measure.

I was taught that and believed it, and it was said that marriage here on earth between a man and a woman is a shadow of marriage in Heaven and therefore meet and competent and to be entered into not lightly. That I accepted and told myself I believed, and from that belief came the other and final one, the belief that would calm and reassure my understanding and acceptance. It would let me draw breath in ease and confidence, and it was this. My husband would know me, would fathom the depth of my essence, and could say to me with certainty you are Maude and this is what Maude is and I can explain yourself to you.

I wanted that to be a true and perfect understanding for me, and I thought it must be. And I wanted that settled faith, and I longed for it the way I longed for the touch of my first husband, my true love, Valery Blackstock, the father of Richard.

And one longing was solely satisfied by him, and that was what happened each time he touched me, and so I learned to depend on that. I had to depend on that, because the other longing was not fulfilled, though it was the one assured by God's word proclaimed in His book.

And there were times I thought I would give up the satisfaction that came to me as Valery's wife with what happened when we touched if I could have that other, that promise made by God that the husband would know the self of the wife and the wife know the self of the husband. But that never was, even at the beginning when I said to myself wait, wait, wait and it will come, and later when I gave over waiting and convinced myself that I could by will create the condition which would allow my husband to know me and show myself to me in finality. But try though I did to crush out of myself all that was solitary and sensed only by me, my husband gave no sign that he was able to know me truly and give me myself.

So when he was dying young as he was, Oh Lord, and I knew that he was, it came to me that God would give me a consolation for that loss of my true love by allowing my husband to know me at the end and present that knowledge to me. So that as I waited for Valery to die, I kept in my mind what I would never be able to admit to another, the thought that on his leaving this world and me in it he would in his last words to me say what he had never before. Here is who you are, Maude, if you translate truly these last words I give you. Hear me speak them.

I waited for them, prepared to write them in flame on my heart, and I made everyone leave the room where he lay dying so that I would not be distracted, so that I could forget all but those words he would speak. But they did not come, beg him though I did to speak one last word to me, one syllable, one sound.

What lasts of this world is one thing, only, and that is water. It comes, it flows, it falls, it washes away, and boils into nothing, but it always returns, and for want of it all things die.

Papa and Mama came across water to Texas, and I remember that, child though I was, and water was a consequence to them, a barrier to be reckoned with, and I knew when we stood on the Texas side of the water we had crossed that a thing of weight had been accomplished.

I learned there is a lie in words, a lie in the very saying of them and in the understanding of what one has said in words by another one not the person who made them to begin with, but the receiver of them. To think you understand is to lie to yourself.

What I had read in all those books, the Bible one of them, and in what I had heard in accounts by others, words thrown out in the air to take into yourself like draughts of clear water in a time of thirst, all that was not discovered truth, but manufactured dreams intended by nature to deceive and entertain.

Since there is no shape and no meaning to give comfort to the one left alone and bereft, there is nothing to do but lie. Let us invent what we think we need. And so I begged my dying husband, the first and true love of my heart, to give me words, to tell me a story which began and prospered and declined and meant, but he could not. I do not fault him. I fault words.

Water crossed is water gone, never to be seen as it first was in that place and in that precision, but there is water ahead still, and who can tell the difference?

They are speaking about me now, Abigail mentioning Valery and how I came to know and love and marry and lose him, and she is fitting all that into a pattern to serve her purpose, but I will not correct or contradict what she needs to believe is true. She must have that as she wants it, and what business is it of mine to deny my sister the shaping of the world which will feed her the nourishment she craves? I grant her that.

I open my eyes. And I will smile, and I will speak, and Abigail will lose part of the story she intends to tell, not because of interruption, but because it is a story and as such subject to amendment as a new hearer appears, particularly this hearer, the one at the heart of the account she's shaping.

"Well, look who's waking up to listen," my sister says. "Maude, we were all just talking about you, and must have got to carrying on so much we woke you up."

"Yes, Abigail," I say, "I've been hearing you, but it's nice to wake up and have people in the room."

"Great-Aunt Abigail was remembering grandfather for us," Dicia says. "Telling us about when you two first met and your early days together."

"It was at a dance," I say, turning my head on the pillow to look toward Dicia. I can hear the sound in my head, though well-contained and not loud, and I believe it will not move outside me into the room, at least for a while longer, and that will give some space to talk.

"It was at Trot Monroe's place," Abigail says, "that you met Valery at the dance. It was a Saturday night, in October of 1884. I forget the date, but Trot and Lucinda Monroe never had a problem with letting young folks come to their place to socialize, and that's where it was."

It's still containable, the sound, and when I touch it a bit, it doesn't flare. I listen again to Abigail.

"Maude," she is saying, "had not even wanted to go to Louselle Monroe's house that night, and so I'd had to talk her into it."

"Abigail," I break in before she gets into full stride, "I'd like to ask one of the girls to go get me a fresh glass of water. This one's been sitting here, and I'd like some cooler, if you please."

"I'll do it," Nola Mae says, springing up from her chair as though she'd been waiting for a signal.

"Please go with your cousin, Dicia," I say. "Help her find me a middle sized glass in that cupboard, the big one."

The sound has picked up in intensity in my head, and I'm afraid it might get outside into the room, though I know that's foolishness. You alone know what's in your head, no other can, even though it's so strong at times, the sound and the thoughts beneath and around it, that I can't believe others can't hear it, too. Maybe they're just being kind, not wanting to acknowledge the sound announcing something of what's inside me, hiding their knowledge out of politeness, the way you look aside when someone begins to weep and the tears come from their eyes with no sobs or any other sign of pain or sorrow. Ignore it, and it isn't there. Even Abigail does that. I know she prefers more of a show of sorrow. That's easier to discount.

Nola Mae has come back into my bedroom, and loud as the sound in my head has become, I can hear her through it, speaking to Abigail in a loud voice, asking her a question about where some place is, a name she's heard on the radio.

Nola Mae brings me a glass of water. I don't know how the child knows I'm thirsty, sometimes she can be thoughtful, too, like Dicia always is, but Nola Mae has to work at that, poor thing, thinking about the situations of others not coming naturally to her in the way it seems to do for Dicia. But maybe there's more virtue in doing something you have to spend effort on than there is in being naturally sympathetic the way Dicia is, though I wouldn't fault Richard's daughter ever for being spontaneously sweet and good.

It must have been easier for Jesus to turn the other cheek and never require recognition than it was for Peter to have to deny Him three times in the garden before the cock crew, and I was not there and could not know, but I can imagine the sweat on Peter's face and the agony in his voice when he had to tell the Roman soldiers he did not know Jesus, when he had to deny his savior, and he did that, said no to the good because it was not in his power to be anything but a man, and men are weak and women are as well, but of course we are stronger than men ever can be, though a man who has worked in the timber woods and had to lift logs and stumps and use his muscles and back and legs can if he has to, in extremity, lift great weights and move loads in this world that no woman could even consider.

Her strengths are not of the world, and neither was that of Jesus, and that is why His task in the garden was no greater than that of Peter's, and the task of a woman weak in her body and in the things of the world which are subject to strength is greater than that of a man's. I would not say such a thing to my husbands, my first and my true love Valery, and my second, a man I married because I had my children to raise and care for and provide for, and oh I had Richard's child Dicia, too, all that was left of him to me, and I was a good wife to him, and I labored at that, and I accomplished the task before me, struggle though I did to lift the load it represented, and my responsibility in being his woman was akin to that of Peter's in the garden, and there was sweat of the brow and agony of the spirit and failure of the heart in it, and I did not let that show.

And that was my strength, and it did not partake of the natural goodness of Jesus whose task was the easier because it came pure from the heart and met no resistance of the will and was not of this world where loads are heavy and immovable and set in stone and defended with briars.

"Great-Aunt Maude," Nola Mae is saying as she holds the glass of water toward me, "Can you tell me where it is and what it is? The water looks cool, there are not bubbles in it in the way they gather in a glass that has set too long still in the heart of a closed room, and I want to reach out and take it from her, but my hand will not do what I'm telling it that it must, and the sound is roaring again inside my head now and it's hard for me to hear her well enough to understand what her words mean that she wants an answer about.

"What?" I am able to make my lips form the word though I can't tell whether I've said it or not because of the sound, and Nola Mae seems to understand because she leans closer to me, now lifting the glass toward my mouth, and I can see Dicia behind her, her eyes open so wide I can see white all around the brown center. I can't drink the water from the glass.

"Pearl Harbor," Nola Mae is saying. "Where's Pearl Harbor?" and I can see the words in my head, but I can see the sound, too, now, and that is something I've never been able to do before, see sound as well as hear it, and I can tell what my great-niece is asking me, and I can open my lips to answer, but all that comes out is a word, a single one of the many I want to say, and I say that and what I'm able to utter of those many is "ocean," and the sound inside is now loud, now I can see only it, not Nola Mae's face, nor Dicia's eyes, nor the glass of water, nor the question she has asked me, nor the words I would give her in return, but only the sound.

It is all I hear now and all I see, and I'm not afraid now of the sound, as I've always been before, I'm not afraid. I'm not.

THE MUMMY IN OUR MIDST

We knew our mummy was Mississippian, in some sense, for several reasons. None of us were around when the remains of the mummy were first deposited in the archival holdings, that having occurred in the 1880's, as far as anyone could determine. H. L. Egerman's history of Bonar University has no mummy mention in 1928, but the mummy's having been found near the Mississippi River meant that he had lived and died an inhabitant of the Mississippi Valley and like anyone, ancient or modern, was classifiable by his habitual location. If one is born, reared and dies in the state of Illinois, he is by definition an Illinoisan. Ergo hoc, propter hoc.

But it wasn't until Dr. James Lanier assumed his appointment at the university as an assistant professor of anthropology that we learned the true scientific weight of the title Mississippian for the mummy which had lain in our archives for over a century. I say "lain in the archives," but to be more accurate, I should say lain most of the time. He was in and out of the archives over the years for quite a number of reasons. He was carried around to various public schools in the area for display on propitious occasions, for example. During the centennial celebration of Mascoutah, Illinois, a city named for a vanished tribe of Native Americans and just a few miles from the university here in Palestine, he was displayed in a place of honor during the Memorial Celebration and was quite a sensation.

I could list several other occasions on which the only formerly living human being in our archives was transported to a location for public viewing, but I will not, save for one. When the University of Illinois in Urbana celebrated its centennial in 1967, he was the focus of attention for a fit audience, though few, at that signal event. That was a moment of some pride for many of us, though we did not make a loud noise about it. True significance need not trumpet itself.

But it was Dr. Lanier, a newly minted PhD from St. Louis University, in his initial year of appointment at our own institution, who made known to the intellectually curious the true nature and import of the label Mississippian for our ancient treasure. Looking at the face of the mummy, whom students in the long ago had assigned a jesting name I will not repeat, Dr. Lanier informed all in his hearing of the true nature of what was before us by saying, "Note the tracery of light blue lines forming a design on each cheek. Note also the single dot of blue on the forehead."

"Is that a design?" Dr. Peter Osmole asked. "I had noticed that before, but I assumed it was something drawn in ballpoint pen during the time when one of the fraternities had stolen Old Orangey for a prank."

"The last group to do that was the Pikes, wasn't it?" Dr. Dudley said, our most elderly senior professor of history in terms of years served if not in actual age.

"No," said the registrar. "It was the Peeps. I believe it was in 1972. Fall term."

"I knew it started with a P," Dr. Dudley said in a jolly tone, causing all there assembled to chuckle, save for Dr. James Lanier in whose field of expertise we all stood as innocents.

"No," he said, calmly but in a tone which revealed the professional excitement he was experiencing. "Those markings were not made by any dyes currently in use. And they are not accidental, despite what Dennis Ryan at Chicago concludes in his paper on Cahokian remains. Those designs, when fresh, would have stood out boldly in color and execution more prominently than any you would encounter in any tattoo shop in St. Louis."

"Are they that unusual?" Dr. Nancy Oldham asked.

"They are not only unusual," Dr. Lanier said, his eyes blazing like a prairie fire. "They are remarkable."

"Are they in fact tattoos, then?" one of the visiting faculty asked, nameless now in memory since his academic appointment was not permanent.

"In a manner of speaking, yes," Dr. Lanier said. "But these designs were meant to serve much more than a decorative function."

"No," someone said in a quietly awed voice, and we all seemed to draw together in the archives room in the basement of the chapel, as though to seek warmth from a welcoming hearth on a winter's day in Illinois. No one actually moved physically, but there was a perceptible psychic gathering sensible to all in attendance. There was a strong sense of intellectual community there established in the moment.

"These markings, this design, its location, its delicacy of line and form," Dr. Lanier announced, "all these are typically Mississippian."

"So our friend was from Cahokia," Dr. Dudley said. "We can now locate his origin."

"If not from Cahokia proper," Dr. James Lanier said, "certainly from one of the inferior outlying mounds. This design marks the subject as of high social and perhaps religious caste. Is there any record of his provenance?"

"Provenance?" Dr. Nancy Oldham remarked, not comprehending immediately the import of the term, since her field of academic endeavor was contemporary cultural phenomenology, quite distant in time from the days when the mummy before us lived, moved, and had his being in the vast prairies of the Mound Builders of Cahokia.

At that, Dr. Dudley spoke and we all gave attendance, as was his due as senior professor in the group. "I have seen no written record of this surmise," he said, "but oral history, with all its limitations of accuracy, tells us that a farmer from the Olive Mound area just east of Palestine discovered the burial during an excavation for a privy he had projected to build."

That was common knowledge, certainly, for all of us at the university, but most of us upon hearing the account repeated over the years, had discounted it as unsupported by solid evidence. In particular, the detail about the connection with the construction of a privy for use by a farm family seemed farfetched and probably the result of someone's crudely awkward attempt at a bit of rural humor.

But Dr. Dudley's remark led all of us there gathered about the archival mummy to add what we knew, had heard, and perhaps believed, in partial bits and pieces. Standing with his hands folded, his gaze fixed upon the facial designs of the mummy and his expression one of rumination and deep thought, Dr. Lanier listened to what we had to tell him, as best we could.

"Was there," he asked at one point, "a series of flat stones placed over the body to serve as a cover for burial?"

"There were rocks, all right," some one replied, who at this point I do not recall, but the identity is not relevant. I'm certain it was not a tenured member of our faculty. "The farmer who found our friend here in fact took the time to dig because he was surprised by them. There are typically no stones in the soil of the area."

"That's because the glaciers of long ago deposited a vast amount of top soil all across this entire valley," Dr. Dudley said in a sage tone, "most of what used to be the tillable part of Canada, I would wager."

We all chuckled again, as colleagues who know and appreciate one another's wit will do. That expression of community seemed to draw us even closer together as we focused as a group on the intellectual import of the mummy at the center of our attention.

"Was there a fibrous material over the body itself, once the stones were removed?" Dr. Lanier asked, his continuing pursuit of fact and truth much in evidence. "Is that a part of the record?"

We all agreed that we had seen nothing of that sort ever mentioned in writing, but oral history tugged at the memory of one there, myself I must confess. I spoke for the first and only time in that session, never having been one to venture unsupported comment when need did not exist. "It is my recollection that some material, something resembling a web of plant matter did in fact constitute part of the lore handed down by word of mouth."

"Remarkable," Dr. James Lanier said. "I would hazard that a robe of woven material was discovered when the farmer lifted the stones from the sarcophagus, as well."

"In fact," Dr. Dudley offered comment, "when I first saw the mummy upon my arrival in Palestine as a pup still wet behind the ears lo these many years ago, there were still remnants of a cloth-like material covering part of the body."

At this remark, our new young assistant professor of anthropology displayed every manifestation of great intellectual excitement, turning his gaze away from where it had been fastened upon the mummy and looking into Dr. Dudley's face as he though he were gazing upon a prophet. "Sir, can you recall precisely what you saw of the garment covering the body? Were there designs worked into the fabric? Were there small shells, as of marine life, contained in any pattern in the material? In what direction was the head pointed. Toward the east and the dawn? Reversed, perhaps?"

"Would that I could be more precisely detailed," Dr. Dudley exclaimed. "But I must admit my interest was not an informed one, and I was much more attentive to the young woman who was conducting me on a tour of the archives than I was to the dead."

Bertram Magel chirped in laughter at that confession by Dr. Dudley, knowing as all we senior faculty did, that Dr. Dudley was in due time to wed that young woman, Samantha Spreng, still his wife and for many years the longtime president of the Women's Club of Palestine, Illinois. None of us joined Bertram in his chortle, however, a much bigger game afoot in our collective mind now.

"Where is that material that covered the body of this pre-historic Mississippian at the discovery?" Dr. Lanier said. "Pray don't inform me that it's lost."

We all lamented that indeed that was the case, that the necklace of shells adorning the mummy, the fibrous material just under the stones, the rude leather foot coverings, the cloak of interwoven cloth-like material, that all save the body itself, had vanished during the years of handling by fraternity pranksters, displayers of the ancient one at various civic events, and assorted others.

"What an immense shame and disappointment," Dr. Lanier said in a tone of restrained sorrow. "Just those elements of the find would constitute true anthropological significance, and they are now dust."

"Is the mummy worth nothing now in an academically useful sense?" Dr. Oldham asked.

"I'm afraid this relic is now little more than a curiosity for the idle and the uninformed to gawk at," Dr. Lanier said, his voice tremulous. "What we can learn in a scholarly sense is gone. At this point, this object is simply an unburied corpse in an advanced stage of desiccation and mishandling."

Sympathetic remarks of regret and disappointment at this verdict were made by all in attendance, and we drifted away from the archives room one by one to our separate duties, thinking, if we considered the matter at all, that the box containing the relic would be covered again by its lid and that the subject would lapse into its usual status as being the object of good-natured, though careless, comments about the fact that the university owned a mummy. We had learned one thing, though, and to learn one true thing on any given day is a blessing in the academy. Our mummy was typically Mississippian.

Later on the evening of that day, a small gathering took place in the home of Dr. Swat Meredith, holder of the Sadie Overstreet Chair in Applied Religion at the university, at which I was not present. My class in Extemporaneous Argument and Celebratory Laudation happened to be scheduled for a nocturnal gathering at which students were to make formal presentations, and I would not have been able to attend the wine and cheese gathering at Dr. Meredith's, had I been included. I assume I would have been, of course, and that my not receiving a formal invitation was due to Dr. Swat Meredith's knowledge of my teaching schedule and its conflicting obligation.

That aside, all which followed in respect to the mummy came from the wine and cheese affair at Swat's home on Hannah More Street that evening. Great events from small causes spring, says the poet, and the truth of that observation was proven that night.

Not being constrained by the need to report first-hand observation of the literal facts of that meeting, I am therefore able to provide the coloring of the discussion and its conclusions by reference to a larger truth, one not tied to the dreary flatness of specific detail. Here then is my surmise of how mere discussion led to plan, plan to implementation, and implementation to vivid action. I do so in dramatic fashion, by showing rather than by simply telling. Here then the scene on Hannah More Street, shades of night falling, in the living room of a tastefully appointed bungalow, long the residence of a series of faculty members at Bonar University over the decades, as I imagine it.

Dr. Dudley. "Today's discovery of the true significance of the university's possession of a Native-American mummy puts me in mind of a story."

Dr. Gwen Simmons. "Please don't inflict it upon us." (Laughter ensues, glasses are raised, cheese is taken.)

Dr. Nancy Oldham: "Ha, ha. But I do love to hear Dr. Dudley's anecdotes. May he be allowed to tell us one?"

Dr. Gwen Simmons: "Easy for you to say, Nancy. You've only been at the university a few years." (More laughter.)

Dr. Swat Meredith: "I must say, venturing a more somber response, I am disturbed by what our new young anthropologist has told us about the mummy. I speak of the implications of several facts. One is that the mummy was of a high social caste, and that is important in itself, since that has been ignored. He was not a Cahokian of low estate. More significant, though, is the representation made by Dr. James Lanier that the facial markings on the mummy speak of a religious role our unnamed friend fulfilled in life."

Dr. Barbara Mostooth: "I concur. But beyond that, I am made most uneasy by the generations of our community over the years who have misjudged and maligned that Native-American who has resided in the archives of the university."

Dr. Dudley: "Be more specific, Barbara, if you will. I do not follow the logic of your statement, nor its drift. How has he resided in misjudgment at Bonar? How has he suffered insult?"

Dr. Mostooth: "That mummy, as we have all called it for generations, is not an archival object. He is not a shard of pottery, not an arrow head, nor a page of leathery material on which have been inscribed designs of a tattooed nature. He is, or was, a human being." (A silence of an appreciable length ensues, broken by several speaking at once with one voice rising above all others.)

Dr. Dudley: "Are you saying, Barbara, that when that nineteenth century rustic dug up Old Orangey from his cornfield at Olive Mound that he was disturbing a grave?"

Dr. Mostooth: "Precisely. I am saying that the mummy, and please don't use that hideous term Old Orangey – I find it unspeakably offensive – I say that the mummy was not dug up, but exhumed. That is my settled opinion."

Dr. Gwen Simmons: "I am devastated. The truth of Dr. Mostooth's insight strikes to the very core of my being, both as a professional sociologist and a human being, one who is fellow in species to this, this …"

Dr. Roderick Surge: "I think the term you want is "this displaced person."

(Sounds of approbation and agreement arise from most persons. Wine glasses are recharged. Cheese is taken.)

Dr. Swat Meredith: "I feel as occupant of the Sadie Overstreet Endowed Chair in Applied Religion that I must make this assertion. The mummy belonging to our university was not only a human being. He was a possessor of an immortal soul."

Dr. Dudley: "Was he a Methodist, do you think?" (An audible intake of breath by most. Laughter from Dr. Peter Osmole, who finding himself not joined by others, breaks off in mid-chuckle.)

Dr. Meredith: "I think we can all agree that the human being we speak of was condemned by circumstance to live in darkness. He was not Christian, of course. He was neither of our faith nor dispensation. Yet who are we to doubt or dismiss his spirituality, his reaching toward a larger insubstantial unknown?"

Dr. Barbara Mostooth: "I am no theologian, and I profess no creed, save that of the human. Yet as Swat has so eloquently put it, this was a man, more than the sum of his purely physical parts. To ignore that is to deny him status as anything other than the poor collection of remains which have constituted his selfhood since the spark of life departed his flesh over eight centuries ago." (Applause from all and expressions of fervent agreement. A lifting of glasses, a further taking of cheese.)

I cannot claim that the actual dialogue I imagined above took place in the detail and manner presented, but I do know what occurred in the meeting of the Faculty Executive Committee on the following Thursday at 3:30 p.m., the usual hour for the monthly coming together of the duly elected representatives of that group. Some faculty call the Committee the brain trust, some term us the gurus of governance, some use less polite labels, but none dare doubt the centrality of what we do. None take our deliberations lightly. As a longstanding member of the FEC, I may aver and swear to that.

I will forgo a full recitation of the progress of the FEC meeting, except to say that the stated agenda was addressed and dispatched in a workmanlike manner, that the chair of FEC, Dr. Monica Thrice-Todt, led us expeditiously through our business, and that when the committee reached the category of new business Dr. Morgan Saucier announced a new item which he would have us consider.

With a graceful gesture of acknowledgment, Dr. Thrice-Todt invited Dr. Saucier to speak his piece. I noted that as Dr. Thrice-Todt turned in her chair to focus attention on Dr. Saucier that a pleasant tinkling sound arose from the elaborate necklace she frequently wore to noteworthy meetings of the university faculty. Knowing what was to come from Dr. Saucier, since I had been forewarned by Dr. Barbara Mostooth, my colleague in the department of language, literature, communication and cultural supposition, of the nature of the topic about to be introduced, I took comfort in the familiar musical note from Dr. Monica Thrice-Todt's necklace. My doing so was illogical, but genuine.

"Dr. Saucier," the chairwoman said. "Please proceed." At that, he did so, explaining the recent increase of knowledge about the mummy in our midst and the moral demands now laid upon us by such expansion of our understanding. With increase of knowledge comes increase of sorrow, as the poet has said. Alas, thoughts that lie too deep for poetry.

At the conclusion of Dr. Saucier's statement, a moment of silence fell, broken finally by a series of questions from almost all members of the FEC, seeking further factual elucidation and context. I alone of the group did not speak, as is my wont, preferring to reserve comment until full comprehension of an issue is reached. Then I will express a summative opinion. Numerous persons have thanked me for such a rhetorical habit over the years, mainly in gratifyingly private asides. "You constantly repeat and sum up in a most detailed and concise fashion what has already been said," Dr. Faith Lee Sung, now sadly no longer with us, once remarked to me.

"Let me put in a word," Dr. Peter Osmole said, his posture and manner of address quietly thoughtful, so unlike the liveliness and exuberance of his conduct in social situations. At the FEC meeting, he was wearing a dark suit and a white shirt with a tasteful splash of color in the tie mounting to his collar. "If we are to be able to continue to consider ourselves as Bonar University faculty to be a morally driven body, it is incumbent upon us to make amends for the cultural insensitivity heretofore displayed toward the mummy in our archives."

"I will violate the usual proper silence of the chair," Dr. Monica Thrice-Todt said, "to express my total agreement with Dr. Osmole."

The discussion which followed was in full accord with the sentiment expressed by our chairwoman, and in not more than thirty minutes the FEC had concluded that it would bring to the meeting of the full faculty our recommendation that appropriate amends should be made to the mummy and the burden of cultural, spiritual, and historical meaning he bore. We would make a lasting statement, one in keeping with our mission and identity as an institution of higher learning. The nature of our reconciliation, our gesture of amends, would be thrashed out in a caucus of the whole.

I had coughed gently to signal that I wished to speak in summation of what had been discussed and decided by the Faculty Executive Committee, and all had fallen silent, when Dr. Peter Osmole spoke up just as I was commencing my commentary.

"Yeah," Dr. Osmole interrupted, the abruptness of that harsh syllable stopping me in mid sentence and causing a perceptible start in all those in attendance, "all this is well and good, but what will He say about it?"

He was the president of Bonar University, the sole person in our academic community whose name never needed to be spoken, the masculine third-person singular pronoun always sufficing for clear and immediate reference and identification for us all. He was He, and the word He was spoken always as though in upper case letters.

"Will he discover a complicating issue arising from the matter?" said Dr. Saucier, looking at no one, but speaking as though to address each of us, his tone modulated though querulous.

"When, pray tell me, has he not?" responded our chairwoman.

"Surely in this proposal there is little to offend the most timid of souls," Dr. Peter Osmole said. "The matter is a private one, is it not? We intend only to redress a longstanding wrong done a dead man."

"Not simply a dead man," Dr. Saucier said. "But an entire culture, a representative of all peoples who lived, worked, worshipped and died in this land before White Europeans invaded and occupied it. We speak for a plundered and destroyed civilization."

"I do not quarrel with your interpretation, Morgan," Dr. Osmole said. "But if we present it to him in such fashion he shall deem it counterproductive to the ongoing growth and success of Bonar University."

"Would that we thought less of gross profit at this institution and more of truth, if I may venture a comment as chair of this committee," Dr. Monica Thrice-Todt said. "But Peter is accurate in his assessment, I fear."

"He will not allow a display which in his opinion reflects any iota of flaw, fault, or lack in the conduct of business at Bonar," Dr. Patrice Kitchens said, her first assertion of the day. "He will consider any such admission tantamount to an act of treason."

"Perhaps," Dr. Saucier said, his gaze directed at the ceiling of Room 211, Founder's Hall, "if we were to design a ceremony with a stated purpose masking a subtext, he would not recognize it for what it actually is."

"Build upon that notion," Dr. Thrice-Todt said, "if you will, Morgan. What do you propose?"

From that exchange grew the seed which blossomed into all that followed. Dinners cooled and iced drinks melted in several homes that day as we worked as a committee well past our usual time of adjournment. Just before the chapel bell tolled the hour of six, I spoke up to summarize what had been proposed as project, how it would be presented to him, and what steps were appropriately next in our plans in the matter of the typically Mississippian mummy in the Bonar University archives. I never like to use the crutch of written notes in my summations, preferring the organic liveliness and texture of extempore, but I must confess I was forced that day by the sheer volume of materials invented in that session of the Faculty Executive Committee to resort to written aid. Yet what I said was characterized to me later by Dr. Patrice Kitchens as "eloquently put," her words and her judgment, not my own. Self praise does not compliment one. It condemns.

Had I but world enough, and time, I would record the exquisite progress of the proposed plan for our mummy arising from the Faculty Executive Committee deliberations as its way was won though not one but two caucuses of the full faculty, thence to the official faculty meeting chaired by our president, and subsequently into the eve of implementation. But I have not space of time nor inclination to recount that remarkable journey from impetus to idea to fruition. My strength of expression is summative, not narrative. I am pleased to condense a mass and morass of information into sharp honing of purpose and direction. The circuitous route through the wandering paths and byways of an example of human enterprise does not tempt me. To the point, I declare. Seek purpose, define it, bring it into focus, then move on to the next stage in truth-telling.

There are mountains before us. Let us begin the climb. Let us seek not the valleys, but the peaks.

My words of preface prepare then for my next attempt at showing, rather than telling. I present, as does the dramatist, a scene rather than a recounting.

Picture a spring morning on the campus of Bonar University, a day early in May, close on to the 176th graduation commencement of a class of seniors from our institution. The gardens are magnificent, abloom with flowering plants, brought by the Latino workers of Buildings and Grounds to a state of high readiness for this year's celebration of academic achievement and farewell. The songbirds themselves, the wrens and finches and robins and all the other feathered choristers of our community, seem in the intensity of their song aware of the moment. All of nature and of human-kind at Bonar University are in accord in jubilance.

On the stroke of the ninth hour, the bell in the chapel tower commences its announcement of the beginning of a ceremony never before in evidence in that place and in the history of our university. A single voice is heard, that of Dr. Peter Osmole, faculty crier of Bonar University. Its tone is deep, its sound is far-reaching, its purpose calls all within the range of hearing to account and attention. It speaks of past practice, current purpose, and due culmination.

"Here ye, hear ye, all within the sound of these, my words," our faculty crier chants, "attend thee, attend thee."

As the chapel bell tolls, it reaches the hour of nine and then continues beyond, a solemn and august signal of ceremony and import. The central doors of Old Main open together as though from an invisible source of command. Lo, however, one sees Dr. Peter Osmole alone in full academic regalia proceed in slow and dignified pace from the interior of the building into the beauty and freshness of the May morning. He cradles the official Mace of Adornment of Bonar University in his arm, a signal as of yore to any who would offer attack or besiegement to the seat of learning which the Mace of Adornment represents.

"Beware," is the visual statement of the Mace in Dr. Osmole's firm grip. "Hold and be advised, ye who may challenge academic freedom. A great knocking will ensue, dare you approach with evil intent."

Viewers in witness of the advance of Dr. Peter Osmole, Mace Bearer, may observe that his regal and imposing beard has been trimmed and combed into a neat arrangement announcing his seniority and years of service in the halls of academe. One such viewer, myself I must confess, breathes an inaudible sigh of relief at this evidence of due preparation on the part of Dr. Osmole's good wife and helpmate, Victoria Eugenia, who has realized and supported the significance of this ceremony unfolding before us. It has been my observation at times that the hirsute announcement of masculinity and seniority made by Dr. Osmole's beard has not been always pristinely kempt. Not so now. I applaud inwardly.

Rapping the butt of the Mace of Adornment on the walk before him thrice, the Bonar University Faculty Crier and Mace Bearer speaks thrillingly. "Let the procession begin."

As he steps forward, behind him follow four faculty members, two male and two female, bearing an elaborately decorated wooden box, streaming with ribbons in the color of Bonar, the orange and the purple. These bearers are senior, tenured, and holders of the rank of full professor in their respective disciplines. Drs. Swat Meredith, Barbara Mostooth, Monica Thrice-Todt, and Morgan Saucier advance in solemn steps, their burden physically light (the mummy weighs less than a good-sized pork ham), but symbolically as heavy as earth.

I note that the female professors are wearing flat shoes, lest there be accidental slippage or totter by fault of a more stylish footwear, and I am relieved. Beauty must yield at times to use. The men, of course, wear the foot coverings customary in academe, a modified athletic shoe dark in color.

As all in procession gain the open air, a single trumpet makes announcement from a window in the second floor of Grumman Hall, its player properly invisible, though all there know it is a senior music major, Jack Streete from Waterloo, Illinois, a hamlet not far distant from Palestine. Jack is the pride and joy of the Bonar student orchestra, and has won prizes for the silver snarling sound he coaxes from his instrument. The air he plays now is of his own creation, special for the occasion of the Inhumation of the Bonar Mummy, and based upon the flute melodies of Native American musicians of the Southwest as imagined by current interpreters.

The course of the procession is toward a previously prepared opening into the earth at the center of the quadrangle formed by Old Main, Grumman Hall, and the Cafeteria, now termed the Dining Commons in all official Bonar publications. Though covered decently by a sheet of green plastic, the dark color of the rich soil of Illinois is much in evidence near the mummy's final resting place.

I think of corn, betassled and moving in the breeze, I think of soy beans, in a deep green bow to the earth, I think of birth, growth, death and resurrection, and I feel a few natural tears on the verge of welling in my eyes. It is a good and sound moment.

He, our president, is waiting at the edge of the opening into the earth at the center of the Bonar academic quadrangle. If He were not to be waiting, there would have been no ceremony of Inhumation of the Bonar Mummy, of course. I give all credit to Dr. Dudley for the stroke of genius arising from his fertile and politic mind which led to the invitation to Him to preside at the heart of the ceremony.

"Of course," Dr. Monica Thrice-Todt had exclaimed at the moment when Dr. Dudley had made his proposal. "If it were the burial of a prize hog, He would be pleased to allow it, were He allowed to preside and address the throng."

As the four official bearers of the bier reach the appointed place of inhumation, resplendent in their full regalia, complete with cords of undergraduate honor societies, medals of award for teaching and service, sashes of significance for committee assignments and attendance at meetings of importance, the remainder of those processing in the march halt to form a half-circle about the focus of attention. Though invited by the core committee to process with the second rank of faculty, I declined the offer and now stand at a vantage point which allows full witness to all stages of the ceremony.

I wear my regalia, my pins and cords and sashes and a cap constructed on the model of those in use for six centuries at the University of Bologna, the oldest institution of higher education in the Western world, and I consider myself duly recognized for rank, status, and accomplishment. I will not march with the category of faculty made up not only of the tenured, but also those on temporary and non-renewable contracts. I do not require a numbering in that group. Know thyself, said Socrates. I do, and I am satisfied.

Someone speaks to me, and I recognize the voice as that of Sam Probely, one whose dissertation is not yet complete. A simple

ABD, he calls himself in jocular fashion, despite knowing as we all do that he is a doomed man. I do not acknowledge his comment to me, hoping that he will assume my attention is so focused on the ceremony unfolding near the mound of earth that I do not hear.

He repeats, in a louder tone, words I cannot ignore if I am to avoid appearing to others as one engaged in conversation with this erstwhile Young Turk. "I beg your pardon," I say in a modulated voice. "I cannot understand what you are saying. I'm intent on the ceremony."

"That's all right, Doctor R," he says. "I can speak up. I just said I wonder if there's going to be an open or a closed casket deal here today for Old Orangey. I deign to look in his direction, thinking that if I do so, he might be satisfied and hush.

"Certainly there's no need for an open casket, as you call it, Sam," I say in a controlled whisper. "We're not a bunch of Baptists, and we've all had our chance over the years to examine the mummy remains as closely as we wanted."

"But that's true of anybody who dies, isn't it? I had looked at my old aunts and uncles when they were alive thousands of times, but I still had to walk by every open coffin and admire how they all looked just as natural as could be before we put them in the ground."

I take a step to the right, a small one, so as not to invite a following movement from this ABD, but he does not let that signal stop him. No, he leans in toward me and speaks again. "I mean this is a funeral, right? We're finally admitting at long last that Old Orangey has died, aren't we? He has joined the Great Majority of the Bonar Family. Just wait and see if somebody doesn't say that."

"My word," I say in exasperation, perhaps speaking a bit louder than I intended, since I notice some of the second line of faculty looking toward where I stand by this oaf. "Please let me participate in this moment."

"Why, sure," Sam Probely has the gall to say, "whatever you say, Doctor R. Just as long as you don't crawl in the casket with the mummy when they pop the lid."

This behavior is typical of those who fail to complete the work necessary to earn the doctorate and thus make themselves eligible for membership in the living body of the faculty of an institution of higher education. I am not surprised by Sam Probely's highly inappropriate behavior, but I want to say to him that if he has no more respect for the rite in process before us, why his attendance. I do not speak further, knowing that what he and his ilk desperately crave are ongoing recognition and interaction from one like me, one who has earned membership in that august company. And if I continue this verbal response, others will assume I am in some sense party to Sam Probely and what he represents.

A last silver note from the trumpet of Jack Streete hangs in the air like a banner, and a moment of silence fraught with meaning ensues. Even the winged messengers of the air have ceased their singing, and all hovers on the edge of ongoing significance, naught but a cough and a throat-clearing or two disturbing the pause.

The president of Bonar University shifts his weight from one foot to the other, creating an anticipatory movement that some wag in years past defined to general amusement as "the executive sway and shuffle." All there assembled wait, and He begins to speak, mouthing the inevitable verbal identifiers of presidential ceremony. I attempt to listen to what He is saying, but having heard such speech from Him for so long, I cannot focus on the substance of His statement. Instead, as always, I allow my mind to go where it will, and on this occasion it seeks sanctuary in a habitual remembrance of a past event in my personal history, one which both comforts and dismays and one which I share with no other. But that was in another country, and besides the whore is dead, as a minor Elizabethan dramatist once wrote.

After a proper space of time, He ceases the oration, and Dr. Swat Meredith steps forward to frame for the company assembled the meaning of the event unfolding before us all. What is it that we are doing, why are we doing it, and what will be its import in the long procession of history and the meaningful relationship between events?

Like all the auditors of Swat's comments, I am attentive, focused, and thrilled at my participation in the ceremony of the Inhumation of the Bonar Mummy. But unlike all others there, I am able to hark back to moments of personal contact with Dr. Swat Meredith, his warm breath on my throat, the sensation of his hair brushing against my face, and the deeply felt and powerfully realized physical consummation of our relationship in days gone by. Alas, all done, all completed, all resolved and all now but a memory. But what I hold in my mind belongs alone to me, sustains me, and allows me a continuing devotion to the professional duties of a tenured professor at Bonar University.

The actual lowering of the mummy in our midst into its final resting place at the heart of the quadrangle is quickly accomplished, though with due dignity and reverence for the life once present in the remains. The recession of the robed participants goes off without a hitch, and only a few of us remain to observe the Latino crew from Building and Grounds replace the dark soil into the grave. I am one of those in attendance, never found wanting in seeing a thing to its end, and I am the last one present fully robed in academic regalia.

When the last shovelful is added to the mound, I advance to read the inscription on the brass memorial set into cement some days earlier and unveiled at the conclusion of the ceremony of Inhumation. Yet unblemished by time's passage, it glows as a golden fire as I lean forward to read it, and I discover that I must shade my eyes to be able to pick out the words in memorial chosen by Dr. Swat Meredith and approved by all faculty by acclamation.

A single note of song from one last feathered chorister sounds in the clear air as I read the words inscribed, my eyes misting over, I must confess, as I do so.

"All peoples," states the inscription which will mark for eternity the gesture of respect and recognition at long last accorded the Bonar mummy, "deserve final burial."

"Yes," I say aloud, the words bursting forth from me, "all that is dead shall be covered, and all that decays will be dust."

"Doctor R," Samuel Probely says from where he has been standing somewhere in a planting of bushes behind me, "some fun, huh?"

"Why don't you just go work on your thesis, Sam?" I say. "I am proud to say I finished mine years ago."

THE LIGHT IN MEMPHIS

They would be coming, Beulahdene Jackson knew, and she knew that fact in her bones, the same way she could predict the onset of heavy weather even on a day the sun was shining bright and the air tasted clear and sweet in Memphis on the river. Something inside whispered to her not in words but a feeling, and Beulahdene had come to trust the truth in that feeling over the years, that thing like a small sickness or pressure around her heart. And it had a color, and that color was a shade of light yellow. Words could and would lie, but that feeling did not. Falsehood was not in it.

Whether they would come more than one at the time, Beulahdene Jackson did not know. It could be two, three, four, not likely more than that. It could be just the one. And if only one, that would carry the most weight and the greatest menace. Knowing that was a feeling, too.

They would not have come a few years before, not there to

the corner of Montgomery and Peach, where Beulahdene had been able to buy the little house where she had lived these years since. The government check had started coming back then, and with what she had saved from the money she had made working for all the white ladies in their houses in Midtown over the years, she had been able to put enough down to move into the brown house on the corner, the one with siding and the front porch and the backyard where she had grown tomatoes and okra for a long time. Not any more now, though.

When Beulahdene Jackson moved in, many of the Jewish people who walked to their church each Saturday, what they called a synagogue, had lived in the neighborhood still. Some of them, anyway, and everything was kept up, and the yards were mowed, and any window that was broken in any house was always replaced the next day. Walls were painted, new roofs were put on, the sidewalks were not all broken up by sycamore and oak tree roots, no pieces of glass scattered in the street got left there long.

But a new synagogue was built by the Jewish people, somewhere out in East Memphis, and they all moved away so they could walk to that new one on the weekends, since they couldn't drive their cars to it. Why they couldn't drive to church in all the big cars they owned and drove everywhere else Beulahdene never did get straight. But they couldn't for some reason, and that was their business and none of hers. So she didn't let that worry her mind.

But they had left, almost all at once, and everything changed in the neighborhood. The old synagogue was now where the white Baptist young folks went to learn how to be preachers, though it looked the same as it ever did, except for the signs in the front of the building. The foreign writing the Jewish people had carved on the building itself was still there, saying whatever it said that nobody could read but them. But they weren't there to read it anymore, the Jewish people, and Montgomery and Peach was not the same place it had been when Beulahdene Jackson moved into the little brown house. No more tomatoes in the backyard, no more families walking to the synagogue at the end of the week, no more okra in the hot Memphis summer, sticky to the touch when you cut it off the stalk.

A little boy knocked on the front door first thing that morning, right before seven o'clock. Beulahdene Jackson didn't open her door to see what he wanted, knowing better, but she got a chance to study him close by looking through a crack between the lace window curtain and the edge of the window frame off to the side.

He was a light-skinned boy, and he looked nice, even sweet in his face as he stood turning his head from side to side trying to look through the pane of glass cut into the door. That was not a good thing to have in your door when the house was located where it was, on the corner of Montgomery and Peach. The policeman who had had the meeting with the neighbors that still lived there had told Beulahdene that directly when he had done the inspection for security measures on everybody's house, the ones still being lived in. That's what he called it, security measures. And he called it community outreach, too.

"That there piece of glass is an entry way, Ma'am," he said to her, pointing at Beulahdene's door and writing it down on the piece of paper which he had left with her later on. Everybody got their own piece of paper, everybody living there who went to the meeting with the police officer. Beulahdene put the form, the inspection report, in that top drawer of the chest in the bedroom where she slept, the place she kept all of her important papers. The letters from the Social Security, the insurance form for her house, the agreement she paid on every month for the burial arrangements for when the time would come when the Lord decided to finally do what He had to do. There were letters there, too, from kinfolks and from David, but she didn't read them anymore much. They were in her head already and had been for a long time. She didn't have to look at letters now.

"I'd say you need to get you a new door, Mrs. Jackson," the policeman said. "A steel one, like the one you got in back. That'd be my recommendation."

"Yes sir," Beulahdene told him, smiling at herself for calling somebody "sir" who looked no older than a child, and knowing she wouldn't do what the policeman recommended about the front door to her house. That pane of glass was small, but it let in the light, and you could look through it and see whoever was passing on the street outside, going up and down Montgomery, summer and winter. If you wanted to, that is, though there weren't many people going by a person would want to see anymore these days, not on Montgomery Street.

The little boy was wearing those pants like they do now, too big by several sizes for what would fit him, almost falling off of him as he stood on the front porch, his hand up the pane of glass to shade his eyes so he could see inside Beulahdene's house into the front room. He didn't look long, though, and as he left the porch, hopping down on the sidewalk without using the steps, Beulahdene could see through the crack beside the curtain that his big pants were so long in the leg the cuffs were frayed and worn out from dragging on the concrete wherever he walked.

"Lord Jesus," Beulahdene Jackson said out loud, "hold my hand."

He is little, she told herself, he's just a child trying to find a little yard work to do to make him some spare change to jingle in his pocket. Or to buy him a treat, an ice cream or a bottle of pop in this hot weather, that's what he wants, what he's looking for, that's all it is to it.

But as she washed the dishes she had used for breakfast and ironed herself a blouse and a house dress and the towels she had been meaning to get around to for a week, she sang over and over a hymn, He Comes to the Garden Alone, to keep her mind occupied.

I'll look at all my papers in that drawer this morning, she told herself, check on everything being where it ought to be. I will dust every surface in my house this morning where it ain't been touched for two weeks. I've been letting down too much here lately. A bad habit will come on you before you know it if you don't keep things up to where they ought to be.

He's real young, she said to herself, he's a little boy, he don't mean nothing, he's just working his way down old Montgomery Street this morning, door to door to door, looking for an odd job.

Randall Eugene McNeill felt the braided wire pulling him slowly but steadily toward the mouth of the cave, struggle against it however much he did or could do. The wire was fastened somehow to his feet, around both ankles, with enough slack to allow him to move his feet apart eight or ten inches, but no more than that.

Although he couldn't see the wire in the dark, Randall Eugene McNeill knew its colors, three strands to the braid – one red, one black, one green – and he knew that if he were pulled feet first through the opening of the cave into the passage into the earth, dark and musty and cold behind it, that he'd never see light or feel fresh air moving across his face again.

A whine was forced through his lips without Randall Eugene willing it, and that frightened him more than anything else about what was happening, more than the wire braided red, black, and green, more than the hole of the cave mouth, framed by boards like those set around a window, more than the dank, dark passage leading somewhere beneath the ground, more than the fact that he couldn't move and his arms lay dead beside him no matter how much he told them to push his hands down toward his feet. Take it off, unwind it, Randall Eugene begged his arms and hands, get it away from my feet. Don't let it pull me, don't let it drag me underneath the ground.

Calling on all he could of his waning strength, forcing his lips apart as far as he could manage, Randall Eugene tried to cry out, but the sound he was able to make was weaker than the whine that had been pried from him, and he felt a sickening lurch as the braid of wire pulled him further toward the window into the cave, the dark mouth into the earth, the teeth of boards framing it.

"Why can't you get up, sleepy-head?" his mother was saying. "I'm about to pull your little toe off, Randall Eugene, and you still won't stop trying to sleep."

"Mama," Randall Eugene McNeill said, "it's you, it's just only you."

"Who'd you think it was, baby? One of your girlfriends?"

"No, I ain't got no girlfriends," Randall Eugene said, pushing his hand toward the foot of the bed where his mother stood. She was dressed for work and ready to leave the house, a raincoat covering all of her uniform and her purse hanging from a strap on her shoulder. Her hair was combed out straight, and her make-up was on.

"Don't talk like that, son," she said. "You know better than that."

"Well, I ain't got no girlfriend. I'm just telling the truth."

"Don't say ain't no. Who're you trying to fool? You weren't raised to speak that way, and you do know better. Anybody hearing you who didn't know any different would never believe you're in that gifted and talented program."

"All right, I'll do it," Randall Eugene said. "I'll get up."

"You've got a lot to do today, remember, Sugar. You have the counselor to see this afternoon, and don't you forget to tell her what I said about your meds."

Randall Eugene began to speak, but didn't, stopped by the way the wall of his room across from his bed looked different somehow. Had his mother changed it in some way, put different paper on it, painted a design where there was only a pale blank space before? There was a pattern evident now, regular small squares in alternating colors, black and red, changing as he watched them to separate shades of gray.

"Why did you do that?" Randall Eugene said, pointing toward the wall by lifting his head as though to indicate with his chin what he wanted her to see.

"Do what? What're you talking about? That picture over there? The one of LaFrance? Is that what you mean?"

"No, nothing," Randall Eugene said, watching the pattern on the wall shift from squares of gray back toward white, fading quickly into blankness again as though to vanish before his mother would be able to see what was happening before her in her own house. Another thing that he knew only he could detect, a state of change which always eluded everybody but him. She couldn't see it. She wouldn't see it, and if she did, she'd be afraid to admit it. "I guess it's just the way the light's doing."

"As little light as you let get in this room, I don't know how you see to find your way around. When you were little, you couldn't let enough light get through your windows to satisfy you. Now you act like an old bear trying to hibernate."

Randall Eugene picked up the shirt his mother had put across the foot of his bed while he was asleep and looked at her.

"You're allowed to speak, young man," she said. "The polite thing would be to say mama I need to get dressed now. And if you did that, I'd leave the room. But I know if I do, you'll just crawl back under the covers and go to sleep."

"No, I wouldn't," Randall Eugene said. "I used to would've done that, but not no more."

"You couldn't sleep again last night, honey?"

"I could sleep all right, but I didn't want to. What I'd like to be able to do is never go back to sleep again. That's what'd satisfy me."

"If you keep going to that counselor lady and taking your meds, you'll grow out of this, Randall Eugene. I know you would. It's just a stage of development."

"Don't call it meds. I hate it when you call them that. And don't say development."

"You hate it when I say anything these days. Meds is what it is. I know what I'm talking about. Now get up and get dressed and do it quick now. Eat your breakfast and be ready in fifteen minutes. I've got to be in the surgical unit in less than an hour. Move it, Randall."

I know why the window, Randall Eugene told himself as he watched his mother leave the room, I know that part all right, up and down and sideways and backwards. But why the rest of it? A cave, a cave? A frame around the hole? Wires on my feet? The wall moving?

I have got to cool down, he lectured himself as he dressed and walked by the plate on the table in the kitchen where she'd left something for his breakfast. He picked it up, not looking at whatever was there, and succeeding in scraping it into the garbage pail under the sink without having to see what it was. He couldn't avoid hearing the sound it made, though, as it hit something flat in the garbage container, a piece of cardboard maybe. It splatted, it sounded heavy and wet, and Randall Eugene's stomach dipped and rose as though it was headed all the way to his throat.

I have got to cool down. I've got to get something else into my head, something big enough that nothing can get around it, nothing can make me think, not a sound, not a sight, not a smell.

They'd said he wouldn't do it. Antwan mainly, standing there laughing, his teeth so white when he threw back his head to show how funny he thought it was.

"Dog," he said, "you ain't going to do shit. You too much of a white man to do nothing but talk."

"Naw, naw, wait a minute," Damon said. "Do Run Run be going to show us something. Show us some shit, ain't you, Do Run Run?"

"You got that right," Randall Eugene said, all of them standing there on the steps going up to the big doors in front, the ones under the stone carved with the Gothic letters spelling out Central High of Memphis. "You just watch my natural ass."

"Oh yeah, oh yeah," Damon said, "Do Run Run going to show us something, all right. He going to show us his vocabulary."

Then they all laughed and fell about the steps, spinning and staggering like they were about to fall, hands thrown up in the air, pushing, pushing, pushing. Three white girls coming up the steps toward them changed the way they were walking to take a path further away, and Randall Eugene saw that Amy Amonette was one of them. She looked right at him, and he looked off as though he didn't see her, but he knew she could tell he did. He turned his back to her, but he could feel her eyes sliding off of him, and he heard her say something to one of the other ones, Elizabeth Hubbard, maybe.

"Fuck that monkey shit," Randall Eugene McNeill said to Damon. "Dog, you don't know what's up with me." The street in front of the steps was doing it again, slow this time, but Randall Eugene knew if he let it know he saw it, the street would do it more and more quickly, too fast for him to keep up and hold it contained in his eyes and then the sound would start up. He couldn't afford the sound this morning, not today. Don't look at it, move your eyes away and face the building, but don't hurry so it'll be able to know you see. Look at the words cut into the stone above the door. Let the stone keep your eyes. It's not moving.

"Unh uh," Antwan said. "That ain't the word, that ain't what we waiting to hear you say. Don't say fuck. Say something like molecule. Say economic trend, Do Run Run, say economic trend. Say honors program."

That's when they really laughed, and he walked off down the steps, taking them three at a time, and by the time he was down to the street, all of them had turned to head into the building, Damon saying over and over, monkey shit, monkey shit, fool, fool, fool.

When Randall Eugene stepped up on the porch, he could see her peeping at him from where she was looking out from a crack in her curtains, thinking she was hidden from anybody standing in front of the door. The light of the early morning sun hit her glasses, and he couldn't see her eyes, and he was glad of that.

Randall Eugene kept looking straight ahead, but he was still able to see the curtain to his left move just a hair, so he leaned forward and put his hand up to shade the glass part of the heavy wooden door. It was too dark to see anything inside, standing as he was in the bright sunlight, but the old lady couldn't tell that.

Seeing him do that would scare her, Randall Eugene thought, and it would keep her indoors with all her locks fastened. When he went back to school, getting there late and coming into the class-room where the officers of the Bones Family, Antwan and Damon and Ja'Nce, would be sitting against the back wall in a row, one-two-three, he'd be able to tell them the house he'd picked out had somebody in it, watching too close for him to go inside.

"Motherfuck," he'd say, "if I'm going to have some old bitch call the blue knockers on me for busting out a window. I want it to count for something when I be breaking in. I want to be able to take my time, do a little shopping for a thing to show you dogs, something worth something, to prove out where I been. Word up."

Yeah, Randall Eugene told himself trotting across Montgom-ery to the other side of the street, that'll work, get them notified I mean business. I ain't just moving my mouth up and down to keep the flies off my face. I be meaning to show I'm Bones material, and I mean to do it big.

He'd just hit the curb with the sole of his shoe, when it hap-pened and it caught him before he could get up all the way onto the sidewalk and out of the hold of the pattern in the cement of the street. How had it happened so fast that he couldn't see it taking place? That was the fastest it had ever been, and that told Ran-dall Eugene that the pattern had been deceiving him ever since it started up. It had always been able to move too fast for him to stop it, to hold and contain it, and put himself at a distance from it. When the pattern wanted to set up like cement in the sun, it could have done that, and the reason it hadn't was that it wasn't ready yet. It was waiting until he stopped being so afraid of the pattern and had come to believe he could live with it, and it would move then when it was ready.

Here on Montgomery Street the pattern this morning had de-cided it was time, and it let him get almost all the way out of the street and up onto the sidewalk before it took him. But now it had, and he was in a pawn's position, and the hand when it wanted to move him would do that. It would give him up for an advantage or not for one, maybe throwing him away just to fool the white king and make him think he was winning. The question is not where it will move me, Randall Eugene said to himself. I know that. The jar the curb gave me traveled up my leg and told me that. What I don't know is when, and the pattern knows that, and it wants to think about that, along with the message it told the muscles and blood and bone of my leg.

I know a thing and I know it is true, from the sole of my foot to the pit of my stomach to the top of my head, Randall Eugene whispered to himself, straining to listen to the one talking to him. The message lodged in a spot just behind a part of his skull directly above his eyes, and it brought with it the look they would have on their faces as he tried to explain why he still hadn't done it, still hadn't done the deed he had to do before they'd let him in, before he would be able to feel both parts of his brain come together and touch and be one with each other like the white and yolk of an egg in the same shell.

"Do Run Run," Antwan would say, "go sit over yonder with the rest of the bitches and read some shit out of a book. Read it real loud and nice, say it like a white girl doing a book report."

Randall Eugene could see himself listening to them laugh at what Antwan said and waiting for the next one to say what he'd thought up, something even better than that, all of them ready to call him what he was.

He stepped off the sidewalk on Montgomery Street, taking himself away from the broken shards of clear glass and the cracked pieces of concrete, now part of the pattern which had been following him and waiting for him to know and allow he was part of it. Randall Eugene lifted both hands to his forehead to press the scene he'd imagined to come at Central High School back into his head along with the other ones already there, all the ones telling him he was a freak and a misfit and a white boy and a bitch and a final piece of the pattern waiting to step into the pawn position and be one with it. He looked up into the hot blast of sun hanging over Midtown Memphis, and he spoke out loud to it.

"Fuck it," Randall Eugene McNeill said. "I'm going back over to that lady's house, and I'm going in, and I'm bringing something back out with me to show their punk asses what kind of a man they messing with."

And that he said out loud, and the other words he whispered to the evidence of the pattern on the wall in his room and in the concrete of the street and in all the tools and formulas and equations and translations in the world, and those words he said but could not hear and heard but could speak and understood but could not know.

But when Randall Eugene got inside after the pattern had moved him there, the inner side of the door behind him, the air in the house smelling of where an old lady lived – paper flowers, some kind of chemical, maybe a floor cleaner, old toast, stale and burnt, a still dead odor of things shut up and sealed away in plastic wrap – nobody was home. Nothing told him to be quiet getting in, so he hadn't tried to be, breaking the window set in the door with a brick from the ones lining a flower bed, hammering it hard and hearing the glass fall inside to the floor, snaking the wire of the coat hanger down, down to where it caught the deadbolt and flipped it up, a hard sharp sound in the middle of the morning.

He went directly to the small dark colored table against the wall, watching his hands pick through the accumulation of things set there, placed by somebody in a shape to show them off. Pictures of men and women and children in funny clothes, everybody dressed up pretending to be young but showing they couldn't be by the way their eyes looked staring into the camera lens, dead for years but trying not to be and fooling nobody. A framed letter, medals with ribbons fastened to them, a coin, a necklace, a pin carved with a white woman's head. Paper weights made of colored glass with flower petals frozen in the center of them, blooming forever, but dead, dead, dead.

From all this collection, Randall Eugene's hand picked up one thing, a book bound in leather with two words made of curlicued letters on its cover, and his hand lifted the book to show it to his eyes to read, and the words said Precious Memories, and his eyes read that but his brain would not tell him what that meant, and he knew he had to understand it, and he believed if he looked a little harder and longer, the meaning would come to him and say its name.

It hung there on the surface of his sight, almost connecting, but it never did, because she was in the room now, and Randall Eugene knew he would never be able to take its meaning now because she spoke, and her words got in the way of letting him know what Precious Memories meant.

"Son," she was saying, "son, don't touch that, don't take my book, you hadn't got any use for that."

She held a butcher knife in her hand, and it should have been trembling because the woman was old and afraid, but it wasn't. A shaft of sunlight from the window broken in the door touched the edge of the blade, and it hung there steady as a stone set in a ring, winking with light, and Randall Eugene watched himself step toward her and take the knife out of her hand.

What will it do now, he wondered, my hand with the knife in it, the wink of the sun gone now from the blade edge, and then it showed him, all the light in the room did, gathered into one beam, like it does when someone is on a stage ready to begin an act or sing or dance or play an instrument, and it showed him what he would do and it let him see him doing it.

And then the old woman was lying on her sofa, but it wasn't like she was asleep. No, she was falling halfway off the piece of furniture, but her fall was frozen in a way it couldn't be, a way gravity wouldn't allow. How could she do that, Randall Eugene said to himself, amazed by the act the old woman could perform, stop in mid-air halfway to the floor, holding, holding, holding everything in the room fixed and set and captured like one of the pictures on the table of the old people pretending to be young and alive and smiling, though they were dead.

"Go on, now," a man said in a deep voice. "You've done what you came to do, son. You've got what you wanted. It's in your hand now. You have it to carry all by yourself."

Randall Eugene knew the voice, and he knew the man, and he

had for as long as he could remember, and the man was standing in the entry way to another room.

Randall Eugene had not seen that room before, how had it gotten there, he had looked that direction before, hadn't he, when he came into the place where he found himself now?

He was dressed like he always was, the man in the entry way – a dark suit, a shirt so white you wanted to look away from it to save your eyesight, a tie with broad muted stripes – and he was solid and bulky across the face and forehead, and his cheeks and chin shone from being freshly shaved, the thin mustache two precise lines above his lips, large and prominent and parted to speak.

"Dr. King," Randall Eugene McNeill said. "I have always wanted to meet you, but I thought I never would be able to."

The man nodded once, but his eyes did not move from where they were fixed on Randall Eugene's eyes, and then he lifted one hand and held it out as though to take the leather book from Randall Eugene.

"My name is Randall Eugene McNeill," he said, speaking as if he was introducing someone whose name he had heard only once and had to concentrate to remember. "Dr. King, I'm Randall Eugene, that's me."

"No," the man in the entry way to the other room said, "you're not him, young man. Your name is Do Run Run."

And then the blood, just a thin line, began to come from the knot of the man's striped tie, the place where the bullet had struck Dr. King on that balcony in Memphis, the one at the Lorraine Motel, and Randall Eugene watched it grow like a flower blossom, a red carnation like the ones in the corsages the girls wore to the Central High prom, and it was stronger and wider and deeper, and the blood was a stream now, not a flower at all, and it moved in steady spurts.

All the light in the room began to gather into one point, which twisted and glowed so brightly that Randall Eugene had to close his eyes or be blind, but he could still see it through his lids, moving past his face now, and he followed it as it floated up and out a window set high in the wall, and Randall Eugene knew he must follow, and he did, and he watched himself take two strong steps and leap from the floor, the leather book held before him as he went through the glass and frame of the window, following the ball of light outside, and now it was gone, and the sky was as black as midnight, as dark as Dr. King's suit and the blood against it.

The light was gone forever, and Randall Eugene knew that, he knew that was true, as true as the leather book he now had to carry in his hands into the pattern worked into the street that ran through Memphis and now through all the world before him.

ENJAMBMENT

David Will's first wife had published a book of poems, and he was afraid that several of them were about him. Standing in Words on Walls Bookstore just off the square in Mount Olive, he discovered that by reading the table of contents in the stack of books he had noticed with her name on each one, but the most telling signal was by a tightening that began somewhere in his lower belly, threatening to move up as it twisted a significant organ just below where his belt bit tightly into his waistline. He emitted an involuntary grunt as he leaned closer to the small yellow book to study the titles Martha had assigned her individual works.

The grunt was much like the ones he quietly allowed himself whenever he saw an attractive woman walking toward him in a shopping mall or on a sidewalk. No one could hear these tributes of admiration he voiced so modestly, but he had grown to depend on the salutary effect they had on his system. He was not obnoxious or obvious enough to make his regard of these women visible by these acts. He was simply reminding himself that he was still a male animal, capable of recognizing lust-worthy females, and quite capable of doing something about it, if circumstances would allow. It was a relief from a momentary pang of longing and served as an interior announcement of an ongoing set of working hormones, pheromones, and testicular potential.

What it says, David sometimes remarked to himself silently, is that I've had a sexual past, and by God I could have a future if need and opportunity should arise. A memory of riding in his car with his father years before on a highway in Tennessee, after the old man had been living in a nursing home for a couple of years, would at times intrude when David glimpsed some woman of that kind. He always immediately tried to squelch the calling up of the scene from a time somewhere during the Ronald Reagan administration, but he wasn't always able to do that.

He had driven from Nashville to visit the old man, accompanied by one of his friends from college, Raymond Bell, who was fascinated by David's father. "Your dad is one of the old timers," Raymond often said. "He was raised in the country and acts like it, doesn't he? He says what he means, by Jesus, huh?"

"Yeah," David would answer, "he has worn me out all my life by the stuff he's pulled and the way he talks about it."

"You ought to be glad about that. My old man never lets you know what he's thinking. What makes him tick I'll never figure out. Ham radios and woodworking, I guess. That's all he's ever had a word to say to me about anything, except to ask how my grades are and what I'm planning to do with myself."

David's father had never given any indication he even knew what grades in college courses were, and he showed no signs of spending a minute's time worrying about what his son would do with his life. Or if he even possessed a life to do anything with. Why would a man think about something he could not do a thing about? It wasn't his business, his father would have said, if asked. David's a man in his own right now.

As he always did when he visited his father in the nursing home, David had intended to stop at a liquor store to buy a bottle of whiskey for the old man, careful not to get anything larger than a half pint of the cheapest brand available. He had made the mistake of getting a full pint for his father right after he had convinced the nursing facility to take him in, and the old man had drunk the whole thing before they got back from their drive in the country, the obligatory trip to what his father called "the old country. There had been hell to pay when he unloaded him and tried to get him back into his room at the home. Drunk as he was, and talking about being that way, how glad he was about being that way, and about who had gotten the whiskey for him, Mr. Will had almost got himself evicted from BelClair Rest Facility.

David had had to spend two hours talking to the director, taking blame for the incident, and begging for his father to be allowed to stay where he and his brother and sister had finally found a place for the old man before the director, a Mr. Spurger, grudgingly allowed him another chance.

So the day he and Raymond picked up David's father, having to guide him into the Buick because his sight had worsened so much since David had last seen him, David thanked his lucky stars he hadn't stopped to buy any whiskey of any quality or any amount, no matter how small, when they pulled out of the parking lot and headed for Maury County and the ramshackle Will family place in the "old country.

He hadn't driven two miles before Raymond, leaning from the back seat of the car to listen to Mr. Will tell stories about his pipelining days, let David know that he hadn't forgotten to make a purchase. "Mr. Will," Raymond said, "Do you like Old Crow or do you prefer a sourmash based whiskey?"

"Hell, Ronnie," David's father said, "who am I to give a good goddamn about its parentage? Whatever's around is my favorite brand. And don't be calling me Mr. Will. I'll think you're talking to David here."

"His name is Raymond," David said. "Not Ronnie."

"I bet he'll answer to anything," the old man said. "Long as it involves whiskey. Ain't that right, Ronnie?"

Raymond allowed that was true in a gleeful voice, and he and Mr. Will laughed like hyenas as the bottle of whiskey Raymond had brought with him was produced. "Want me to open it for you, Jesse?" Raymond said. "This pint I'm holding in my hand's got a screw top on it."

"Let me do it," David's father said. "I love to break the seal on a bottle. Hell, I love to break the seal on anything."

"Be the first one to taste it, huh?" Raymond said, handing the pint to the old man. "Here it is."

"Be the first one to get into it is more like it," Jesse Will said. "Whatever it happens to be I'm about to bust into."

"Don't start drinking that whiskey until we get off this main highway," David said. "The last thing we need is some highway patrolman to stop us. You'd never get readmitted to BelClair again."

"If that's the case, let me lean out of the window and take me a big swig," David's father said. "Let them take a picture of it with their radar guns. Get the real goods on me this time." Raymond laughed at that until he had to wipe tears away.

By the time they left the state highway and got to the county road which led to the unpaved road to the old Will family place, Raymond and David's father had killed most of the pint of Old Crow, and Jesse Will was deep into a story about a female resident of the BelClair Nursing facility.

"Let me tell you boys one thing," he announced in the sincere tones a man might use in declaring himself to be a born-again Christian of the first water. "If she keeps coming around me, offering me bites of banana pudding and slices of pineapple upside down cake, I'm going to make her pay the price."

"You think she's coming on to you, Jesse?" Raymond said, leaning over the back of David's seat to punch him on the shoulder. "Is she looking for some action?"

"If she is, I don't care how old she is," Jesse Will said and then uttered the words which David had never been able to banish from memory. "That girl is going to find out I ain't up Dead Dick Creek yet."

What happened on the rest of the trip to the Will place in the "old country" David had forgotten completely, the words his father had said about Dead Dick Creek so thoroughly burning into his brainpan that nothing else from that day's expedition had stayed. The old man was dead and gone and buried with the rest of the clan in the cemetery in the old country years ago, and David had lost track of the whereabouts of Raymond Bell soon after his father's funeral which Raymond had attended, teary-eyed and drunk as he told stories about "that good old boy" as he called him.

What still came up in David's mind these days when he emitted his silent grunts of tribute on noticing sexually attractive women was the sinking realization that he wasn't much different from his ignorant old father bragging about not yet being up Dead Dick Creek. What did it take to get over being what you used to be? Why can't memories be reassuring and positive once in a while?

And now a book of poems had been published by his ex-wife, a woman who never when he knew her read anything heavier than a historical novel about one of the wives of Henry the VIII. What would lead Martha into arranging her thoughts in jagged lines on a piece of paper? Not only the miracle of that, but she had published them in a book from a well-known press, one several ranks above any house that had ever taken on any of his work.

David groaned aloud at the thought, remembering all the networking and brown-nosing and kowtowing he'd had to do to get any one of his books published. The last one, Mealtimes in Minneapolis, had cost him a direct cash subsidy to get it launched, a payment he'd had to hide from Celia by hook and by crook and by third party silent intervention to keep her beady accountant's eyes blindfolded.

"If you can't get your stuff published without paying somebody to do it," she'd said about an earlier bit of angeling he had resorted to, the deal he'd cut for Old Story, New Love, which should have done much better than it did, at least with the reviewers, "why publish the damn thing? Aren't people supposed to want to read what a writer publishes? Can't you expect the publisher to at least pay for your little book?"

David forgave her for that, but it had not been easy or immediate. She didn't know the literary world, the ins and out. of quality work, the fact that even Robert Frost had self-published his first. collection. Jesus, if a writer doesn't believe in himself, how can he expect anyone else to? She worked in a world of facts and figures and bricks and mortar, and nothing was real to her that wasn't verifiable by the physical senses. How could she know what it took to persist as an artist?

One thing he knew, though. He had to tell her about Martha's book of poems from Coequal Press before Celia discovered it herself. He could imagine her marching into the kitchen/den/great room area brandishing the book and chortling. She wouldn't let him forget she had discovered the literary triumph of wife number one unless he beat her to it.

He picked up one copy of the yellow volume from the stack on the first table in Words on Walls Bookstore . the first display table, for Christ's sake! the one immediate to the door – and walked toward the cashier. No, he thought, and turned back. Better get two copies of Dead Cities by Martha Foster. One for Celia to see me throw in the waste basket and one to slip into my bookbag to take to my office for deconstruction. He noted that the photo of Martha on the dust jacket was recent and that she had lost weight and changed her hair. It was curly now. She was smiling, and her teeth were blindingly white. David couldn't bear to read the blurbs surrounding her likeness.

Celia was making cooking noises in the kitchen when David entered the house through the door to the garage, scraping away with a knife at some root vegetable while a pot of water boiled away on the range, and she didn't look up before speaking.

"Turn that burner down," she said. "No, better yet, just turn it off and take it off the heat."

David did that and turned with Martha's book of poems lifted up in his right hand as though it were a host being presented to a congregation at worship. Take, eat, I am the Resurrection and the Life. Let no man cometh to the reader but by me. "Look here, Sweetie, what I found in the bookstore."

"I haven't got time. I'm about to let dinner get away from me."

"Okay, but you'll want to see this," he said in a tone he intended to be both jocular and dismissive. It didn't come out right, though, he judged, more of a hint of complaint in his voice than he'd wanted. He tried again, louder this time. "I could not, by God, believe it." He leaned against the back of a chair in a careless pose, waiting for Celia to regard him.

"What? You didn't buy another book, did you? Can't you go to the library once in a while? What do all those books of poetry cost by the line, I wonder? It's worse than gasoline."

"I can't go to the library. Not for this one," David said. "It will never end up in the stacks of any library I might use."

Martha looked up from the vegetable she was peeling, an eggplant David guessed from its color, but a strangely shaped one. He wondered if that was going to be it for dinner. "What is it?"

"It," David announced, his voice in smooth control this time, "is a thin volume of verse entitled Dead Cities."

"What's it about? Iraq?"

"I don't think so, but I know who it's by," David said, pausing to let his wife ask for the author's name. She didn't, head down again as she renewed her attack on the purple root vegetable. "It's by," he went on, "one Martha Foster, a new poet as far as I can tell, whose work I've not seen before."

"Not the Martha Foster? Not your Martha."

"She is not my Martha Foster, as she'd be the first to tell you, but yes it is by the woman to whom I used to be wed."

"You're shitting me," Celia said, moving toward the electric range to reach for the pot David had taken off the heat. "Has she got into the poetry racket, too? Why would she do that? I thought she'd have more sense."

"I don't think she would consider it a racket, as I myself do not, and why do you think she'd have more sense?"

"I'd think she'd have more sense," Celia said, making an adjustment to the heat control panel, "because she showed enough sense before to do some things I'd call smart."

"Oh, what would that be?" David said, waiting to see how far Celia would take things in this direction. "Pray tell me."

"Mrs. Will number one did leave the field of high school English teaching, for one thing," Celia said. "And she started making some money, among other things. That in my opinion was smart."

David didn't take that bait, though he refrained from comment at some pang of immediate emotional cost. I will not goad her into saying Martha was smart enough to leave me, he promised himself, not with this book from Coequal Press in my hand. I can prove Celia mistaken in her thinking and wrong in her logic, to my satisfaction, but it's not worth the downside just now.

"Don't you want to look at the book Martha has published? Aren't you ready to investigate the gripping topic of dead cities?" He shifted the book to his left hand and began flipping the first few pages, noting there was an epigraph and after that a dedication alone on a page. Oh, God. It was generic. "To all my sisters in silent bondage. May your chains become heavy enough to float away in smoke."

"Read me a poem," Celia said. "I know you're dying to."

"Oh, no. You can look at it later. Need some help with chopping?"

"Read me a poem by your old lover, David," Celia said. "Pick out one that'll move me."

Flipping quickly through the first few pages, David saw a title which looked harmless enough to satisfy. If he read Celia one or two innocuous bits of the drivel his first wife had written, he knew she'd get bored and never pick up the book again except probably to look at the photo of Martha on the back dust jacket and make a catty remark about her hair. Then he would have dodged the bullet and lived to fight another day, as his father might have said, but in terms much more colorful than that cliché.

"All right, you asked for it," David said, assuming his teaching voice and holding the volume at arm's length before him. "Here's one. Promises to be a travelogue, perhaps."

"Amsterdam," he read with poised resonance, and then added in a small voice meant to entertain and denigrate. "That there's the title, see, Sweetie."

"Hit it," Celia said, dumping the vegetable cubes into the reheating water in the pot. "Let's hear it, and do it with style, Professor."

"Amsterdam," David said. "That first night on Prinsengracht, you pointed her out to me, standing alone near a booth of tulips, petals reflected in the canal, asking us in as we stared past the stamens, deeper and deeper into the seducing waters of that ancient city, place of shadow and light, captured by the old masters in tints that outlast the graves of love."

David stopped reading, and looked up at a corner of the kitchen as though he'd heard the scrabbling of some small animal behind a wall and was waiting to test the perception. Had he imagined it? Was something there? What was moving somewhere in a hollow space?

"That's it?" Celia said. "Surely not. Keep going."

"I don't think this one is a good one to read out loud," David said, closing the book but leaving a finger to mark the place. "It's not rhymed, and it's not in a regular meter. And the lines are enjambed. It's much more visual than it is aural. It doesn't work right when you read it aloud and can't see it."

"Enjambed? What's enjambed mean? Are you trying to snow me with scholarly lingo here, Professor? Do you want me to use some financial terms on you, see who can out-nomenclature each other while the eggplant cooks?"

"Enjambment," David said in a careful tone, "is the running of a syntactical unit across the end of the line so that the endstops don't occur at the strong position in the line."

"Explain that explanation, Professor," Celia said, turned now to face him as she leaned against the counter, holding a wooden spoon in her hand, as though about to focus the attention of an orchestra. "What is it again, and pray tell me what is this strong position in the line business?"

"The strong positions are the beginning and the end of lines," David said. "But the end is the strongest of them all."

"Read the rest of it," Celia said. "Read all of the travel poem about Amsterdam. Let me hear all the poet has to say about Amsterdam and the depths and the water and the old masters."

"No," David said. "I've already told you the enjambment works against the sense of the line. It's hard to tell what follows what when you just hear it told to you. You have to see it. The context is crucial, Sweetie. It means everything, Nothing means anything unless you understand the context. That makes it clear. It explains and justifies. You can't just pull one single thing out of its environment and expect it to mean anything."

"It's clear all right," Celia said in the tone of someone accustomed to balance sheets. "Especially the woman you see standing by the booth full of tulips. And her stamens reflected in the water."

"It wasn't like that," David said. "It's just a verbal construct, some words on a page, arranged as the poet wants it. It doesn't mean anything outside its own being."

"Let me hear what slant Martha Foster puts on it, David," Celia said. The eggplant cubes were rolling in the boiling water on the stove, and the steam rising in a cloud. "Let Martha's poem tell me how it really was with the two of you and the flower girl in the hands of the old masters. I've heard your reading of that poetic moment. I want another one. Say the next line aloud."

"It's enjambed, I tell you," David said, looking down at the poem written by his first wife, the lines jagged and scattered against the white space of the page, straining against the control of meaning. "It doesn't mean what it sounds like."

"Let me read it to you," Celia said, taking the book from David's hand. "You listen to me while I take care of the enjambment."

The cooking eggplant cubes rolled and simmered toward softness and dissolving, sinking and losing definition in the pot as the steam rose toward the wall from where the scrabbling noise came again, a small sound in a dark hollow space. Celia read the next line aloud. "Liar, this is the city we didn't hate. This is the woman we took to our bed."

"Wait, no. That was a different time. And that was in a different city."

"And I guess next you're going to say 'and besides the whore is dead.'"

No, Celia, David said to himself, knowing she wouldn't listen if he spoke aloud. It's not real. It's just a poem. The strength of the line doesn't matter, not at all, not at all, when there's no context, only enjambment. It's nothing but that. The sense of the line is lost, lost for good.

BLOOD COUSIN

I woke recently from a dream about my cousin, Winston, a relative I haven't thought about in years. I woke the way you do when you're trying to escape a nightmare, a situation so disturbingly dire and real that your mind tells you to find a way to leave it as soon as possible. It's only a dream, you want to be able to say. This is not really happening. I'm not here. I'm in my bed asleep, and if I try hard enough I'll be conscious again in a place where I'm not dreaming.

I jerked awake, in a cool room with covers over me and my wife asleep beside me, and I waited for the calm of reality to reassure that all was well, no matter what my unconscious mind was telling me. The after effects of the dream lasted, though, much longer than ordinary, and even after I'd gone back to sleep, something worked inside me to remind of where I had been and how badly I had wanted to leave that place.

In the dream, Winston and I possessed a stolen car, a luxury auto of some sort, massive, sleek and dark in color, and we were in a parking garage planning how we'd convert what we had into cash. My cousin had stolen the car, but I had arranged the theft and now I was terribly afraid I'd be found out. In the dream I was conscious of being myself in my current situation in life, a dean of a college with a reputation and social status to protect. A black man was there in the garage, colluding with us in this criminal act. He had jerri curls, a ruined face, and he reeked of danger.

Winston was himself, as I had last seen him, a day over twenty years ago when he had come to my father's funeral in East Texas in a cemetery named Menard Chapel where members of the Holt family have been buried for generations, all the way back to the first family member in Texas, Winston's and my great-grandfather who had come to the state from Louisiana after his participation in the Civil War. He had become a Baptist preacher after the war, he founded the church at Menard Chapel, and he spawned a large family.

Winston and I were the only sons of two brothers of the clan. I was four or five years older than Winston, and my first memory of him is as a child in my family's house in Nederland, a town on the Texas Gulf Coast. He had been left for my mother to look after, and he had a cold so severe that snot was running down his face as he stood in our living room, looking up at me, his older cousin, and trying to snuffle stuff back into his head.

"Look at Winston," I said to my mother. "Fix him. He's all messed up."

She tended to that, and I left the room, not wanting to be around somebody who looked like him, who was so repulsive and who wanted to follow me around in such a leaking condition.

Our family moved a lot, from one rent house to another in whatever location in the petro-chemical area of Texas my father could find work, and Winston's family was worse in that respect than we were. My sightings of Joseph Winston Holt were scattered and infrequent, but always memorable, due largely to the fact that his father, my father's brother and my Uncle Lewis, was a notorious drunk, liable to show up at any time of the day or night at the homes of his brothers and sisters in search of somewhere to lay his head and particularly to look for something to drink. Often he had Winston with him.

Uncle Lewis's only son was the fifth child born in the family, and his arrival was so momentous to Uncle Lewis – a boy at last, after the succession of daughters Emily, Betty, Doris, and Nola Mae – that he was given a special name. It wasn't until I was well along in my education that I realized why my cousin was named Joseph Winston, and I was amazed to recognize the source of his first and middle names. He was born during one of the monumental diplomatic meetings of the Allies during World War II, and the name chosen for him by his father came from those of Joseph Stalin and Winston Churchill in light of their gathering with Roosevelt in Yalta to divide up Europe on the verge of the Allied victory over Germany.

Winston's naming was Faulknerian, I came to realize, akin to the sardonic name slapped on the character Wall Street Panic Snopes by the novelist in one of his lesser books, and it reflected not thought, but a desire by an ignorant parent to lend an infant significance by labeling the child after a stray element in the Zeitgeist. It would have been embarrassingly laughable to anyone with a semblance of education and awareness, but that fact did not apply in the case of Lewis Holt, father of Joseph Winston. The names he chose for his only son sounded important, even august, I imagine, to him, and he intended by the naming of his son to bestow a mark of due respect and an homage to greatness by the act.

Joseph Winston had been singled out, and he had the label to prove it. He didn't realize that fact, but those in the social classes above him could be mildly entertained by what he was called, if they happened to notice it. That amusement of his superiors would be an expression of contempt for him and his kind, but he was not likely ever to know that.

I was around Winston, off and on, until my family moved

from the Gulf Coast to the pine barrens of Polk County in East Texas after my father lost his job with the Sun Oil Company and retreated to his home ground to sulk and plot vengeance. It wasn't until after we returned to the Golden Triangle, so-called, eight or nine years later, that I saw Winston for more than a couple of hours at a time.

My family, brought low by my father's inability to find regular work at a living wage, came back to Nederland so that my father could seek employment in a place that had jobs, and we stayed for a couple of weeks with Uncle Lewis and Aunt Myrtie and their children still at home. Those were Virginia Anne and Winston. Ginny Anne was a child still, but Winston had grown into a rangy, wide-shouldered youth, hungry for a different kind of food, real and metaphorical.

"Winston," I said to him soon after we'd moved in, "will your daddy let us use his lawn mower to go around and ask folks if we can cut their grass and make some money?"

"I don't see why not," my cousin said. "He ain't going to be using it."

We took off every morning then with a gas can and the beat-up rotary mower, walking the streets of Nederland, Texas, and looking for unmowed yards. Sure enough, we found a few people, old ladies living alone mainly with a few younger ones with husbands who either didn't own a mower or wouldn't use it, willing to hire us to mow their weedy San Augustine grass filled yards. Our most likely takers, we soon learned, were on the low end of the economic scale of the city, and they didn't want to pay much.

The nicer looking yards belonged to people who gave us hard looks and short answers, no matter how badly their grass needed cutting, and we quickly learned to judge our low likelihood of success with this class of people and to keep moving when we saw signs of affluence. A nice car parked in the driveway, matching curtains in the windows, houses neatly painted, well-dressed children, women whose hair showed signs of having been messed with in beauty parlors, unbroken toys in the yard, planted flowers in beds.

A typical rate for a grass cutting of the yards of people who would hire us was two or three dollars, and as soon as we got paid for a job, we took a break from employment by going to the drugstore. There we bought milk shakes, candy bars, and Pall Mall cigarettes. We chose that brand because it provided smokes that were longer and stronger than most others. We repaired then to the closest empty lot, ate our candy, smoked our cigarettes, and talked about what we'd do when we were old enough to escape home and live on our own.

"You know one thing I will have," Winston once told me, puffing hard on his Pall Mall, and taking hits off a quart sized Coke, "once I get grown?"

"What?" I said, drawing my own dose of smoke deep into my lungs and holding my cigarette the way James Dean did in *Rebel Without a Cause*. "What's that, Winston?"

"I will have my goddamn cigarettes, that's what," he said. "As many as I want to."

"You're goddamn right," I said and flipped my butt into the street. "Let's see if that old lady on Detroit Street will let us cut her grass again. It's as high as my knees."

What we really wanted was access to beer, but that was hard to come by. At age sixteen, I had already been introduced to the pleasures of alcohol by my cousin on my mother's side of the family, Addison Irwin in Maryland. I realized vaguely that I was to Addison Irwin, an older cousin from real people as opposed to the Holt bunch, as Winston was to me, but I didn't let myself think about that at the time. The comparison made me uncomfortable. If Addison considered my status and worth in the light I considered Winston's, I was on shaky ground. I didn't like the terms of the equation, and the way it figured socially, given the conditions of the relationship.

I knew one thing clearly, though. I would never want Addison, my exalted cousin, to meet Winston, my low class one, or to know I was related to someone like him. In the meantime, though, I liked cutting grass with Winston, eating sweets and smoking cigarettes with the money we made from our efforts, and having him look up to me as older, wiser, and more sophisticated. I wanted and needed the unconditional approval he gave me, and I would take all of that he had to offer. He thought I was something, though I and the rest of the world knew different.

My family went back to East Texas later that summer, but in a few months my father did find a job on the Gulf Coast, working for the City of Nederland in the Streets and Alleys Department (which meant picking up garbage and digging ditches), and we moved out of the pine barrens for good. By that time I was in my senior year of high school, and Winston was living with his family in a town named Fannett, twenty or so miles from where we were located.

I finished high school, enrolled as a commuter student at Lamar State College of Technology in Beaumont (a third rate institution called by its students Pecker Tech because its mascot was the Cardinal and because we all knew why we were there rather than at the University of Texas or Texas A&M or some other real college), and I had little reason to be around Winston, my young cousin living in the sticks.

But then Uncle Lewis moved his clan back to Nederland, Winston enrolled in the high school, which had been a power in Texas school boy football for years, and he proved to be a defensive end of note. One of the coaches told me years later what made Winston so formidable at his position.

"When we played any team," he said, "they would run Winston's end sometime early on in the game. Let me tell you, hoss, once they ran it that one time, they didn't run it again for the rest of the game."

"He was that good?" I said.

"He was that mean," the coach said. "He wasn't that big, but nobody could stop him from getting to the ball carrier. He would do whatever it took to get there."

"And he took the ball carrier down."

"Winston Holt took it as a personal insult that somebody carrying a football would try to get around his end of the line. He made that back pay his dues."

Winston got enough public notice in that football crazed part of the world that people at Lamar began asking me if I was kin to him, and I allowed that I was. I even invited him to come to a retreat held by the fraternity to which I belonged, a collection of people too poor financially or ethnically or intellectually to be members of any other social organization, even of the ones at Lamar. We had Japanese in the fraternity, and Arabs, and dolts, and others recognized to be misfits of many stripes and colors. But we did wear fraternity pins, and have meetings, and we did get drunk every chance we got.

Winston was a great hit at the fraternity retreat, held on someone's abandoned farm north of Beaumont in the palmettos and pines, and fueled with kegs of beer and random bottles of cheap liquor. At age sixteen, he drank with the best of them, not falling down and not throwing up, telling jokes and stories about playing football, and making his older cousin proud of him, a football end for the Nederland Bulldogs, destined to be recruited to play for a real university in the Southwest Conference someday.

That drunken weekend in and around the only building still standing on an abandoned and overgrown farm in Jefferson County, Texas, a tin roofed barn full of drunken college boys, proved to be the height of Winston Holt's public regard and career, in my estimation, as I look back over the years.

Within a month's time, Winston's father moved his family north to Corrigan, a played out sawmill town in rumpsprung Polk County, and he took Winston with him. The head coach of the Nederland football team begged Lewis Holt to allow Winston to remain in the high school and on the team (which would have been illegal, but we're talking Nederland Bulldog football), living with him and his family in a subdivision tract house, in progress and on course to play out his eligibility and have a shot at attendance at a big time Texas university where use might be found for him on the defensive end of some line in a large stadium in autumns to come.

My uncle would not allow that separation of his only son from the family, called on all the ties of kinship which bound his boy to him, and obliterated any chance for Joseph Winston Holt to escape the fate laid down for him by circumstance and blood. Winston listened to his father, accompanied the family to Corrigan, played football there in the obscurity of smalltime East Texas, and dropped out of high school in his senior year, assuring that no ray of light would ever chance to fall upon him again.

The next time I saw Winston was at my mother's funeral at Menard Chapel in 1961. I was newly married, in graduate school out of state, and Winston was working as a journeyman carpenter in the Beaumont area. He came up to me as soon as I arrived in the procession of cars escorting my mother's coffin into the woods of East Texas. He was wider in the shoulders than ever, rangy in the leg, and he was with a young pregnant blonde whose bra size looked to be larger than her IQ.

"Calvin," Winston said, embracing me. "Aunt Dorothy was always so good to me when I was a kid and would come to y'all's house .This here is Jeanette. We're going to get married, I guess." And then to the blonde, "This here is my cousin Calvin, Jeanette. He's studying to be a college professor."

"Hidy," Jeanette said, staring over my shoulder at the woods behind me, proving that I was still not attractive to Texas women with big breasts. Talking to Winston, I was pained to see that his teeth had gotten bad, decay clearly visible on a couple of incisors, and more painful than that to me was that Winston was aware of the fact, holding his mouth funny and throwing a hand up to hide his teeth when he smiled or laughed.

"I bet you can't guess how much money I made last year," Winston said at one point, "contracting to build kitchen cabinets in new houses."

"How much?" I said, and then naming a figure I thought would be low enough to give him bragging rights when he answered the question he'd put to me, "six thousand?"

"I made over eleven thousand dollars," my cousin said. "And that was only what I had to declare to the government because of the paper they had on it. I really made a couple of more."

"Damn, Winston," I said, truly amazed at the amount of his earnings in that year of 1961, "you're really making out all right."

He beamed, even forgetting to hide his teeth in his pride. During the funeral itself, Winston sat by me as I wept and mourned the death of my mother from cancer at age fifty-two, and I was glad to have him to lean on, literally and metaphorically that cold gray day in November on the burying ground of Menard Chapel.

It was not until several years later that I heard of Winston again. I was living in Nashville, teaching at Vanderbilt University, when my sister called me to bring me up on Holt family news. "Too bad about Winston," she said. "I guess you heard already."

"What? Is Winston dead?" I said, imagining a car wreck or an accident at work, something involving sudden violence and blood and finality.

"He might as well be," Nancy said. "He's about to go to the penitentiary in Huntsville. I don't know for how long, but it's got to be for years."

"What did he do?" I asked, knowing Nancy would string out her telling of the tale for dramatic effect, true to the narrative sense of the Holt family, a clan relishing stories of disaster, loss, and abandonment. "Did he get caught robbing somebody?"

"No, Calvin," my sister said, exasperated at my leap to conclusion. "My goodness. Winston would never steal anything from anybody. He killed a couple of black guys outside some honky tonk up in the Big Thicket, that's what."

"He shot them?"

"No, good lord. Winston wouldn't shoot anybody or stab them or anything like that. They got into some kind of argument or something inside the honky tonk and when Winston went outside and got into his pickup to leave, these guys were waiting for him, I guess to beat him up, and Winston ran over them with the truck."

"And they put him in prison for murder for that? It wasn't called self defense?"

"I guess Winston could've got off with something like that, if that was all there was to it. But the thing is, see, after he knocked them down with the pickup, he backed up and ran over them again two or three times. That showed premeditation, the way the jury and judge saw it."

"Jesus," I said. "And now he's in the pen. How stupid could he have been?"

"I expect he was drunk, too," Nancy said. "Not just stupid. So our cousin is a convict. How do you like that?"

"I don't," I said. "I don't like it at all."

"I'm not going to visit him, either," Nancy said. "Are you?"

"How could I? I live in Tennessee."

"I'm just not going to think about it, my cousin in the pen," my sister said. "I've got enough on my mind as it."

"Me too, Nancy," I said, "me too."

After then, I went back to Texas many times over the years for visits and anniversaries and graduations and deaths, but I never tried to see Winston in the state penitentiary in Huntsville, and I never asked any member of the family for any news about him. What news could there be? He had killed two men, been convicted and sentenced to confinement, and to think about him in that situation was something I would not allow myself to do. How would he look at me if I visited him in some special room for that in the prison? What would he say to me? What would he expect me to say back to him? What would he need from me that I was not prepared to give? Did he believe I had resources inside me that I could call on? I didn't think so. I didn't believe I did, no matter what my cousin might think.

I didn't want to have to try to summon up anything responsive to Winston's emotional need. I didn't want to discover what was inside me. Or what wasn't. I suspected I knew already how I would act, and I didn't want to admit that I could not and would not do my cousin any good in this time of his greatest need.

After getting credit for good time served, Winston was released early from the Texas State Penitentiary in Huntsville on a probationary status, and he returned to his work as a carpenter. I learned about his release indirectly, and I didn't try to find out where he was living and what he was doing. I did not want to contact him. I had told the woman who was my wife at the time about him, about my growing up with him, and what happened to put him in prison, and she made me swear not to let such a relative know anything about where we were living, where I worked, and who she was.

"Just what we need," she said. "A convicted murderer showing up in Gambier, Ohio, looking to establish old family ties."

I agreed with her, imagining Winston asking around Kenyon College in a search for his cousin. He'd be toothless, I figured, dressed in keeping with his social status, driving either a wreck of a car or a new pickup, and eager to see me. That reminder of my family and my origins I didn't need and could not have borne. I just won't think about him, I told myself. Winston couldn't find me anyway, and he'd never appear at my door, expecting me to respond to him as an older cousin from East Texas ought to do by reason of blood ties and memory.

I was right. Winston never wrote me, never called me, and never came to my door. I was never put to that test of blood. I did hear about him, intermittently, though, again from my sister who had also risen socially and economically, in her case by marriage to a successful computer programmer in Houston.

"Calvin," she said one night in a phone call, "guess what Winston did when he got back home to Buna?"

"Violated probation?" I said. "Ran over some more people? Stuck up a convenience store?"

"You know he's not like that. He wouldn't commit a crime. No, what he did was find out that that wife of his, Jeanette, had been messing around with Johnny Pauling while Winston was in the pen, and he beat the hell out of him. Broke the bones around one of Johnny's eye sockets. That's all he did."

"Johnny Pauling?" I said, "Betty's husband?"

Betty was one of Winston's sisters, and it was in her home

with her husband Johnny that Winston had been directed to stay by the Texas State Department of Corrections while he served out his probation. His wife Jeanette had been living there with her two children by Winston while he was in Huntsville. I was not surprised to learn that Johnny had put a move on his brother-in-law's wife or that she had responded to him. The only thing out of the ordinary, I considered, was that Johnny had been stupid enough to think he could get away with it. He was not thinking at all, obviously. As my father would have said, Johnny was thinking with the little head.

"Did Johnny put the law on Winston?" I said. "Will the probation people send Winston back to the pen?"

"I don't expect Winston has anything to worry about from Johnny Pauling," my sister said. "Johnny knows what would happen to him if he breathed a word to anybody that could get Winston put back inside."

"Is Winston still staying at Betty's and Johnny's?" I said, knowing Nancy was right about Johnny Pauling taking his beating in silence. One would be enough.

"Winston has to until he gets permission to go off to live on his own, but that wife is gone now."

"Did Winston beat her up?"

"No," Nancy said in a disgusted tone. "You know Holts don't hit women. They've not been raised like that."

"No," I agreed. "A Holt from East Texas will not physically whip up on a woman. He'll just wreak havoc on her mind."

Yet years later when I saw Winston for what I think will be the final time, he was still living with his sister Betty and her husband Johnny Pauling, together somewhere in a small house in a dying town on the Gulf Coast. As usual, that encounter with Winston took place at a funeral, the only event that ever draws all the extended Holt family together, this one the burial of my father in Menard Chapel with the rest of the clan and their connections by marriage and happenstance.

I was even more of a curiosity to them than ever by then,

though I had always been an oddity among the Holt bunch, as we were known in Polk County, Texas. As a child, I was strange because I stuttered and talked at a hyperactive rate, I spent most of my time reading, impervious to calls for attention by other people, I was not athletic like most of my rangy, self-confident, supple cousins, people who shrugged off physical pain and emotional slights as they fought for possession of various kinds of balls, earning approval and admiration in the process. I was easily dissuaded, subject to fears and extended expressions of them, not prepared to be knocked down and get up again with blood in my mouth and the intention to get payback for injury.

My father's funeral was not nearly so riven with depression and foreboding for me as had been my mother's. When she died, she did so from cancer at age fifty two, leaving a twelve year old daughter to be raised alone by my father, a man supremely unsuited for such a task. I was in my first year of graduate school, my bipolar wife pregnant with our first child, no financial prospects in view, my older sister Nancy living in Seattle with her husband in a time when air flight to and from Texas and paying for it were comparable to sending a man to the moon. I was alone.

The time had been November, leafless, wet, and dark. The coffin was cheap, and it was open for all to see my mother dead inside it. She had not wanted to be buried in those woods, as she called the graveyard, and she had asked me to promise her she wouldn't be. But that's where my father put her, since it was free of charge. The preacher for my mother's service was a cousin ordained as a Baptist minister, trying his best to justify what God had chosen to do by subjecting Aunt Dorothy to such suffering and early death.

On that desperate day in 1961, I wept and staggered about the graveyard physically supported by Cousin Winston as he tried to speak consoling words into my ear. He repeated my name over and over as though to convince me I was still myself, capable to survive the day and meet the others to come, unknown and perilous as they might be.

At the funeral service for my father, dead at eighty-seven, by then I was secure in my work. I was dean of Rhodes College in Memphis, I was the father of two accomplished and educated children, I was married to the woman right for me, I owned property, and I held title to university degrees and to professional respect. I had not been in my home country for longer than a day or two at a time in almost thirty years. I had worked myself free of the place I had come from, and I was only technically a member of that Holt bunch in Polk County, Texas.

Yet when I saw Joseph Winston Holt standing in the shade of a sycamore at Menard Chapel on that hot day in August, I knew him instantly. And he knew me.

I was wearing a pin stripe suit and a dark tie, chosen from my closet by my wife because it was right for a funeral. She was not there, but back in our home in Memphis, because I didn't want her to see in one gathering in one place the clan of people I belonged to. She had expected to accompany me, since that was what family members of her class did in Alabama when someone died.

"You wouldn't like it," I told her. "You don't want to meet those people."

"What's to like or not like at a funeral?" she said. "Wives go with their husbands to the funerals of their husbands' parents. Don't they?"

"They all do go all right. All of the family goes. That's the problem. If they didn't go, I could take you with me. But they do go, and that's why I can't bear to have you there."

"Something's badly wrong," she said.

"Oh, yes. Badly wrong."

"With you, I mean," she had said.

Standing under the sycamore tree, old when our great-grandfather preached at Menard Chapel, Winston looked at me with a quizzical tilt to his head, waiting to see if I would recognize him. He was wearing a blue jean jacket, a striped shirt, khaki pants, and his sleeked back hair was showing signs of graying. Next to him were his sister Betty and her husband Johnny Pauling, the man who had seduced Winston's wife while he was in prison. All had been forgiven or at least forgotten. The wife and children were long gone, but the Holt sister and brother were together.

"Winston," I said, and we embraced for the first time in our lives, such demonstrations of affection and relationship not having been cool those years ago in the middle of the century. I greeted Betty and her husband, and Johnny reminded me of when he had fixed something gone wrong with my 1952 Dodge, a broken windshield wiper which had to function for me to be able to get a license plate. We laughed and joked, as people in East Texas do at funerals for the dead old enough to be considered to have had a long life. My mother had not been that age, but my father was. The tone of the service was different, as a result, and my cousins felt free to josh and pick at me.

I remember two exchanges from that day, apart from my talk with Winston. Both were with Richardson brothers, first cousins to me and older by a couple of decades, both were basketball stars in high school and college, and both had careers as coaches of the sport.

Jesse Lee, the greater of the two in reputation and at one point coach of the basketball team in my high school, said to a group of relatives gathered around me in the graveyard, "Y'all might not know this, but Calvin tried to play basketball in high school."

"Naw," one of my aunts said, "Calvin was always a book worm. He wasn't interested in ball."

"Yes, he was," Jesse Lee Richardson, onetime Texas all state center, said. "He was a book worm, all right, but he wanted and tried to play basketball. Didn't you, Calvin?"

"I did," I admitted. "Jesse Lee's right, but I wasn't any good."

"He couldn't play a lick," my cousin said. "But look at him now. He is a self-made man, if anybody ever was."

A little later in the day, after the service was over, and people had begun to drift away to drive back to town, the other brother, Wilson, asked me if I could hire him to coach basketball at Rhodes College. "I know how to handle inner city black players, Calvin," he said. "That's what y'all use in Memphis, and it takes special handling to get anything out of them."

I told Wilson to send his resume to my office, though I had nothing to do with hiring coaches and Rhodes College was an institution for upper class white students who couldn't get into the likes of Vanderbilt and Duke, not a place for inner city blacks to run up and down the basketball court. He never did, and I knew he wouldn't, since getting a resume together would have involved writing something down on paper.

Winston and I talked about the time I had taken him to the drunken Lamar fraternity retreat, about our cutting grass together to be able to buy cigarettes and ice cream, and finally he brought up the subject lurking behind all we were saying to each other.

"Calvin," he said, just after telling me that the most important thing my father, his Uncle Willie, had taught him was the use of Copenhagen snuff in the place of cigarettes, "I guess you heard about me and them niggers."

I couldn't look him in the eye after he had said that. Not because he had called the men he had killed the term he used, the epithet for blacks still the only designation current in that place and with its people, but because I didn't want him to tell me about it. I did not want to know the details, I did not want to hear his story, I did not want his version of reality to be offered me. Let all I knew about it just be what my sister had told me during our telephone conversations over the years. "Winston killed some black men. He ran over them with his truck. He's in the penitentiary. He's out now. He beat up Johnny Pauling for taking his wife to bed. He's living with Betty and Johnny now."

"I did hear that, Winston," I said. "I was sorry to hear about it."

Winston looked at my face, trying to get me to meet his gaze, and at that moment, our cousin Jewel walked up to join what she thought was an ordinary conversation in the graveyard at Menard Chapel. It was not that. It was a confession, a remembrance, a reminder of blood, a plea for kinship. It was all that I did not want.

I jumped on the chance to accept the definition of the moment as Jewel imagined it to be, turning away from Winston's eyes and looking into hers.

"Jewel," I said. "Remember when you used to read to me when I was a kid? You would read whole novels to me and Nancy while we sat on the floor listening."

"I do remember," she said. "I can't believe now we all had the patience for that. Or the energy."

"It was a different time," I said, desperate to change the focus from what Winston had been wanting to say to me. "Kids wouldn't sit still for that now, would they?"

"No, they wouldn't," Jewel said. "What were y'all talking about when I walked up? Don't let me interrupt."

"Jewel," Winston said, his eyes still on me, "Calvin and I were just talking about the old days."

"The old days. What do you two boys know about the old days?"

"Yeah, Calvin was real important to me when I was a kid."

"How was that?" Jewel said.

"Calvin taught me how to be bad," Winston said. "That's what he did for me. He was my model. He let me know how to be bad."

"Winston," Jewel said in a tone of dismissal and shock, "Surely not. You shouldn't say things like that. Don't make jokes. Calvin did not teach you how to be bad."

There in the graveyard at Menard Chapel, my father newly placed at rest in the earth for the long sleep that never ends, my kin all around the three of us, I knew in my bones and blood which of the three cousins was telling the truth. It was not the retired schoolteacher. It was not the college dean. It was the convicted slaughterer of men, the boy who had pushed a lawn mower alongside me through the streets of Nederland, Texas, those years ago in the bright past, grown now into the only speaker of truth on that burying ground.

That recent dream about Winston and me from which I woke, that scene of him and me and a black man involved in a criminal act, had broken at the point where Winston was being led away in handcuffs. Just before he turned to enter the police car, he looked at me and made a gesture with his manacled hands, a sign of the kind you can interpret and believe only in dreams, since the waking world is never clearly seen. What he meant by the gesture was that he would take the blame. I was not to be afraid. I would not be found out. My cousin would be the sacrifice. In the dream I was grateful to my cousin, and I was determined to let him shoulder all burden of guilt. I would walk free, unsoiled and whole and in the light of day. He would dwell in darkness and shame.

When I woke, I told myself that it was only a dream. It did not pertain to my life in this waking world, and it would slide away into obscurity, fade into nothing, as the days wear on. I will likely never see Winston again. I have never been complicit with him in anyway. I never taught him anything. He has nothing to do with me. It's all an accident of blood relationship. It will fade, it will vanish, it will go.

It has not.

Win/Place/Show

"That little bitch looks fast," she says, nodding toward a lemon-colored dog standing close to the leg of its handler, a black kid in a burnt orange T shirt. "It's not too heavy to run."

He watches her watching the dog and doesn't say anything until she looks over at him and then back at the lemon bitch.

"Is that better, you think?" he says. "Not heavy? Not heavy can mean not strong, right?"

"I wouldn't know," she says. "I go by looks, not theories."

"You go by names," he says. "Whatever sounds cute."

"You bastard," she says just as her nephew walks up. He's her sister's boy from Florida, just graduated and jobless. He's in Memphis, wanting her to help him get on at Federal Express, where she's an expediter on the line. His problems are that numbers make him dizzy and he's so homesick for Jacksonville that he sobs himself to sleep every night on the sofa where he sleeps in their den. They've taken him to the Southland Grayhound Park across the river in Arkansas to watch the dogs, bet a few dollars, maybe even win a little. There's always the chance. She's just found out her husband's been having a thing with a girl at work. The girl's divorced, two kids, big bills, all of it.

"Go buy us all a beer, Ronnie," he says to the nephew and gives him a ten. "Coors Light for you, honey?"

He looks over at his wife who's still studying the number on the blanket on the lemon-colored dog.

"Whatever," she says. "Yeah, Coors."

"Light?"

"Yes," she says. "Jesus. Coors Light."

It's time to put them in the starting boxes, so the black kid pulls the lemon dog away and joins the other handlers who are putting their dogs into the enclosed metal pens. A few try to stay out, like always, and the handlers have to push against them with their knees and feet until they're all inside and the automatic doors close with a bang. All the dogs bark and yip and will until the doors jerk open to start the race.

When the loudspeaker comes on to announce the race, the fifth of the night, you can't hear the noise of the dogs any more, and the mechanical rabbit comes flying around the rail, going like blazes, and when it's just in front of the dog boxes, the announcer says "Here comes Rusty," in a drawn-out, excited way, and the doors open together so that everybody at Southland Grayhound Park in West Memphis can scream with one voice.

By the time Ronnie gets back with the Coors Light, the race is over and the lemon dog has come in second.

"Did you bet her?" the husband asks.

"Yes," she says. "What do you think? That's why I'm here."

"To show or to place?"

"Not to show and not to place," she says. "To win."

"You always try for too much," he says and sips the Coors.

She doesn't answer and walks off to look at the next group of dogs being brought up by their black handlers. She wants to pick out a light fast mover, one that won't get left at the gate or jump over the fence before the race is through, or get shouldered out by something heavier.

"Find a good one," he calls out. "Something cute."

When the last race is run, they'll get in the front seat of the car and Ronnie will get in the back, and they'll join the hundreds of people looking for a lane back to the interstate out of Arkansas. A few will have fender-benders in the parking lot, but there probably won't be a real wreck or breakdown until the Southland crowd hits the approaches to the Hernando DeSoto Bridge to Tennessee. Nothing major.

Later that night while Ronnie is trying not to think about Florida and getting on at Federal Express and finally be able to fall asleep, he'll hear his aunt call her husband terrible names as they undress to lie down together again back across the river, there in the king-sized bed, home in Memphis.

YOU WILL NEED ONE EGG

I will tell you what gets me about this situation. It is not the fact that Kevin is going through a phase of acting out and seeking attention. I figure that comes with the territory. After all, my little boy has just turned thirteen, and according to all the experts those hormones are just raging through his system, making him do things that are not really part of his personality and his upbringing. So, all right, he locks himself in his room and drags his chest of drawers across the floor to barricade the door. And he won't let us in until his father breaks through the door and pushes the chest out of the way. He's done that twice now in the last week, and it is getting old. Why even fix the lock any more if it has to be broken every third day?

He will not do his English homework. He has singled the subject of English out for failure. Why that, I do not know. He will,

however, do all his assignments in the rest of his eighth grade classes, he's turned vegetarian, and he wears sunglasses morning, noon,
and night and even when he's sleeping. I've seen that when I sneak
into his room after I can tell he's gone to bed. He has made a little
arrangement with a rubber band to keep his glasses on even when
he might turn over and flop around in the bed. He always was a
restless child, even back when he was a baby, knocking his head
against the crib when he was asleep and later when he had graduated to his own bed, he would just hammer his little head against
the wall where the bed was shoved up against it.

So he's asserting his independence and marking out territorial
limits for his sense of self. What's wrong with that, pray tell me? It's
simply something Kevin is going through, medicated though he is,
and we need to give it room to work its way out. That's the way I
see it, anyway, and I'm an educated and experienced woman. The
other day I counted up how many jobs I have held, full and part
time, starting as a teenager in high school, then in college, and
then after Bertram and I got married in Little Rock, then moved to
Texas and then to Salt Lake when he got transferred. Thirteen was
the number I came up with.

That is not a small number, in anybody's book. And some of
them lasted almost as long as a year, too, I'll have any busy-body
know, especially Bertram's father and that step-mother he's married to. Even now with the excellent salary Bertram makes, though
it doesn't go far enough, I would be the first to admit, I am present-
ly on permanent call for a small firm as executive assistant. Sometimes I will work as much as nine hours a week when Suzanne has
need for me, and if she ever gets a client again, there'll be a lot more
than that she'll be requiring from me.

What I'm really doing is waiting for that to happen, her client
list growing from where it is now to at least one signed on, and
then I'll just tell her I've got to have a promotion if she expects me
to continue contributing my insights and expertise. The problem
with her now, as I see it, is that she's not motivated to get ahead, to
do something, to dream of what might be and make it happen. She

has just let herself go physically, to the point now where she wears big smocks and mu mus most of the day. Of course when she rides that horse she keeps in the paddock behind her and her husband's place there in the valley, she puts on a blue overall outfit, but even that looks like it's about to burst at the seams when she mounts up on Thunder Girl for a canter.

I'm waiting my time on that new client business, and I'm not about to let my investment of commitment and mental energy on behalf of Blue Doll, Inc just slip away through impatience. I can wait out anybody or anything when I put my mind to it. I am the soul of biding my time. And I'm not about to look for other employment while things at Blue Doll, Inc keep wallowing along. What if I took a job elsewhere and then Suzanne found that client we've been waiting for? There I'd be doing prep at Godfather's Pizza, chopping onions and peppers and sausage rolls and being on my feet all day when I could be sitting in an air conditioned office talking on the phone to business reps making pitches to Blue Doll.

Nope. Not this girl. Nuh uh. I will wait and reap the benefits of patience, and Bertram can heave long sighs until he turns blue in the face in the meantime. I will not be badgered and bluffed into taking a job beneath me. I am a college graduate, and I am owed big time for the work I've put in to get to where I am. I will above all things not betray the trust and confidence of my poor mother, recently deceased, in me and what she knew I could do.

She was a Southern lady, a person of style and elegance and grace, and my boys did get to know her for the first several years of their lives before she was taken from us. I am eternally grateful for that blessing which will color all their lives, whether they realize it or not.

Of course, she loved her wine and cocktails, and she was drunk most every night that rolled, and sometimes even in the middle of the day, considering the time of the year it happened to be. Christmas, New Year's, Thanksgiving, Independence Day, Derby Day, her birthday and mine and the boys, to list a few. I've left some out, I'm sure. Not Bertram's birthday, though. Birthdays for men don't mean much, and he doesn't even know how old he is. If I were to walk up to him today and ask how long he'd been in this world, he'd be likely to be off by a year or two either direction.

Now, Mother, or as I taught Kevin and Roland to call her, Grand MaMa, with equal emphasis on both syllables of MaMa and a continental value to the vowel a in Grand, she knew always to the minute how old she was, how old I was, events such as what dates she went to the Peabody Hotel Roof Terrace in Memphis to a fraternity ball with Townsend Daughball or Luke Lanier when she was a student at Millsaps and dating boys from Ole Miss every weekend of the school year, the date when she was installed in the Kappa Kappa Gamma chapter at Millsaps, and any other occasion of significance in her life. It was a full one, her life, and she lived it to the limit. She documented in her diaries all of it that she could remember or was aware of.

She even renamed herself, as a girl not ten years old, changing it from the family one her mother gave her, Mattie Lou, if you can believe that, to Maureen Louise. She went by the nickname Mo when she was in college.

She would act out, though, when she had had a little too much to handle of an evening or afternoon. I must admit that, and I am not embarrassed to do so. She came of a class and a time when attractive, talented, vivacious Southern women had a good time and led all around them to do the same. Alcohol was the depressant of choice in those days, and she remained loyal to that drug.

"Roseanne," she would tell me when the topic of drink arose, "when you're feeling a little uncertain as a woman, challenged in some way because maybe you think you're getting a little older than you want to admit to, or some other female in the room has the edge on you in years or looks or dress or quality of the man she's with, I have found over the years, and I'll swear to its merits, that a little sip or two of wine or the harder stuff will be a great enabler."

"An enabler?" I'd say, knowing what she meant but pretending I didn't because I loved my mother and wanted to give her every opportunity to perform, which she always did so well, "what do you mean by enabler, MaMa?"

"I mean a little help, dear," she would say, "in allowing you to lose the restraint of a dangerous lack of self confidence. When you doubt yourself, how can you expect others to do anything but dismiss or ignore you? So that little boost in esteem which a drink or two gives you is a blessing. It says directly to that old reptile part of the brain, that old naysayer, that it's time to let you strut your stuff. Speak up, be playful, be assertive, be witty, be charming, be what you're capable of being. Let's do it, lady."

Then she would smile, showing that wonderful expression of friendly self assurance she possessed in such abundance, turning her head to the side in that cute way she had, and anyone watching would know she was thinking positive thoughts as she sat there, her drink held so gracefully in her hand with her rings and bracelets sparkling in concert with her perfect nail job. "But," she would add, "you must be careful not to let the power of the drink take you too far. Control, control, control, that's the ticket."

I wished she had listened to her advice to me and taken it to heart more than she did, I've got to say. As she got further along in life's career . that's the way she would speak of what gross people call getting old . She did tend to let the drink take her further than was wise at times. You could always tell when she'd reached that point, of course, by the way she'd begin blinking too much and opening her mouth too wide when she'd talk. I hated to witness that, particularly when I'd be sitting at an angle which allowed me to see into her mouth, sometimes so far I could spot that little lump of flesh, that little organ that hangs down in the back of the oral cavity. When it started dangling in full view, my mother was either about to say something embarrassing or laugh too loud and long or start leaning up too tight against whichever man was close and convenient, no matter his age or his marital status or who he was with.

And after reaching that point of enablement, she would demand that music be put on or if it was already coming from a speaker in the room that it be turned up louder. "Let there be harmony," she'd say. "Put on something we can dance to, somebody. Let's have some fun." And then she'd grab some man's hand and lead him out into the middle of the room and start doing her dance thing in front of him, whether he was willing to move or not. I hated that.

But she's gone now, to a better place, I guess, according to what Christian teachings tell us, and I don't have to worry about what my mother might do next when she reaches her limit and gladly goes over it. Which she would do almost every time she got near the stuff.

No, now my problems don't include her, and I don't have to try to keep up with her any more. She was better looking than I am, as she always would tell anybody who was in range, whether they were listening or not. She was petite and well shaped and graceful, when she hadn't had too much to handle. And she was musically talented, she would say, to a degree that I'm not. "Roseanne," she would announce, "has not got one speck of musical talent. Oh, she's studied all right, and she's learned to play the piano the way a high school girl can who practices two hours a day. But it's all mechanical for her. I've got the spontaneous sense of rhythm and musicality, and she just hammers along one note at the time. But bless her heart, she does try. I don't have to try, on the contrary. It's a gift, and I've got it. Come on, somebody, get out on that floor with me. Let's dance!"

No, my problem now is with my sweet little love bug of a son, my second one, my baby, and my last one I'll ever have, I fear. I have just the two, both boys, and I love them to death, of course, and who wouldn't? But I've got to admit, I do wish I had a little girl, a sweetheart I could dress up in frills and lace and, as MaMa always called it, buttons and bows.

I say I don't have a daughter, and the situation argues that I never will have now, given my age and my and Bertram's financial and family situation, but I mean that in the physical sense only, what could be called the literal, the earthbound, the here and now as lived on the ground, which is to say where it's all rocks and desert vegetation and dry high mountain climate as we have in Salt Lake. All that's true. There is no daughter of mine in the sense of a being who has to be fed and have her diapers changed and baby teeth saved and her sent to school dressed real cute and all that day to day activity which just eats up a woman's time in her role as a mother.

But I will say this, and I know it is a truth, as real as that Play Station game the boys spend all their time on. I do have a daughter in another sense, a more real sense in a manner of speaking, and she is always with me. How do I know? How did it come to me that I do have a baby daughter in spite of what the literal minded among us would have us believe? How can I make that statement with such certainty? I will give the credit where it's due.

Ramona Spatts told me. She did more than that, I'll confess. She showed me that truth, and I'll believe it as long as I live on this earth, and I'll reap the benefits when I enter the world that comes after this one, this old flat earthly one where all the problems exist every hour of the day and night and just take up all your energy and strength.

I met Ramona at the first gathering of a bunch of people devoted to the realm of music, specifically to chamber groups. I am a flautist of some ability, no matter what my mother always said about my lack of talent, and I was sought out by a girl at church, just a real cute person, to meet with some people in Salt Lake who were interested in forming a group to play together, just for fun and fellowship, and if the chance arose, maybe some gigs at Christian churches, not LDS certainly, and weddings and what have you.

When I arrived at the home of Betsy Flummerfelt, a pretty blonde but with legs too big for her torso, that night I was a little late, and they were all off in the den already. So I was greeted at the door by a stranger, Ramona, a woman who I knew I had never encountered before, how could I have? Yet when she reached out her hand to me, I felt a spark of communication between us that seemed a memory rather than an introduction. Ramona felt it, too, need I say.

"You have a deep soul," she said to me, fixing me with that wonderful expression she possesses, that look which invites confidence and open sharing. "I feel it in the aura of your blood flow."

"My blood flow?" I said, looking down to see if I had a scratch on my hand or a bug bite or a wound or something. High mountain or not, Salt Lake is just full of biting insects except in the dead of winter, and it's a constant struggle to keep your hands nice. I have the bills for hand care to prove it.

"The pulse of your heartbeat," this wonderful and mysterious woman said. "What loss have you experienced recently? Has there been a death in your family?"

That was well before MaMa was taken from me, so I couldn't think of anybody who'd died that meant a thing to me, just Bertram's grandfather but I didn't really know him, as old as he was and in a nursing home and all. So let me tell you, I was at a loss. "No," I said, not meaning to go any further with this weirdly exciting conversation, but then the words just burst out of me.

"I've lost no one, but I've recently realized I'll never have a baby girl to call my own." I felt like breaking into tears when I admitted that to a stranger, but I was strong and didn't.

"Oh, you do have a baby girl," Ramona said, still holding my hand in hers and then turning my arm to look at my wrist. I had just had a manicure, so my nails looked at their best. Not to brag, but I have been complimented all my life on the appearance of my hands, all parts of them, not just the nails. "See the pattern of the vein from your heart? That is a certain sign of the fact."

"The fact?"

"Yes, the fact that you have a baby girl, a spirit child not yet embodied to you, but as real as that lovely ring on your index finger."

I looked down at the vein Ramona was studying so closely, and I swear I could see it pulsing as she spoke. "Where is my baby girl?" I asked. "Where is she? Can you tell me?"

"She is with the spirits yet, and she wants her mother. She wants to come to you. She wants to be at home in your arms."

Naturally, I burst into tears at that revelation and had to be led to a sofa to sit down and have my cry out, but the tears were joyful and fulfilling, not like the ones that come with marital spats and the ups and downs of raising two boys. Everyone there in Betsy Flummerfelt's den was perfectly sweet and nice to me as I sat there just bawling my eyes out, and in a few minutes I calmed down and we started the meeting and eventually got out our instruments and began to play. I don't remember what piece I played on the flute, but people there told me later that it sounded perfectly inspired. I think that was true because I was playing from the heart and not my mind.

And then to cap that first meeting with Ramona Spatts and the message she had given to me, you'll never guess what happened next. A knock came on my door not two days later, at about ten in the morning when the boys were in school and Bertram was at work and I was watching the food channel for want of something better to do. Besides, since I've become a vegetarian, I do find a good reason to watch food shows on the chance I'll find something tasty to cook which is not bought at the price of the death of some harmless imprisoned animal. I do not consider that time on the tube wasted, and those that would are meat-eaters whose opinions mean less than nothing to me.

But the doorbell rang right in the middle of a talk on tofu I wanted to hear, and I peeped through the side window to see who it could be, not expecting anybody that morning and certainly not wanting to be the victim of some LDS missionary practicing at home before he took off for Guatemala or Peru or somewhere to peddle that philosophy they teach in their temples. They are entitled to freedom of speech and religion and all the Bill of Rights stuff we have in this great nation, I understand, but they do not have the right to try to sell good Christians that bill of goods called the Book of Mormon. I mean, for goodness sake. I admit I did flirt with the idea of the Mormon worldview when we first moved here from Houston, being unconnected and alone, but I learned soon enough it was nothing but a cult which denies women the right to be fun loving and live independent lives. The only thing I had found about the LDS when I first arrived in Salt Lake, I concede, is that they will talk to you and pay attention to you as an individual the way some so-called Christians won't.

The Mormons don't like to look you in the eye, though, aiming their gaze just a little above the brow line, I noticed as soon as that first young woman to talk to me, Sister Sarah she called herself, began her series of sessions designed supposedly to inform, but really meant to indoctrinate and seduce. Yes, I use the sexual term, because that's what it came to feel like to me as they kept sending different people to come to my house for those little friendly talks which they've got down to a science. I won't say any more about that, the seduction analogy, thank you. They know what they're doing, the LDS. They hold seminars to polish their pitches.

So I'm always leery of unwanted solicitations at the door of my house. I swear these LDS missionarie. wear out people's yards all over Salt Lake and Sandy and Harriman walking from one house to the other trying to get you to sign up for a one-way ticket to a place no Christian wants to visit, much less spend eternity in. But that morning, it wasn't two young guys in black trousers and short-sleeved white shirts with dark ties and real short haircuts knocking on my door. That would've been a dead giveaway. No, it was a guy in brown shorts and a brown shirt and a baseball style cap, and he had a UPS package for me.

After I signed for it, puzzled as I could be because I didn't re-member ordering anything online in the last several weeks, I tore into the box to see what I had and who it had come from. What I discovered made me drop to my knees in surprise and if there had been somebody there in my house that morning besides me I would have burst into tears. There wasn't, though, so I didn't waste the time or effort to convince myself that I was overwhelmed, touched, overjoyed, and simply transfixed by what I found in that UPS package addressed to me. I knew that already and nobody was there to share the moment with me and that I'd have to demonstrate my emotions in front of. I have saved the package itself that the gift came in, given what it contained and what it conveyed to me. It was this.

A precious pink outfit for a newborn baby girl, of high quality material, and it was accompanied by a note signed by Ramona Spatts. From your spirit baby to her mother, it said in green ink on a pink sheet of stationery. I'm wanting and needing my mama, and I want to be in your arms.

I was totally knocked over, and I just ran in circles through every downstairs room of my house, holding to my breast the simply precious outfit, sized for infant wear, with the cutest little red lady bug appliqué against the pink background, and I felt the palpable presence of my baby girl moving with me with each step I took.

After I calmed down enough to talk on the phone, I called the cell that Ramona had given me the number to, knowing she'd be out and about and not likely at her home phone. She does maintain an office of sorts, as she calls it, but she spends most of the daytime hours here and there, meeting with people individually at their homes for the conclaves, her term, which she conducts. I've learned all this as time's gone by, but when I got the gift of a garment for my spirit baby I had no idea that Ramona has devoted her life for the last several years to ministering to women like me, women who to all appearances have a settled and fulfilling life but who inside and not for public consumption feel the want of connection with a child unborn.

Some of these women she helps are completely childless currently, at least in this visible world, while others like me have real children already but are in want of that precious little being, their spirit baby, floating out there in the darkness, alone and not arrived and craving the earthly connection with their mother.

What I'm talking about is not creepy, as some call it, including my own husband who, when I first told him of what Ramona Spatts had revealed to me about my spirit baby, said it sounded "weird and icky," his words. He doesn't use that kind of language now, I assure you. If we do nothing else, Bertram and I communicate. We hold nothing back from the mate we are bound to, and I make it my duty to keep him aware of that fact. Given the nature of his job, which is both real and abstract, he does tend to drift off into his own little world, but I keep yanking him back into reality when I see that he's lost touch. Yes, we need the income from the real world, but that's a given, I tell him. What we are dying to have is not countable and can't be programmed.

Here is what he does, reduced to an explanation which is communicable to ordinary people who live in the real world. He writes code. That's what he calls it, and what the other nerds and geeks like him call it, too. Once when I just forced him to try to explain it to me so I could tell people what it was that my husband did for a living, Bertram got a yellow pad out and began marking on it to show me what he spends all his time doing. If this, then that, he wrote down on one line. Then on the line after that, he wrote if that, then this.

"See?" he said, looking at me with his eyes all bright and eager. "Do you get it?"

"Let's have something a little more specific, Buster," I said. "That does not communicate." So what he did then was start writing a bunch of little symbols, I guess you'd call it, squiggly marks and reversed b's and d's and t's and g's, sprinkled in with some regular words, but you could tell they didn't mean in his little world what they mean in the real one where I live with my children and my dogs and my role as mother and human being.

"What does that do?" I asked, in a calm and receptive tone designed not to get him flustered. "How does the computer deal with that line of marks when you enter them into it? How does it know what to do with all that stuff?" Then he made this statement to me, and after he did, I just simply gave up any hope of his ever being able to explain to a reasonable person what he spent all his hours at work and at home at night and on the weekends doing.

"See, Roseanne," he said. "The computer doesn't know anything. It does not ever do what you want it to do. It does what you tell it to do. That's all it knows and all it needs to know."

"Even a Mac?" I said, having myself always preferred a machine which is friendly and comes in attractive colors, at least in the newer models.

"All of them are the same," Bertram said. "They are stupid."

"Tell me about it," I said, and since then I have never asked him a single thing about what he's up to. I get the shivers and shakes and the creeps enough from trying to live in the real world of 1815 Mountain Mist Road without bothering my head with that kind of spooky nonsense.

Anyway, when Ramona answered her cell that day, and said hello in that wonderful tone of intimate communication she possesses to such a degree, I began by saying, "Thank you, thank you, Ramona." I tried to go on to let her know who I was and what I was thanking her for, but I couldn't continue, naturally, as I couldn't speak further through my tears of gratitude and joy. I would have sounded like a duck quacking. She knew who I was without my having to tell her, calling my name in a soothing yet firm tone, full of a deep promise of communication and connection to come between us.

At the time, I didn't wonder about how she knew it was me, Roseanne Pausewell, instinctively believing she sensed my identity through a means far beyond a simple statement expressed by me over an electronic instrument. Later, Bertram in his cool scientific way responded to my telling him this part of the story by saying Ramona had just read my number off her cell phone, but I did not accept that explanation then and I don't now. Could she have? Yes. Did she? No.

"Roseanne, Roseanne," she said. "I've done nothing for you but convey a message from another. You needn't thank me for that. Thank your spirit child, your precious daughter, for letting you know she's waiting and yearning for her mother. I'm only the messenger, and I sent you the little garment in the same way any friend brings a gift to a baby shower in anticipation of a happy arrival on its way."

My tears at hearing that from Ramona were the most satisfying of my life, up to this moment. I'd always considered that when Bertram announced his agreement to marry me those years ago in our senior year in college that my tears then had set the standard for me in expressing joy, elation, satisfaction, and anticipation of coming fulfillment of the highest order. I was wrong. What has meant the most to me to date is a realization not of this world but of the other, the insubstantial, that realm where my spirit baby waits.

I have not told Bertram of the displacement of feeling which has taken place in me, and I'm afraid to. I'm not afraid of hurting his feelings. I don't mean that. He can get over anything. He's proved that a thousand times. No, I don't fear he'll be hurt by the revelation I've undergone or that he'll be in danger of feeling second best. What I'm afraid of is that he'll not even remember that scene in that old car he always drove on that night after we had left the fraternity party and when I just simply laid down the law to him about obligation and trust and responsibility. What happened did happen, though, whether he remembers it or not and whether he honors that memory or not. Bottom line, he finally just gave it up and said yes he'd marry me. That I don't want to think about right now.

What I would like to think about is my spirit baby, but two things stand in my way. Number one is Bertram's reluctance, even refusal, to entertain the notion of our adding another child to our family. Two kids are plenty, he says, and then he starts writing down numbers on one of his damned old yellow pads to show how we could afford it technically but that we'd have to undergo a life-style change to let that happen.

"Do you want that?" he had the nerve to ask me the first time I brought up the subject of my spirit baby, my sweet little insubstantial doll, floating out there in limbo. "Do you want to have to keep both cars several years longer? Do you want the boys to go to school when the time comes not at a four year university but at some community junior college? Do you want to have to find a fulltime job yourself? Do you want at your age to chance what a birth might bring? How do you know if it's a good one, it won't be just another boy?"

"No, Bertram," I said in a controlled voice and manner. "I want all those good things to go unchanged, but I want my spirit baby, too. She is female, and she's perfectly sound physically, if she gets the chance to be. She's out there, and I must accept her or suffer the consequences of eternal loss."

"How can you lose something you don't have?" Mr. Logical said. "That's not the way having babies works, and you ought to know that, the way you carried on when you gave birth to Kevin and Roland. They couldn't find a drug strong enough to shut up your hollering."

"Do you think I fear the physical task I would face in bringing my spirit baby into the light from out of the darkness? If you think that, Buster, you don't know the girl you're married to." That shut him up, but nothing's happened to change things since Ramona let me know about my spirit baby. I'm still just drifting in the fog and mourning in the shadows. I am a female alone with three males in this household, and until I find a way to let my spirit girl come to me, I'll remain lost and outnumbered.

That's number one on my list of obstacles, the way Bertram has taken a misguided and stubborn stand. Number two is the acting out that my love bug of a baby boy has decided to adopt. Locking himself in his room, refusing to talk to me or his father. Screaming in anger at nothing. Making threats he's much too young to carry out. Keeping a ball peen hammer stuck down between his bed stead and his mattress. He doesn't know that I know that, and I haven't even let his father in on that little secret I discovered. Another thing: Kevin being a real little jerk in the psychologist's office after I'd taken him in for a little tune-up, just a mini-session to let him express his frustrations with what those awful old strong hormones are making him do. Picking up a ceramic paperweight shaped like a nun at prayer and throwing it against the wall hard enough to leave a terrible dent in the sheetrock. After that stunt, my therapist said she would never meet with him again, and I had to practically beg her to keep letting me come in for our weekly talks. Kevin doing all that, mind you, just to assert himself and say no to reason.

What I really want to do is have Bertram realize. his responsibility to our spirit baby, have Kevin act like an ordinary thirteen year old and play with his video games, take his medication every day and do his homework, have Roland keep on being the perfect older brother he is – knock on wood. Don't let him get ideas – and give me a chance to follow that recipe for spirit cake that Ramona has given me. The recipe does not purport to be magic, it's not occult, and it's not nutty. It's a symbolic action that the baking of the spirit cake represents, and if it puts into substantial form an idea, a manifestation of the world beyond this one I'm living in here in this old high desert landscape, what's the harm?

Here are the ingredients for the recipe, and no, it is not for an angel food cake, as cute as that idea might sound to some. It is not silly like that would be, even though it intends to honor an infant existing only in the spiritual realm. You will need one egg. So it's not really a rich dessert. You'll want sugar and cake flour, of course, you'll want butter and cream, you'll need a bundt pan, and a spice the identity of which I'm not at liberty to announce. Ramona Spatts hasn't even revealed that to me yet, saying she'll be here in my kitchen to furnish me with that ingredient when I commit to putting the recipe into action. I am patient when I need to be, and this is one of those occasions. I don't have to know everything immediately each instant of the day.

I have a little secret of my own I'm going to spring on Ramona when she comes by this afternoon to reveal the special ingredient for the spirit cake and we launch into the project. I think it will delight her, and I just know it will surprise her. First, I'm not going to keep calling this wonderful creation a spirit cake, although it is that, without a doubt. No, I'm christening our gateau something a little different and a lot more to the point. It will be named "My Daughter's Unbirthday Cake," and it will be dedicated to her by name and I will speak that name for the first time. So that's the first surprise I'll announce to Ramona Spatts, my wonderful guide to the spirit world, the godmother of my infant-in-waiting.

Here's the other surprise, and it's the biggie. My dear mother, Maureen Louise, will be in the kitchen with us, supervising the mixing, the baking, and the creation of My Daughter's Unbirthday Cake. That's the announcement I'll hit Ramona with.

Do not get me wrong. I don't mean MaMa will be there hovering as a ghostly presence, some kind of half visible woman wearing an apron as transparent as she is. No, I mean she will be spiritually sensible to us, just as much as my daughter, my sweet spirit baby, will be. How do I know that? I'll tell you.

I dreamed it last night, after I had gotten off the phone with Prissy, my dearest and best friend from the time we were children in Little Rock and grew up next door to each other. We have kept up ever since then. We had talked for over an hour – God bless cell phones with unlimited minutes on specified days of the week – and when I fell asleep alone in the bed, since Bertram was in his office writing some more damned old code, I guess, I fell into the deepest and most profound sleep I had ever experienced.

Then the dream started, and I knew it was a dream, but it was realer to me than most events I go through every day here in the high desert. MaMa was in the kitchen in the dream, and it was the old one I grew up in from the time I was five until I went off to college. All the old kitchen furniture was there, oak chairs around the table, the same old bronze refrigerator, the bric a brac on the walls and shelves, the bookcase full of cookbooks, all that was there just as it used to be.

What was different was the range. It wasn't the old bronze electric one we had, the mate to the refrigerator, the one I saw so many meals coming from on the days when MaMa was not too far gone into the cocktail hour to cook, but instead it was a silver gas stove in the exact center of the kitchen. In my dream I knew it was gas because it was making a loud roaring sound and flames were licking out of the door of the oven. It wasn't scary, though, since in the dream that was the way it was supposed to operate when you were doing some baking. MaMa was there, dressed in a wonderful outfit, sparkling with sequins and a silver thread design worked through the material. It was spelling out some words I couldn't read, and I was puzzling over that until MaMa spoke to me.

"Roseanne," she said to me, "do you want to lick the mixing bowl before I put the cake in the oven?"

I did, of course, as I always had as a child, and when I did, the taste was exquisite. I couldn't get enough of the batter to satisfy me, and I begged my mother for more. She told me I'd have to wait until the cake was baked and frosted and then I could have all I wanted, and I began to cry like a baby even though in the dream I was a grown woman. When I began crying, MaMa started getting smaller and smaller, and the more I begged for the raw batter, the littler she got.

"Don't leave, MaMa," I said. "Stay big."

"I have to go, but I'll be back tomorrow and we'll bake a cake for the baby girl. I promise," she said.

Then I woke up, my face just covered with tears. I was alone, and Bertram was still downstairs, I guess, saying to himself inside his head where I can never reach, "if this, then that. If that, then this..

But all in all, I felt good. I felt great, in fact. I wasn't worried about a thing. I knew MaMa would be in the kitchen in the afternoon of the next day and she would guide me and Ramona as we mixed up the spirit cake, added the special spice, and put it in the oven to bake. When it came out, I knew it would be perfect, and I'd tell Ramona the true name for it.

So here I am, bathed and dressed and made up and my hair in place, only a little over two hours to go until Ramona Spatts is scheduled to arrive with the secret spice in her bag. MaMa, wherever she is in the other world waiting for the moment, will be on time as well, never having been late for an appointment close to five o'clock in the afternoon in her life.

Roland, my perfect older son is in school, Bertram's at work, and my little love bug of a boy is in his room making some kind of huge banging noise. I'm not worried about that, though, knowing as I do about the ball peen hammer he's got secreted in his room. I know what it's coming from. He's probably pounding on something, knocking bits and pieces off of it, making a class project for tomorrow if he decides to go to school that day. It's a booming racket, and it is loud, and he's yelling some word or combination of words over and over. I'm not going to worry about that, though. I may get out my flute and play a few pieces or I might put a favorite CD on the player, maybe The Best of Queen, and turn it high enough to drown out the noise from Kevin's room. I have always loved Freddie Mercury. I can't get enough of him. The Bohemian Rhapsody just does it to me, every time I put it on. How can that get old?

All the ingredients for My Daughter's Unbirthday Cake are ready, except for the last special spice, and that's on the way. Ramona's bringing it. MaMa is ready to take charge of the baking. Freddie Mercury may be gone in body, but he's always here in spirit. Nothing's lost. It's all coming together this afternoon, all rising to be baked to perfection, here in the valley where I sit thinking of the truly wonderful name I've chosen for my daughter, here in Salt Lake, here in this high desert where I live.

Power of Attorney

"**G**ranny Sarah, can you tell me what date it is?" Myra said, stealing a glance at the BelClair Senior Home leaflet she was holding behind her purse to be sure she was asking the first question suggested.

"Do you mean today?" her grandmother Sarah said, her head cocked to one side as though she were a robin early on a spring morning deciding whether or not to peck at something it couldn't identify. Was what she was seeing good to eat or not? Myra knew that trick of posture and was not about to respond to it and get distracted. Granny Sarah was using a cute pose, one of many from her arsenal of attractions, a selection that had ceased being reliably effective some years ago, though Granny Sarah was not above trotting it out one more time.

"Yes, today, Granny Sarah. Today's date, the month and year."

"Well, I don't know exactly about today's date, but I do know next week on Tuesday is the Republican primary. And you know what?

"No, what?" Myra said, stealing another look at the directions for questions to put to loved ones in the facility, queries designed to help the old folks stay anchored in the here and now. The next question sought the name of the president of the United States, she noted.

Sarah's cute pose used to be powerful, Myra supposed, aimed at the right person, a man the proper target, one of those old boys from somewhere up in the woods in. Columbus County, now dead and gone and covered up in a country cemetery down some dirt road. Myra paused for a space to consider what it would be best to say to move the dialogue forward a bit. Her grandmother held her cute pose, smiling a little broader to signal she was ready to receive an answer to her question and widening her eyes. I might as well fling in and start, Myra thought. There will be preliminaries, no way around that, and the sooner we get through them, the closer I'll be to getting out of here and back to the office.

"Tell me what," she said.

"They are going to load us up in the van and take us to the poll, that's what. So we'll get due opportunity to exercise our constitutional right to vote. I expect it might take more than one trip to handle all of us, too. I certainly hope so."

"Who is the president now?" Myra asked, putting the next officially approved question to her grandmother.

"Why, Myra, I'm not surprised at that question, but I am curious you in particular would ask it. It seems that every young person who visits anybody at BelClair is worried about who the current occupant of the White House happens to be. Given your accomplishments, I am a little concerned that you would ask. You do mean the president of the United States, don't you, dear?"

She's playing for time, probably, Myra thought, remembering the warning included on the sheet of appropriate questions. They say the loved ones will try to trick you into giving them the right answer when they aren't certain about accuracy. It must be like being in a law school class on torts trying to fend off a professor's attempt to show you up by springing some arcane query on you. The best response? Make the questioner talk. Put him on the spot.

"I believe I know, Granny Sarah," Myra said, "but I thought I would just check to see if I'm right."

"And to think of all the time and effort and expense spent on your education," Sarah said with that copyrightable lilt in her voice. "And you say you believe you know. My, my. I remember when you used to lie in your crib as an infant and just giggle and coo, unable to say a word yet, and I'm reminded of that time in your life when you ask me such strangely uninformed questions on a gorgeous spring day like this one."

To hell with it, Myra said to herself. My grandmother might think the sitting president is George the First or Abraham Lincoln, but she still has enough wits about her to convince a questioner she's not that far into a demented state yet. Let's cut to the chase. It's time.

"Granny Sarah," she began, using the label for her grandmother as approved by the designee when Myra first began to babble as an infant, "we need to settle some business for you, and that's why I'm here this morning."

"And I thought you were here just for the sake of a visit or to improve your knowledge of current events," Sarah said. "Silly me."

Touche, Myra thought, watching her grandmother make a sad face by pulling the corners of her mouth down and glancing to the side as though to stifle a tear, a point for you, old girl.

"Well, of course I'm here to see you, like I always am when I drive way out here, but I thought we could take care of some business, too, some matters that've been pending. After our nice visit."

"Pending. What a nice word. I believe it must be related to pendant, like some little piece of jewelry a lady would wear to perk up her outfit."

"I think you must be right about that," Myra said, thinking about another variant of the root word, pendejo, a term some of her Latino clients used when explaining to her why they had committed some act of violence that required her services in their legal defense. I think it must mean something like swinging dick to that linguistic group.

"But no," she went on, trying to keep her gaze steadily on her grandmother's eyes, a difficult task at any time, given the coquettish way the woman moved her head around as she carried on a conversation. It was like watching a tennis match between two expert players accomplished at the lob, able to loft the ball just out of reach when you thought it was possible to put it away finally. Nope, oops. I've got to turn tail and run like hell to get to it. "What I mean when I say pending is that we need to attend to some legal requirements in a timely manner."

"You've become so grown-up," Sarah Livingston said with a lilt. "I'm just so proud of you, you little lawyer you. My little granddaughter speaking in such a way and using so many big old words. My goodness. I remember when all you could do was either coo or cry."

"Yeah. I imagine so. But we have to take care of some pressing matters," Myra said, then remembering to add the magic words, "Granny Sarah. And then I'll leave you alone. I promise."

"Oh, sugar, I'm used to being left alone. There's no shortage of that behavior around my room in this facility," Sarah said. She moved her hands apart in a gesture to include her bed, the table beside it, the chest of drawers and the framed photos and knick knacks upon it, the chair in which her granddaughter sat, and the bathroom behind the door with its special bars and oversized commode. "My home, my all, my place in the world."

Jesus H. Christ, Myra said to her self. Here it comes, the thing she always says to everybody who enters her chamber. Let me see if I can say it before she does.

"And here we are," Myra said, just a hair before her grandmother voiced the words, and instantly she regretted beating the old girl to it. Lord, I should let her win again. It means so much to her. Why do I give a damn?

"Yes, here I am," the woman in the bed especially equipped for raising and lowering the comatose said. "For any and all to behold."

Neither said anything for a space, both breaking eye contact and looking in opposite directions, Myra toward the window through which she could see a mockingbird perched on a branch of a crepe myrtle in the courtyard and Sarah, Myra knew without having to check, staring at the photograph of her daughter, Myra's mother, taken over thirty years ago. The young woman in the picture was smiling deliriously in her light summer dress and her hat, and she had a small bouquet in one hand and held the hand of a man in the other. All of the male figure but that single hand had been cut away from the photographic record before Myra ever saw it whole. If technology had allowed at the time, all signs of the hand would been have erased, too.

Sing, damn you, Myra sent a silent command to the mockingbird, or at least flap your wings and fly off somewhere. Make a move, bird. The bird didn't, comfortable where it was.

"All right, Myra," her grandmother said, her voice laden with resignation. "Where's the paper and where do you want me to affix my name?"

Why can't she just say sign? Why does she have to say affix my name, Myra asked herself as she reached for her briefcase, knowing the answer to her silent question even as she posed it. Saying "affix my name" rather "sign the paper" put a gloss on the action, lifted it out of the mundane and at the same time, distanced it from what her grandmother called the real world.

The real world was where most people had to live, grubbing away for a living, shopping for groceries and lugging them home to cook and eat, paying bills, worrying about having enough money to pay those bills, and all the other tiresome facts which tied the common folk to everyday existence.

Once when Granny Sarah was still in her mobile years, she had visited Myra in New York during the time she was still married to Wendell and considered herself an escapee from the Greater Houston Area for good. Her husband, a bright young man she had met in law school in Austin, was just arrived at Goldman Sachs, she was a newly minted attorney this close to being hired by a Manhattan firm, she was secretly planning to get pregnant down the road, and then she would have it all. A career, a husband in love with her and destined for big things, weekends in the Hamptons, crisp falls and snowy winters, a child enrolled in the Ethical Culture School, and never having to go back to Texas, all in one big package. the whole fucking enchilada.

On the way in from picking Granny Sarah up at LaGuardia working her way through traffic to the restored brownstone in Brooklyn which Wendell had gotten them into, determined to turn a big profit when they sold it and moved in two years to Manhattan, Myra had had to drive through a crowd of local residents involved in some kind of loud argument in the street.

"Oh, my," her grandmother had said, "please get us past those hoodlums and into somewhere with a lockable door. I swear I don't know how they stand it."

"Stand what, Granny Sarah? Those kids, you mean?"

"Yes, Oh Lord. Just to think. For them, this is their existence, this is their all. I feel for the poor things. Never to know the real world of River Oaks and Houston, what a fate."

Still in her New York phase, Myra had tried to point out the error in Granny Sarah's thinking about what constituted the real world, arguing her position all the way home and into the brownstone, while her grandmother smiled and tilted her head to one side like a feeding chickadee. Myra argued not to convince, but to make her take on socioeconomic and cultural differences and realities clear to this old lady from Houston, determined at least to let Granny Sarah know how far her granddaughter had come from the southwest section of that unzoned city. Let's get that part straight, she had said within, proud to declare the self she had earned through hard work, denial of ease, and the pursuit of a dream.

And now here I fucking am, Myra said to herself as she pulled legal forms out of her briefcase. Home in Houston, by God, again, all by myself. Before moving toward her grandmother's bed, she stopped to slap at the window to inspire the mockingbird to flap out of the picture. The bird flew lazily to a higher limb, but didn't leave the sweetgum tree. Was he tied to it by an invisible wire?

"Oh," said Granny Sarah, "don't bother the cute bird. The little creature is a friend and a comfort to me, just looking in here to see how I'm doing."

"He's just staring at his reflection in the glass," Myra said. "They all do that. He doesn't know what's him and what isn't. Now let me explain this form to you."

When Myra walked back into the office of Sung, Battle, Morgan, and Grier an hour later, stepping briskly to discourage anybody from thinking she was available for chit chat, Jason Lee Sook was leaning on the receptionist's desk, finishing up the delivery of a witticism that J'Nique Broussard was obliged to giggle at. She was laughing enough to cause her chair to swivel, a move which pleased Jason, but to an informed observer was obviously faked.

"Hey, Myra," Jason said in the middle of J'Nique's performance. "How do it be hanging, girl?"

"That is not the kind of thing you say to a woman, particularly in Harris County, Texas," Myra said, trying to maintain momentum on the way to her office, but forced to break her stride by an adroit spin by Jason which put him in her path. "I hope that's not the kind of language you use on our clients."

"Please pardon my vernacular," Jason Sook said. "It's just a way to say howdy. What's sup?"

"Does he talk that way to you, J'Nique?" Myra said. "Do you let him?"

"Mr. Sook, he says all kinds of stuff, Miz Livingston," the receptionist said, her chair rocking back and forth as she snickered. "He don't mean nothing by it."

"Doesn't mean anything," Myra said. "And yes he does. He just doesn't know what things mean when he says them. He's a verbal loose cannon."

"I know what that means," Jason said. "Bang, bang. Shoot'em

up."

Myra stopped making shuffling motions to indicate a desire to move on, stood dead still, and fixed Jason Lee Sook with a direct stare. He instantly dropped his gaze, shrank in on himself, and began to back toward J'Nique's desk, clutching a file to his chest with both hands, as though he'd just received a gift from one of a higher social order. "Pardon my vernacular."

"That's not the way to use that word," Myra said. "You can't possess a vernacular, for God's sake." Then turning to J'Nique, who had fallen into a close study of her keyboard, "Come to my office when you finish whatever you're doing there. I have something for you to do."

"Yes ma'am," J'Nique said, nodding at her keyboard and not looking up as Jason Lee Sook walked backwards a couple of steps before turning to move at speed down the hall to the inner offices of Sung, Battle, Morgan, and Grier.

I know, I know, Myra conceded to herself as she followed the junior associate down the hall toward her corner office, we have to employ an ethnically diverse group, and I'm totally committed to the concept and practice, but why in Christ's name can't they stay rooted in their cultures, at least linguistically. Why is an associate from Tulane Law named Sook determined to talk like a wannabe Houston gang-banger? And why won't my eighty-three year old grandmother give me a break and stop reminding me I used to lie in a crib and babble?

Behind her J'Nique Broussard answered a phone call, speaking the name of the firm in a clear and completely unspecifiable general American accent. She can act, Myra thought, she can put on the dog when it's called for. Why can't all of them?

Walking into her office and moving toward her computer, Myra promised herself Tex-Mex for lunch, spicy enough to make her forehead sweat. Pardon me, Granny Sarah, she said out loud, ladies don't sweat. They get dewy.

In the bedroom of her townhouse on LaBranch, just at 11 pm,

later than she would have liked by over an hour, given the fact she was scheduled for a court appearance at 9 the next morning, Myra was looking over the right shoulder of Ron Spaulding as he hammered away at her. He was close to getting to that place where he was supposed to be most desirous of arriving, and he was making groaning sounds overlaid by deep wavering intakes of breath. Putting on a show to demonstrate how wonderfully magical and physical it all is, Myra knew, but she wouldn't point that out to him.

Let him think she was where he was, grateful beyond all measure and verging on deep and lasting fulfillment. No reason not to let him have his moment, though it was clear to Myra as she looked over Ron's shoulder that Inez had not cleaned high in the corners of the room where cobwebs appeared regularly every week in the climatic conditions of Greater Houston. Inez knew to tend to that, told by Myra every Thursday to do so, but her knees wouldn't allow her to stand on the ladder Myra had bought her specifically for the task. That was Inez's claim, at least, one of many she made in justification of the limitations of her house cleaning abilities every time she walked through the door.

I swear I'm going to fire her next week, Myra told herself, this time for sure. Why should I keep paying a woman to do the cleaning chores I don't want to do myself and then have to end up following behind her to do the shit jobs? I'll let her go just as soon as she cleans the master bath one more time. I'll write it down so I won't forget.

Ron was reaching some sort of zenith in his breathing, and Myra decided to help things along, forcing a high-pitched mew and a tremulous whimper and twisting away from and out from under where he was hard at work. That would have to satisfy him for the night, ready or not.

"Did you get there?" Ron said in a ragged voice, as he rolled off to collapse beside her.

"Couldn't you tell?" Myra said, pulling the towel that had been beneath her from the bed and heading for the bathroom. He would be lying at ease behind her, his hands beneath his head and a wistful smile on his face, she knew, and she would not respond to his line of questioning further. It is late. Deponent sayeth not.

The next morning in court Myra knew her client would want to take the stand in his own defense, CEO of a start-up company that he was with all the bluster attendant to that role, despite all her arguments to the contrary, and he was now being taken apart by the opposition. Millie Shumacher, counsel for the plaintiff, was doing the questioning, flipping her long swatch of blonde hair as she put her barbs, each time she did so throwing a smirk at Myra out of the corner of her eye.

She swayed in a rhythm, though, which worked to Myra's benefit, giving her ample opportunity to fasten her gaze on the papers before her during each prosecutorial head bob. Millie Shumacher loved the twitch to her hair provided by her flounces enough not to give up a single one of them, and so far Myra had had to suffer only one eye contact with the little bitch during her questioning of Carter Avery, under suit for divorce by his wife and mother of his children. The issue, as always, with persons with residential addresses in this area of Harris County, was child custody and division of property. Ho hum.

"When Belvedere police officers were called to respond to your home on the night in question, they were told that acts of domestic violence had taken place and were in progress. Is that true, Mr. Avery?"

"I imagine so," Myra's client said, shifting in his chair with a roll of his shoulders and trying to catch Myra's eye. "She's always had a habit of telling such lies." Myra fixed her gaze high up on a corner of the court room, no cleaner of cob webs than her own townhouse. Where can you find good help these days?

After the objection from Millie Shumacher and the judge's admonishment, the line of questioning continued, Millie's massive swatch of blonde hair in regular movement as she moved in for the kill.

"Let me show you some photographs, Mr. Avery," she said,

pausing for the objection she expected from Myra. Myra made her wait until the judge looked in her direction and then said her piece. Carter Avery nodded with satisfaction toward his counsel, smiling slightly as though to say "that's my girl. Go get her."

Of course he beat on his wife, Myra said to herself with resignation, half rising from her chair in a display of outrage and shock at the tactics of the plaintiff's attorney. That's how the two of them communicated, and that's why she stayed with the asshole as long as she did. But here goes.

Outside in the hallway after the break in testimony, Carter Avery moved at least a food into Myra's personal space, leaning forward as though to attack a weak tennis return blooped over the net and ready to be put away. As Myra rocked back a step, bumping into somebody behind her hard enough to cause a flutter, Carter Avery of Mogul Inc, spoke into her face. "At least, she didn't get away with that domestic abuse shit, did she?"

"We'll see," Myra said. "Don't say anything else to me now."

"Why?" Carter Avery said in a minty breath through his perfectly white teeth. "Attorney client confidentiality pertains, right? I can say anything I want to you."

"Not in the hall, Carter," Myra said, stepping back another step, this one unimpeded. "Everything's fair game in public."

"Yeah, but I'm going to win, right?"

"There will be a proper disposition of these matters before the court," Myra said. "You can count on that."

"All right," Carter Avery said, rolling his shoulders and jiggling in place. "Let me buy you a cup of coffee."

"No," Myra said. "I don't like the taste."

Her cell phone vibrated.

Myra had told J'Nique to do her a map quest for the hospital as soon as she returned the call, but something electronic had blown up, and she was having to drive in Houston traffic with one hand on the wheel and one holding her cell to her head.

"What exactly did the people at BelClair say?" she asked

J'Nique. The trick with driving in Houston while talking was to keep your speed up enough to avoid being rear-ended, and Myra was having a hard time forcing herself to drive beyond her comfort limits while in a state of divided attention. Pickups and SUVs were roaring up to tailgate her car, swerving to get around her, their drivers shooting her the finger as they passed and mouthing various salutes in her direction in the process. She was able to keep from acknowledging their existence except for one woman, well dressed and neatly coiffed who slowed down as she pulled to within a foot of Myra's car and held it there until Myra looked over. You fucking bitch, Myra lip read the woman say, obviously late for an appointment, as they made eye contact. Bite me, whore, Myra articulated back as clearly as she could while listening to J'Nique explain what had been said by the caller from BelClair.

"All she said," J'Nique reported in her talking-to-clients voice, "was your grandmother had a medical event which required immediate transfer to Ovetta Culp Memorial."

"Was it an infarction?"

"Do what?" J'Nique said, lapsing into her Fifth Ward accent.

"A heart attack," Myra said, telling herself to keep the accelerator depressed, "maybe a stroke."

"She said medical event. That's all I heard her saying. Said to tell the responsible party to get down there to Ovetta Culp."

"All right, I'll talk to you later," Myra said, punching the end button on the cell and goosing the gas on the Acura. Let me get off this damn loop and see what the damage is to Granny Sarah. At least I won't have to hear the Honorable James Lanier announce his judgment rendered on Carter Avery for beating hell out of his estranged wife while tying to keep all of his money and his kids after the dissolution of marriage. Jason Sook can record that news.

When Myra arrived at the hospital, she was given directions to the intensive care unit where she was told her grandmother had been deposited. Naturally, Myra thought as she rode elevators, walked down corridors, and read signs on doors. Where else would she be? Will there be a meteor strike on downtown Houston sometime later this afternoon to complete the scenario? Is she in pain? Will I be able to know it, if she is? Let her be comatose, at least. Don't let her talk to me. Let her be out.

Sarah Livingston was that. Myra could tell by the way her hair was mussed that her grandmother was unaware of any effect by her on others at this point. Her mouth, through which she was sucking and expelling long draughts of air, was wide open, and she had no teeth in the front part of her lower jaw. She has a bridge, Myra realized, and I never knew that. It must have been installed by a damn good dentist to have fooled me all this time. Maybe I never looked at her mouth that close. She found ways to hide the loss, more likely, twisting her face and smiling and popping her eyes whenever she caught me giving her a regard.

The tubes, the wires, the needles in the backs of the hands, the electronic monitors and displays – all the paraphernalia was there in its due and proper place. Each breath, each beat of the heart, each electrical firing of the system was under supervision and measurement. All was being managed, right up to snuff.

"How is she?" Myra said to the nurse who was regarding a plastic bag of clear liquid hanging from a metal stand, its contents dripping through a tube attached to a needle taped to Sarah's hand.

"She's right there," the nurse said.

"I know where she is," Myra said and then realizing that statement may have sounded rude, went on. "I mean what is her medical status. Her prognosis. What happened to her?"

"Doctor Reiman will be here to talk to you," the nurse said, nodding at the plastic bag as though to give it a thumbs-up on its performance. "He'll let you know."

When he arrived, Dr. Reiman appeared to Myra to be about eighteen years old, but he moved into the room with the assurance of a holder of a medical degree, prepared to meet and greet someone imminently beneath him in intellectual fire power and achievement of status. I wish this was an occasion on which I could put him in his place, Myra found herself thinking. Get him on the stand and take the little twerp apart. See how he'd like a female officer of the court putting the brakes on him. Damn, he is short, no matter how straight he's standing in the doorway, the sure tip off to the way a little man declares he knows himself lacking. No, she told herself, don't stray. Stay focused.

"So this nice lady is your grandmother," Dr. Reiman said, reading from the sheaf of notes on the metal clipboard attached to the frame of the hospital bed. "Are you her closest relative?"

"Yes," Myra said, "my grandmother has no other close relatives still alive." Maybe I shouldn't say that word or any other one like it here in the ICU. Such as dying or dead or so long, Granny Sarah. I can't and won't say the word passed, though. "What can we expect at this point?"

"It's difficult to predict," Dr. Reiman said, pursing his mouth and tapping on the top sheet of paper on the clipboard, "with seniors in her condition. From what we can determine, she's suffered an aneurism. Not a stroke as such, though the episodal symptoms are similar."

"Is she likely to recover?"

"Oh," Dr. Reiman said, drawing out the syllable and turning away from the paper work and ending by looking directly at a spot on Myra's forehead. I know that trick, she thought. I use it all the time to make people think I'm noticing them while I'm talking in their direction. Say what you have to say, Short Stuff.

"She's not likely to be with us much longer, I'm sorry to say. The damage is done. She's finished her course."

"It's hopeless?"

"Yeah, well, most likely, yes. She's still breathing on her own, and we can intubate if that stops, and keep her hydrated, but from all indications, she's essentially gone already."

"Gone?" Myra said, looking at the empty spot in her grandmother's lower jaw she'd never seen before. Where were they keeping her bridge? Was it somewhere close? Would they take care of it and give it back? "How long until?"

"I could use a number of medical terms to describe her situation, if you want to listen," Dr. Reiman said. "But I don't know if you want to hear all that. Let's just say it's up to you."

"Up to me?"

"She has a DNR provision, I see," Dr. Reiman said, looking at his clipboard again. "Signed just yesterday. Today is the third of the month, isn't it?"

"Yes. She signed it yesterday when I took the forms to her. That and the power of attorney transfer, all that."

"You're an attorney, then," Dr. Reiman said, giving her the look of a fellow professional who had set for and passed myriad exams, met qualifications, and satisfied judgment, for years. "She was lucky to have you in the family."

Myra nodded, thinking she shouldn't have publicly agreed to the compliment even as she accepted it. "So," she said, recovering from the lapse in modesty, "I have to decide what to do."

"You know the drill," the teenager posing as a doctor said. "Just let us know when you're ready. I'll be around the hospital until noon. If you can't decide anything before then, you can let the staff know what and when."

As Dr. Reiman left Granny Sarah's last room on earth, his back ramrod straight, Myra felt a little buzz start up somewhere deep in her head, loud enough to give her the sensation that the sound was outside her as well. Low blood sugar, she told herself, nothing to eat since six this morning. The stress of all this with her. The lack of any warning. No preparation. All I have to do is give my head a quick shake and sit down in that nasty looking brown chair, and I'll stop feeling dizzy. Then drink a Coke, a real one, and I'll be fine.

I could just catch the little doctor before he leaves the floor and tell him I know it's time to let my grandmother go, so make the arrangements, but shouldn't I make it look like it's taking me longer than thirty seconds to decide to tell them to pull the plug? But what if I faint when I stand up? This is a hospital and they'd probably admit me or something, and I'd find myself coming to in a bed of my own. They'd be confused, but they'd think they were right and I was weak and out of it, and I refuse to have to argue and explain the truth of the matter.

No, first, sit down in that chair, put my head between my knees and let some blood get to my brain. Then when I stop feeling woozy, get a Classic Coke, call J'Nique to let the office know what I'm doing, and then just do it.

Myra took a step toward the bed, putting out a hand to grab the metal bar at its foot for support, and swung around to sit down in the brown leatherette chair. As she did, Sarah Livingston made a sound, different from the previous pattern of deep groans of breath intake and expulsion from her, and by the time Myra reached the chair, her grandmother said something.

"Granny Sarah," Myra said through the light buzz in her head – wasn't it more pronounced outside her now? Didn't the sound seem to be coming from the wall behind the head of the hospital bed? Was it all just internal?

"Did you say something?"

Turning to look at her grandmother, Myra saw that her mouth was now closed and her lips were pursed as they often were when she was about to say something she thought might raise an issue she would have to address further on in her conversation. She would be positioning her argument. Her eyes were open.

"Granny Sarah," Myra said again, giving her head the shake she had promised it to make the swimming sensation stop, "did you say something?" The head shake wasn't working well at first, then suddenly the buzzing sound outside in the room and inside her head lifted as though a sheet were pulled off a bed in which she was lying and a cool burst of air had rushed in to cause her to shiver.

"Myra," Granny Sarah said, but she wasn't talking the way she talked as Granny Sarah but the way she did as Sarah Livingston. "Myra."

"Yes," Myra said. "It's Myra, it's me. Can you hear me?"

"Remember," Sarah Livingston said, stopping to lick her lips as though they were too dry to speak through, "Remember."

"What, Granny Sarah?" Myra said, not hearing the buzz now.

"Remember what?"

"Remember," Sarah Livingston said in a slow and deliberate voice, fixing her gaze on the person listening to her, opening the lids wide enough that the entire pupils and irises could be seen against the whiteness around them, "remember the color of my eyes."

"I will," Myra said, knowing she had to assure her grandmother she would never forget the blue light blazing across the space between them. "I'll remember the color, I will. I'll never forget."

It wasn't until hours later when she was outside in her car, about to make the first of the calls now pending before her, the notification to the medical personnel about the decision to withdraw all artificial life support having been accomplished and the deep breaths of Sarah Livingston now ended, that Myra began losing sure hold on her grasp of the true color of her grandmother's eyes.

Light blue around the pupil, she began listing to herself, a darker blue encircling that. Small specs of dark blue scattered close to the pupil. Wasn't that it? Can't I still see it, the exact colors and the locations and where one shade fades into another. If I focus and close my own eyes and let her eyes rise up before me, I can still do it, can't I?

I know the way things really look, the things I care about, if I want to keep them whole and separate and recoverable. I do that all the time. I can fix things in place. I do it everyday. That's the way I make my living. All I have to do is close my eyes, and whatever I want to remember will come to me, be with me, and stay. It will. It always has. It won't fade. I won't let it.

I'll make a list, she said out loud. I'll write it all down, in steps, so I can remember each part, each shade, each boundary, each beginning, each end and gradation. It can't be that hard. Things aren't that difficult. You just have to focus. Now, she thought, imagining herself touching a pencil point to a sheet of paper and getting ready to write with everything drawn to a hard clarity before her, start in the middle and work out. Start where there's no color. Start where there's nothing. Begin with black.

A More Perfect Union

The Georgia Peanut had already pulled off both of his hull-shaped shoes and was rubbing each foot with something white from an unmarked jar, and it was only the first work break of the day, not even 11 o'clock yet. The sun was up, not a cloud in sight, and like always the Peanut was moaning as he worked on his feet, looking around in hopes another one of us would meet his eye. None of us wanted to do that. It was bad enough as it was with the temperature so high the sky was not even a washed-out blue, but the color of an old sheet that wanted washing.

"How can the sky be yellow?" I said, "and it not be storming?"

Nobody said anything back, but the Georgia Peanut moaned a little louder as he rubbed his left foot. I could tell he was about to take his head off, and that was not allowed during a short break but only at mealtimes when we were all in the commissary with the doors closed and locked so the patrons couldn't see us out of uniform. I have learned to call what we wear a uniform, even when I'm just thinking the words to myself and not about to say them out loud. If you get into slack habits, you will be bitten in the ass for sure.

I learned that the first year I was here, and I don't need to learn it again. Once will do me just fine. What any one of us wears is not a costume. Costumes are what kids wear at Halloween and what clowns put on to be in the circus. We are not costumed. We put on a uniform every morning we come to work, and knowing that makes us be the thing we say we are. In uniform or out of uniform we are what we say we are.

"I got to come out of this head for just a breath or two," the Georgia Peanut said through his mouth hole. "If I don't, I'm going to keel over."

"You better not," the Mississippi Magnolia said, singing the words like she knows how to do so well, the end note starting low and then going up and coming back down again a little lower than where it started out. I could listen to her all day. I'd like to be able to do that, goodness knows, listen to her all day. "You'll get in trouble. Law, law, law."

"That's easy for you to say, Lorene," the Georgia Peanut said, still talking through the mouth hole in the head of his uniform, but it sounding different from what it does usually. He had loosened a strap somewhere, I could tell. The sound is a definite tipoff. The echo is flat.

"Your head is natural," the Peanut went on. "It ain't made of high impact polyethylene. It's just painted-on goo and stuff."

"Well, I never," said the Mississippi Magnolia, "how dare you tell a lady she appears unnatural or artificial in any way, shape, or form?"

"Not only that, my dear," said the South Carolina Gentleman, smiling so his pencil-thin mustache crawled on his lip a little and drawling out his syllables so they sound like they're bubbling up through a whisky toddy full of sugar and mint. "But our friend, the Georgia Peanut here, just spoke your Christian name, if my ears don't deceive me. I swear I didn't hear him call you the Mississippi Magnolia when he spoke to your sweet self."

"The Peanut said Lorene," the Missouri Outlaw said. "I heard him say that, and I hear everything real good, just the way it's said."

"I don't know how you can hear anything at all, Missouri," the Texas Cowboy said, "your ears crammed full of dried manure the way they are."

Both of those bad boys roused up like they were fixing to come at each other with their fists flying in a minute or two, but they sank back down quick enough after making that first sign of belligerence, figuring they'd got their point across. Such attitude presentation was part of the public affect of both of them, so they used every opportunity to keep in practice.

"I swear," said the North Carolina Tarheel, "if y'all would spend as much energy actively fighting instead of getting set to do it, we could sell some tickets and make a little money here."

By that time the Georgia Peanut had worked his head loose enough to pull it off with a wet popping sound, and we all looked at him to see what his true looks had come to by now. They were about the same as ever, a little paler maybe, but for his ears which were red as a radish from the polyethylene rubbing up against them for at least one and sometimes two shifts a day, depending on which state character did or didn't show up in the morning for duty.

"I'm dying in this peanut costume," the Georgia Peanut said. "This thing is going to kill me before it's too much longer."

"Not a costume," sang the Mississississippi Magnolia. "It's your uniform. Can you say that word, Mr. Peanut. Just repeat after me. Uniform, uniform."

"My, oh my, Miz Magnolia," the South Carolina Gentleman said, "I just love to hear you carry on like that."

"Uniform," the Peanut said.

"Too late," several of us said, me one among the Florida Gator, the Kentucky Miner, and the Missouri Outlaw.

The Outlaw went on to put a fine point on it. "You delayed and lost spontaneity. Sounded flat, just like a train running late."

"He's right, Peanut," the Kentucky Miner said, his voice up high like he was about to break into a mountain melody any minute now. "You letting us down when you don't pay close attention to how you say what you say."

"How is ninety percent," the Idaho Potato said, his skin immaculately arranged and all parts of his uniform up to snuff and where they ought to be. "What is not what they're looking for, the patrons I mean. They're interested in manner and method, not content."

You had to give the Potato credit. He was a professional, and rumor was that if in the middle of night when we were all asleep in the dormitory that if a fire flared up or a lunatic with a machete come running through the room or some other disturbance was to break out, the Idaho Potato would be the only one of us fully prepared to jump out of the sack and entertain. The rest of us would be to some degree in some way out of uniform.

The Mississippi Magnolia always said it was because the Potato was a gentleman, Yankee or not, but to my mind the Potato was no more a Yankee than the Florida Gator was a reptile. The Magnolia was born and bred and trained to see two kinds of people from two categories of states: Southerners and Yankees. If you weren't one, you were the other. I argued with her about that a couple of times, but there wasn't a chance of making an indentation in her gray matter about that or anything else she believed in. Not ever. I tried to explain to her that Idaho was in the West and the Potato was not a Yankee by definition.

"Oh, Arkansas," she said. "You are just precious. And I bless you for your warm and open heart. But let me tell you, Hillbilly, when you cross that Ohio or that Mississippi River headed north, all you're going to find are Yankees. Don't get me wrong now. Some are just the salt of the earth and would give you the shirts off their back if they had to go uncovered. But Sweetness, they are still Yankees. Bless their hearts."

It was no use to argue with her, so I just cut a big chew of tobacco off my plug and popped it in my mouth. I knew that would get her mind off Yankees, and it did.

"Oh, goodness," the Mississippi Magnolia said, "I know you people do that and it seems to satisfy some deep physical craving, but please, for the sake of civilization, don't do that in front of me."

"You've read the Adventures of Huckleberry Finn by Mr. Mark Twain, I do expect," I said. "Mr. Twain spends several paragraphs in that book on the manner and use of chewing tobacco among us Arkansans. We are proud of that notice and do uphold the tradition in the Land of Opportunity."

"I thought y'all were the Diamond State," the Tennessee Long Rifle said. "Last time I looked across that river into West Memphis, I do believe I saw a sign on the bridge stating just that phrase."

I was about to rear back and fix him with an Arkansas stare, the facial expression that won the West, and begin to speak in refutation of that ignorant remark, when the door slammed open and we all looked up to see if he was coming in. I could hear the Georgia Peanut scuffling to get his head back on.

"Well," the President said, "how are the states of the Union doing this morning?" He was wearing the pinstripe, the blinding white shirt, and a light blue tie, fixed at his throat with a Windsor knot. We all knew that particular arrangement of cravat meant something was up. I sneaked a look at his shoes. Polished to a mirror finish. "The ones of you that are here, I mean."

We all said fine, fine, up to snuff, feeling dapper, fit as a fiddle, and the rest of the slogan responses to such a question as were approved for voicing. I could tell the Georgia Peanut had his head back on right by the way his words sounded coming out of the mouth hole of the peanut noggin. "Chipper as a jay bird," he was saying.

"Where is the Nutmeg this morning?" the President said, "I don't see his cheerful visage among you."

"I believe to my soul he's ill," the Mississippi Magnolia said, getting that last lift to the ending syllable that made everybody love her. Except for the other female states, that is.

"Dude be hurling, last time I see him," the Michigan Motor Maid said. "Just puking up yesterday's dinner, not even to say getting his breakfast up and out." She drummed her oversized boots on the floor in a syncopated rhythm, not quite up to what she used on stage but close enough to it to show she was keeping in practice. She could dance, I'll give her that. Anybody that doesn't acknowledge that the Motor Maid can get it is betraying a prejudice to my way of thinking, and I've never been one eager to look for insult.

"He's been ill often in this last quarter," the President said, showing us his smile, mouth full of more white teeth than is regulation among the states of the Union. But he was the President, and attendant on that office is executive privilege. "I fear the Nutmeg is in a slowdown."

"Could it be a recession?" the South Carolina Gentleman said gently, "or just a downturn?"

"I don't like to hear that term applied to the natural vicissitudes of the market," the President, that little sound thing he gets in his throat beginning to tune up. I hoped and prayed he wouldn't start bugling. "We are accustomed to gradual perturbations over time. That's all we're witnessing in the current market. A mere challenge."

Yes, sir, you got that right, nothing to fear, a natural phenomenon, ups and downs and ups again, a swing of the pendulum – these and other sentiments came from the mouth holes of all the states in the room. Only the California Hippie didn't add a peep of agreement to the chorus. That wasn't unusual, though, since the Hippie went her own way all the time, that being part of the affect she was obliged to provide.

"What's your take on the situation, Miss California?" the President said, not one to miss a missing voice. He did not suffer suffering, either. "Do your sister states speak for you?"

Let her handle it right, I said to myself. Lord, don't let him get to bugling at us.

"Far out," the California Hippie said, putting a hand up to adjust her headband, the Indian-looking arrangement today, the one with the beadwork and the single feather rising up at the rear of her head. It was more tattered than ever and in a sad droop, but it was there, and that was better than the alternative. "Out of sight," she added.

I could hear the Mississippi Magnolia singing under her breath in a low but pleasing manner, as though to distance herself from hearing such language usage and let everyone of us know she was doing that. She could not abide the Hippie, no matter how much she pretended to enjoy her company, nor how fondly she spoke of how "interesting" and "quaint" and "colorful" the Hippie was. The Magnolia recognized dated material when she saw it, though she never changed her own affect by a hair's difference over any speci-fied length of time. Once when I asked about that constancy, the Mississippi Magnolia gave me a mini-lecture on archetypes.

"Bless your heart, Arkansas," she had explained, "some states need not worry their heads about what's au courant, and my home place is one of those. We are one thing, have been that thing, and will remain that thing in essence as long as that big old river flows down our full length and separates us from the other less fortu-nates on the western bank. Sugar, we are the Magnolia state, and it's our little postage stamp of ground, and will remain as it as long as there's an it to remain. That's an abiding comfort and joy to all of us."

I had listened to her as long as she would talk. Who of the male states wouldn't?

"Who's ready to get out there and show the flag?" the Presi-dent was saying, his tone still mellow but a hint of darkness seeping up around the edges, much in the way water that's leaked from a busted pipe into a room will work its will on any covering, whether it be cloth or veneer or polyethylene floor material. "Who wants to show our citizens what a great and good nation has to offer in all its constituent parts?"

"I'm dying," said the Georgia Peanut, pausing at an unfortu-nate moment to clear his throat by blowing a breath through his mouth hole, "to perform." His little pause and hitch in delivery made us all look down and away, all but the Texas Cowboy who let out a yodel and swung his length of lariat in a small compass, given the size of the area he had to work in.

"There was something in my throat," the Peanut said in deep apology, "that slowed me down. A husk or something. A little piece of legume covering, maybe."

"I expect all of the states have something in their throats at about this hour every day," the President said in a loud voice, edging too damn close to bugling for my taste. "And what is that, I ask you? Tell us, you Tennessee Long Rifle."

"If any of y'all are like me," said the Long Rifle, "you feeling a lump in your throat about now. That's what I got working on me."

You got that right, that's what I'm talking about, yessiree Bob, uh huh, uh huh, tell it on out – these and other protests of joyous agreement began pouring from one and all, enough to calm and reassure, and I ended the chorus by jumping to my feet and yee-hawing like a drunk tourist in Eureka Springs on a scalding day in August.

"The Arkansas Hillbilly's not shy," the President said, poking an arranging and reassuring hand at his perfectly tied Windsor knot. "The Wonder State will be heard from, and what it proclaims will be loud and clear."

We all made beaucoup noise then, and I led the holler, hoping that the rest of them, particularly the Tennessee Long Rifle, had heard what the President had voiced as an identifier for Arkansas. Don't, I said to myself, none of you dummies start yammering about the Land of Opportunity or the Diamond State. He's let you know what he wants to hear. Give that back to him. Every state of the Union, the ones that were there, did, nobody screwed up, and the President left the room, probably on his way to a Cabinet Meeting, and we began to shuffle out of the room, headed for the performance area. Don't call it a stage, damn it. Nobody, please, nobody.

The crowd was small again, as it had been being for longer than any of us wanted to admit. It had dropped substantially since as recently as last week. A few families, mom and pop and kiddies in tow, were gently drifting down the middle path of the park, looking dazed as though they had been gently rapped on the backs of their heads with a hard rubber hammer or slipped a happy pill in their orange slushies. Most of the young ones were that, young enough to be curious about all us uniformed figures moving together to the staging area to prepare for the Entrance of the States, and they were holding tight to the hands of their parental units, but there were three or four adolescents bobbing along in a cluster unto themselves. Old enough to be real trouble, they appeared to be, but few enough in number not to form a real blood clot in the orderly flow of events about to transpire.

Damn them, anyway, I say, when they get to be at that stage of development. The juices are flowing enough to drown out any sense of control of behavior or ability to concentrate, but they haven't reached the point of hormonal surge strong enough to make them pair off or triple off and get genital with each other.

Until they get to that age level of flow, transference, and juice swapping, I swear I wish we could chain every one of them up to separate stanchions for the duration. Let them see how it is to have stand still in one place without electronic support.

"Far out," the California Hippie said to me out of the side of her mouth. "I see tats, I see France, I see bulges in some pants." That was an old poem she claimed to have created and which she liked to mouth, but it wasn't much of one, in my opinion, and I made out like I hadn't heard her.

She would not be denied, though, that persistence bred into her kind as a part of her affect, and she began repeating what she had just tried out on me. We were coming into the staging area for the Entrance of States, though, so I was able to divert California by nodding toward the metal shed we used for forming up. "Look there, Hippie Chick," I said. "Some shade for us before we have to get out there on the midway and strut our stuff."

"Far out," she said, using up fully half of her vocabulary. I wished sometimes the President's Cabinet would rethink the casting they had done before signing her up to represent the Golden

State. I would just as soon have a real California babbler do the job, one of the hardwired breed, I swear, if it wasn't for what the Hippie Chick could and would do for us old boys from the Solid South now and again. Still, though, was it worth the tradeoff? What would I prefer, a west coast blowjob or peace and quiet? The older I got in my role as the Arkansas Hillbilly the more I'd settle for a nap under a shade tree. I declare I would.

"That's for true, yeah," the Louisiana Cajun was saying to the Virginia Cavalier, either warming up his vocal cords for some zydeco honks and whistles or actually carrying on part of a conversation with the Man from the Commonwealth, the Tyro of the Tidewater. I figured what they were discussing was of no merit, if it was a true verbal interchange, but I did hope it was a calm and non-musical sharing of views. The last thing I wanted to hear before we lined up for the Entrance of the States was the Louisiana Cajun launching into Jolie Blonde one more time. No demonstrations of rhythm and rhyme, please.

"What you boys talking about?" I said, aiming to further the conversational aspect of the exchange between the two of them, if I could affect it. The Cavalier was in a sweat, looking as hot as a two-dollar pistol on a Saturday night in Little Rock. That comparison is one of the signifiers I'm to use whenever possible, so I throw it in at this point to keep in practice. I don't want anybody but the citizen/patrons to think I actually use that kind of idiom, and the President, of course. Lord, please let him stay convinced of the authenticity of my Ozark roots. I'm talking it right, boss. I'm talking it right.

"Mr. Labbe here has just advised me of an alarming development, Old Sport," the Virginia Cavalier said, "if it's accurate and verifiably true." I do wish the Son of the Tidewater would deign to sound one or two of the R's in the words he uses now and then, I remark to myself. But I know he won't. He never slips out of character. In public, at least. Does he have to think to leave that consonant out? If he does, is it worth the strain of remembering, and if he doesn't, what could account for that letter of the alphabet being stricken so thoroughly from the vocabulary of his people? Is it just cultural or genetic? Nature or nurture, I'm talking now, but I ain't doing that aloud. Arkansans have not happened on that turn of phrase and the thought processes it represents, at least in the opinion of the President and his Cabinet, and we as a breed are not allowed to wax philosophical.

"What is Eldridge Labbe telling you, Virginia?" I say in a jocular but relaxed tone. "The authentic Louisiana recipe for crab cakes?"

"Hillbilly," the Virginia Cavalier said, "what our friend from the Bayou country is relating is a bit more serious than that."

"Do tell," I said, thinking about the fact that the Virginia Cavalier, the Tyro of the Tidewater, did sound initial R's, just as he had just done with the word relating. That means he can use that sound if he wants, though I will admit that if you tried to pronounce a word beginning with an R without sounding it, you would be thought guilty of lisping or of being of the party of morons. Who wants to say welating? "What does our French friend have on his mind?"

"Them states, yeah," Labbe said, "them ones that begin their name with a I or a O, they say they succeeding. That's for true, yeah."

"Succeeding?" I said. "They think the rest of us ain't doing that?"

"Friend Arkansas," the Virginia Cavalier said, "the gentleman from the Pelican State doesn't mean these states with the initial letters of I and O are making great progress in some venture. He doesn't mean to say succeeding. He is referring to another concept altogether, one which landed us all in the peanut soup some decades back."

"You mean," I said, a light dawning like unto the sun rising on the Mississippi River as one might gaze upon it from the Arkansas shore. Peanut soup, my ass. It was a lot stronger broth than that Virginia delicacy that drowned us that first time.

"I mean that our Cajun companion means to say seceding,"

the Virginia Cavalier said, the sound of the word coming from his mouth much like the word turd would sound if the Mississippi Magnolia for some reason were forced to utter it. Let that never be, and perish the thought of her sweet lips suffering such defilement.

"Seceding," I said. "Secession. Oh, Lord. What a thing to say."

"What I'm saying on about is Illinois, Indiana, Ohio, Iowa, Oregon," the Louisiana Cajun said, keeping in character, I noted, by the way he began his statement with that dislocation of ordinary sentence structure. Credit be given the boy from the bayou. He would continue to misuse English with a vengeance from his own perspective. "Them Midwestern states, yeah. That's for true."

"Oregon is not Midwestern," the Virginia Cavalier said, "but that's by the bye. Let me ask you, Arkansas, have you seen any of these states in the last couple of work shifts?"

"No," I had to admit, "but you know all of us never show up every morning for the Entrance of the States. As long as we've got a voting quorum, the President allows us some leeway and flex. He has so informed the Cabinet of that allowance."

"I'm not speaking of flex time or virtual workplace location online, my roving denizen of the Ozarks," the Cavalier said, using that initial R again. "If you cast your mind back, can you recall such a commonality of absences from the Entrance as closely grouped as these particular states before? Is it just random?"

"Well, let's see," I said, looking straight into the eye of the Virginia Cavalier, not fixing him with the full Arkansas Stare, but reminding him I had it in arsenal. "I haven't seen the Indiana Hoosier or the Ohio Buckeye that I can remember."

"You ain't seen the Iowa Corncob, neither, no," the Louisiana Cajun said in a volume a bit louder than was usual, desired, or allowed. "Not the Oregon Meteor Crater, no. Not him, neither."

"Worse than that," the Virginia Cavalier said, dropping that R in worse so that the word sounded like wuss, "the Illinois Railsplitter has not been at the last several Entrances of the States."

"Not that they just ain't here, no," the Cajun added. "They be talking all together suppertime last night about succeeding one and all in a bunch."

"Seceding," Virginia and Arkansas said as one. "Oh, no."

"If the Railsplitter is talking secession, I am worried," I said. "Entertainment of that concept is completely not part of the affect of Illinois. The Prairie State has made a career out of not countenancing that word."

"Remember the fist fight at the Christmas party between Illinois and the South Carolina Gentleman?" Virginia said. "When South Carolina told the Railsplitter he would break him from sucking eggs?"

"The Railsplitter had to be pulled off of South Carolina before he did lasting harm to that representative of the Palmetto State," I agreed. "He promised to whip his secession licking ass every time he saw him from now on out."

I knew, of course, that the Railsplitter didn't really intend to do that. Eggnog was flowing like water, and I know for a fact that the California Hippie and the New York Trash Mouth had been passing around bodacious joints and a regular snow storm of the white powder at the party. Me, I stuck with moonshine, like always. It hurts me like I'm used to being hurt, and it does get the job done. That's one thing the Tennessee Long Rifle and I agree on right down to the ground. Distilled spirit from corn.

"This secession thing is just talk," the Virginia Cavalier said. "Nothing will come of it. Those states just think they're underpaid and underappreciated. They'll be back in the procession today, tomorrow at the latest. Check out what I'm saying."

"I say uh huh to that, Virginia," I said, lapsing a little into my vernacular niche, the Louisiana Cajun following up with a "that's for true" and some kind of mumble in Swamp French which I couldn't understand the burden of and would never want to.

"I believe it's about time for the Entrance to kick off," I said. "Are we doing order of ratification or alphabetical today?"

"It's Friday," the Cavalier said in a snippy tone. "So it's ratification order, unless things have changed without my knowing it."

I knew what day it was, and I knew it was ratification Friday, but I wanted to get off the topic of secession and back into a pattern familiar enough to all of us that we could shut off our brains and let the muscle memory do the walking. Sure as rain in the Delta in March, here came the Georgia Peanut, hull shoes hitting the ply-wood platform of the staging area with a slapping sound not to be misidentified or ignored. By regulation, he had to wear the loudest and the biggest and the worst looking shoes of any of us, and we never let him forget that.

Children of a certain age loved the Peanut's shoes, but those in the fell grasp of puberty would give the Georgia a lot less respect than he wanted, hooting and hollering at times, even making slap-ping sounds with their hands and their own footwear. The Peanut was good at ignoring such low-level insults, but we all knew he was a proud member of the legume family and took the hoorawing hard.

We all lined up behind him as per usual, roughly in the order of ratification of the constitution if our states had been around at the time and not still owned by France and Spain and Mexico, and after that all us late-blooming orphans struggled into line as the mood hit us. Days we were alphabetical were easy, of course, Tues-days and Thursdays and Saturdays, and we swapped off every other Sunday. So if we could keep straight whose Sunday was last, all was copasetic. MWF could be a booger, though, and the particular day I'm talking about was a Friday.

Being first in line three days and sometimes four days out of the week was important to the Georgia Peanut, and he took it seri-ously, trying his best to lead the Entrance of the States with dig-nity and grace and pride and all those other concepts the President used on us like steel shanked whips. I say the Peanut tried to lead in that fashion, but let me ask any reasonable man if it's truly possible to lead a procession of the United States of America, as portrayed in uniform, with grace and dignity and all that whoop-de-do while you're wearing 18 inch long non-flexible shoes in the shape of a peanut hull, the temperature is over 90 degrees in the shade, and your head is encased in a hard plastic peanut with one tiny mouth hole to breathe through. Add to that you're about 50 pounds over-weight, the administration won't spring for funds to buy you a big-ger uniform to fit what you've become, and you walk around in the attire of the Georgia Peanut so much each day that your skin when revealed is as white as the underside of a catfish belly.

It ain't easy, friend. Give me the rags and barefeet of an Arkan-sas Hillbilly any day. I count myself lucky, being able to live as close to the essence of ignorance as I do.

At any rate, here came the Peanut, the other states behind him in order of ratification, the orphans behind that in a ragtaggle line, and America the Beautiful blasting over the loudspeakers of the Patriot Park of America. At least it was instrumental now since the CD of the Blind Boys of Bessemer had vanished a month or two ago by sheer happenstance, and that was a relief to all of us. I mean bless the blind and the handicapped and let them do all they can to achieve an effect, but a bluesy, low, blind-sounding rendition of America the Beautiful more in keeping with field hollers rath-er than uplifting patriotic strains will bring a procession of states down rather than inspire them to greatness.

It those sentiments don't sound politically correct to some au-ditor, he can kiss my Yell County, Arkansas, country ass.

But we were marching out of the staging area, we were heads-held-high and fully uniformed, one and all, and the patrons had something patriotic to behold. Only a scattering of folks lined the way of our procession to the performance area, hot as it was, but sneaking a peak from under my cone-shaped felt hat with the patches of many hued fabric sewed to it, I could see that maybe thirty or forty were already seated in the open-sided building wait-ing for the Entrance of the States and the Declarations of Selfhood and Allegiance to follow.

The Georgia Peanut was in full waddle, shoes slapping, his peanut head bobbing from side to side, and the ones of the Origi-nal Signers present that Friday were right behind him, dipping and weaving in a good observance of the choreography as prescribed for that segment of our presentation.

I felt encouraged enough by the semblance of order and regularity and predictability there on display before me to let out an Arkansas yodel as I wheeled left to follow the Alabama Only Child into the performance venue. The clump of citizen/patrons by the entrance appreciated what I had just uttered, and not only that I had made a sound, but the content of it as well. A couple of parental units pointed me out to assorted offspring, one of them saying loud enough for me to hear, "Look, Jonah Eugene, that Arkansas hick just had to holler."

I appreciated the notice, but the use of the term hick instead of hillbilly did grate a bit. They knew better than that what my true label happens to be. It's printed in bold letters in the program that every citizen receives at the main gate and ticket office, and there's no excuse not to use the appellations assigned to the representatives of the States of the Union. They like to say hick, though, these chicken-shit Midwesterners, which was all we were getting those days at Patriot's Park of America, and hearing that insulting term always made me think two things. One is "kiss my hillbilly ass, you RV driving service worker from Akron," and the other is "this is another telling clue about our relentless demographic slide."

The paying customers by the door liked what I did with the Arkansas yodel, but the Alabama Only Child did not. She hated such displays of uncontrolled exuberance, considered them false, designed to mislead, and way yonder out of keeping with what she was accustomed to experience in the polite society of Birmingham. She would call it Buhminham, of course, as bad in her own Alabama way as the Virginia Cavalier at dropping internal R's and G's, so I added a modified and shortened Woo Pig, Sooie to get her blood up.

The Alabama Only Child pretended not to hear that, naturally, but she did give a flounce to her outfit, a beautifully detailed ball gown built on a 1950's model, and at that some of the patrons gasped in admiration. She knew how to make an entrance, I'll give her that, since that's been bred into them for generations, ever since Jefferson Davis stood on the Capitol steps in Montgomery and got the Great Mischief kicked off back in that 19th century spasm.

I was thinking to myself that maybe by some further strategic Arkansas yells and verbal flapdoodle I might be able to push the Alabama Only Child and the Mississippi Magnolia into a flounce-off once we all reached the performance area and got lined up for our Declarations when the whole thing began to happen. I was so deep into my session of Ozark scheming that I didn't realize what was going on until the sudden stoppage of the Entrance of the States before me caused me to step on the trailing tail of the Alabama Only Child's gown.

I was sorry I'd done that, since I knew what hell it had become to get any damage to an elaborate uniform repaired, and nobody knew that better than our two belles of the beauty states, the representatives of Alabama and Mississippi. That was the only thing those two lovelies agreed on, constitutionally despising each other as they did.

"Damn you, Arkansas," the Alabama Only Child said over her shoulder in a low and venomous tone, "keep your ignorant dirty feet to yourself." She was as preoccupied by my misstep as I was, and consequently we were the last states to realize what was happening at the head of the procession.

What finally caught my full attention was a low booming sound, a repetition with a bounce in it, and it didn't take me two seconds to identify it. I had heard it before many times and with increasing frequency as the Georgia Peanut deteriorated in the heat of summer, his increasing need for more oxygen to get to him through his insufficiently sized mouth hole, and his waning physical strength and endurance.

The little boom was the sound his hard plastic peanut head made when Georgia would let it drop to the floor after he'd popped it off for some relief. That sound I knew and was used to. What puzzled me was the repetition and the louder than usual bounce in the sound of the peanut head hitting the floor. With a gesture toward apology, I worked my way past the Southern Belle in front of me, saying, "Please pardon me, Alabama. I think the Peanut is in trouble."

"I do hope not, whatever could be…" the Alabama Only Child said, beginning her traditional verbal expression of Southern female concern about the misfortune of another, and then stopped midcareer in her speech. "Good God," she said in full voice, "I think they're trying to kill him."

It was the head of the Georgia Peanut giving forth that series of bouncing, booming sounds, but it wasn't the result of the Peanut's having popped off his noggin holder for relief. What I saw as I worked my way past Alabama, first in line alphabetically after the Original Signers, was the Georgia Peanut in complete captivity and control of the work hardened hands of the Illinois Railsplitter, on the floor and tipped on his side as the Railsplitter bounced the Peanut head up and down against the plywood of the center aisle. Dancing around the two was the Iowa Corncob, aiming kicks with his kernel shaped shoes against the Peanut hull of Georgia's hard plastic torso.

"Help me, Tennessee," I called out, not seeing the Long Rifle, but knowing he'd be the first to volunteer to aid me in rescuing the Peanut from the onslaught of the two I states from the Midwest. He did that, knocking the Idaho Potato aside in his rush to catch up to me, the Potato falling into a row of empty seats, blaspheming loudly as he fell.

"You bastards leave the Peanut alone," Tennessee yelled, just as I seized the Railsplitter by his leather suspenders where they crossed his back in support of his ragged and strategically shortened denim breeches. "Have you Yankee son of a bitches gone crazy?"

Giving a long and strong and heavy jerk to the Railsplitter's well made suspenders – let's hear it for authentic leatherwork – I got Illinois pulled away from the bashing he was laying on the Georgia Peanut, and straightened the Railsplitter up to his full height. He was long and tall, naturally, since he was representing an archetypal Lincoln as a young field hand, so he towered over me, not a shortie myself by any stretch of the imagination. Ignorant, yes, and backwoods with a vengeance the Arkansan may be, but he is not a little man. We are not talking about the Delaware Rutabaga or the Rhode Island Red here.

"Looky here, House Divided," I said to the Railsplitter, grabbing a suspender in one hand, and making a gesture of threat with my other one. "What has come over you? Have you lost your corn-fed mind?"

"Don't lay your traitorous hold on me, Hillbilly," the Illinois Railsplitter said, knocking my hand loose from his suspender. "There comes a time when parley and compromise will not suffice."

The crowd of citizen/patrons were beginning to stand up to see what was going on, the ones closest to me and the scene of the attack of the I states on the Georgia Peanut quailing back a bit from the action. The Iowa Corncob, now able to get a better purchase for putting his kernel shoes into the ribs of the Peanut, had stopped skipping around now that I had pulled the Young Lincoln away from his hold on Georgia. I could see he was loading up for some heavy footwork, and about the time I noted the impending stomp about to be launched, the Tennessee Long Rifle barreled into the Corncob with a whoop and a holler and a clothesline forearm.

The Railsplitter aimed a looping blow with not much on it at my face, which I was able to dodge, just before I put my head into the chest of the lanky field hand impersonator in front of me. I hardly had time to feel good about my maneuver, though, before somebody hit me from behind with a body block that sent me flying onto the back of the Georgia Peanut. Trying to scramble off the groaning promoter of the official legume of the Peach State, I saw that who had hit me was the back-stabbing Indiana Hoosier, living up to the lowest implication of his name.

The Texas Cowboy and the Missouri Outlaw let out twin bellows of threat and mayhem, and here they came pounding their way to the clot of us at the heart of the action, running full tilt into the Mississippi Magnolia and knocking her to the floor, the sight of which hurt me much more than any sneak assault by a lowlife Hoosier ever could.

Things became general at that point, the bays of alarm and joy from the citizens drowning out most of the language of threat, calumny, and promises of immediate and lasting damage from the nation's representatives rolling, struggling, biting, and begging for help from sister states as they fought. Straining up to see if I could spot the Mississippi Magnolia, I caught a good hard right hand from the famed peacemaker of our nation of laws and not men, the Illinois Railsplitter, and a light blossomed before my eyes, coming at me like a flood on the White River in Arkansas in late March. I tried to utter the name of the Mississippi Magnolia, but I sank deep into the flood, tired enough to sleep for a week before I was able to get past sounding the second S in the name of her home state.

The next morning all of us sat in the Room of the States in the stressed plastic chairs, lined up in order before the President, dressed in the suit he wore to receive visiting dignitaries, potential investors, public school administrators, stray historians, and announced visitors from foreign lands, and all others in the sphere of influence.

"Fisticuffs," he said, beginning his remarks in a softly voiced manner touched with sorrow and wonder. "Physical expressions of hostility in and among the states of the republic." We all stared straight at the chief executive's face, knowing better than to invite a remark from him about downcast eyes and dropped heads. He did not abide and would not endure a public lack of attention to his every word. We knew that from the marrow of our bones all the way out to our tiniest arm hairs.

The point of my chin did not ache exactly, but felt a bit numb with a buzz to it, a reminder of yesterday's hard right from the Illinois Railsplitter. I was pleased to note he was favoring his chest area, plucking now and then at the rough material of his linsey-woolsey shirt as though to ward off as much as possible anything touching his sternum but air. I took little comfort from that, though. He had put my lights out, and I did not rouse from slumber until I had been carried by one of the states back to my bunk. That was true embarrassment for a native of the Land of Opportunity, to have been shut down by one blow from a Prairie state resident. At least, though, I thought as the President worked his way into his address of remonstrance, I hadn't been decked by the Indiana Hoosier.

We sat, one and all, save for Maine, who was in the infirmary I had heard with a persistent cough, waiting for the bugling to begin. But it didn't.

"I speak to you assembled representatives of the United States of Patriot's Park after the events of yesterday to deliver my thinking on where we go from here," the President said. "I do so not in sorrow but with resolve. This is a time for truth-telling and facing up to the predicament in which we find ourselves." The president smiled, he touched his Windsor knot, he leaned forward manfully, he stepped from behind the podium, he held his hands palms up in a gesture of supplication. He scared the fire out of me.

"We are and have been in a downturn. We have touched the face of recession and found it dour and befouled with untended and wanton growth of a noxious nature. Let's just say it. You have witnessed the decline in patronage, you have experienced the empty venues before you as you have performed so bravely with so little reward, you have seen the darkness looming and enveloping Patriot's Park. It is time for a change."

"Hear, hear," the Massachusetts Minuteman said in a timid little voice, sidling up to authority in his lobster sucking way. Others joined in, from here and there in the gallery of assembled states. I heard Maryland, I heard New Jersey, I heard the Utah Jello second the sentiments. I didn't say a word, but I kept my gaze on the President's forehead in a constant fix.

"Yesterday's event may have seemed to many of you lamentable, a foretelling of doom for you and what you stand for and for Patriot's Park itself."

Yessir, too bad, oh pitiable, a day of infamy, desolation, and assorted other yips of agreement arose from all points of the compass, but the President held up a hand to quell the expressions of like-mindedness.

"I do not. I saw yesterday in that struggle among you a ray of light. More than that, a new direction and a pointer toward prosperity. I saw the future crook a finger of invitation and promise. I saw the response of the citizens to what they witnessed in that dust-up."

"Oh, shit," the Tennessee Long Rifle whispered in my direction, "what he's going to make us do?" The Long Rifle's face was badly battered, and his buckskin tunic was torn. He had lost a moccasin. My jaw flared with pain as though somebody had just inserted an icepick in my lower gum and leaned on it. I did not try to answer Tennessee.

In tonight's match, I am facing the Illinois Railsplitter, as happens every week or so. It has proved to be a popular pairing for a couple of reasons. We have a history of resentment and hostility, dating back to Independence Friday, and to what Illinois was able to do to Arkansas on that date. Add to that the disparity in physical makeup between the long-armed, long-legged, ham-fisted Railsplitter and the regulation sized Hillbilly, and you have a nice contrast in physical advantages and downsides.

What Arkansas lacks in reach, he makes up for in Hillbilly trickery and downhome clinch wrestling. He uses his feet in clever and unorthodox ways as well, sliding to the mat and lashing out with a dirty bare foot to trip up the essentially honest upstandingness of the Illinois Railsplitter. The verbal exchanges between the two leave the citizens both angry beyond measure and tickled half to death by the things Arkansas and Illinois say to one another. The Railsplitter will announce his intent to win the match by skill and aboveboard effort, saying something like "in fourscore seconds I will demonstrate not what I say here, but what I do here," and the Hillbilly will spit into the coffee can in his corner, and say something crude back.

He has been known to call the Railsplitter a jerked-up, slack-twisted handful of used corncobs, and to show the citizens what he means by the phrase used corncobs by vulgar movements of his illclad body. The citizens go mad, with joy, hate, and patriotism, and by the time the bout is over, no matter who wins this time, they rise as one and sing in pride the Anthem in accompaniment to the current version blasted over the loudspeaker. Every other week, a rap version is broadcast.

The President himself makes appearances at key matches, even refereeing important ones, such as the Georgia Peanut versus the Wisconsin Cheesehead or the Florida Gator matched up against the Maryland Crab. Another character has been added, not a state, but the District of Columbia Bullet. When the Bullet and the New York Trash Mouth lock up, watch out!

Business is booming for Patriot's Park, Old Man Recession is on the run, and new uniforms with tear-away parts for the matches have been issued to every State. Word is that the President himself may suit up in the near future and take on Old Man Recession in a grudge match.

And it's always something new, something different, something uplifting and fun at the same time, in store. Last week, the Mississippi Magnolia took the California Hippie apart in a sectional battle. She may talk sweet, she may be beautiful, she may smell like a roomful of flowers, but when Mississippi clamps her Rolling River hold on the peace loving, dopesmoking, green seeking Hippie, it is a sight to see. The Hippie begs and cries like a Buddhist.

Tonight is the first meeting between the loveliest representatives of all the states, the Mississippi Magnolia coming off her victory over the California Hippie up agains. the Alabama Only Child, who intends as she puts it "to show Mississippi how a lady can fight, not get her hair mussed, and still pull every faded petal off that magnolia. Bless her heart."

The Arkansas Hillbilly will referee the match and promises to make those belles keep it clean. "These lovely ladies represent the best of our nation," the Hillbilly said. "And they will fight like pit bulls to show it. Bless their hearts, and God bless the United States."

I feel good about it all. I really do. Woo pig, sooie.

Meat Shoot

It seems to me that you should have to be able to do more than just blink an eye to pull a trigger. Disabled is disabled, I understand that. But, Lord have mercy, when the fully able-bodied spinal cord therapist is the one that squeezes off the shot, it's a real stretch to say that the contestant she's pulling it for is playing on the same field level as the rest of us.

I know they claim she's been given the sign to pull trigger by the contestant himself. Jerome Miller has squinched up that right eye, and that's supposed to signify due intent, as they call it and as it says in the rule book, but hell, Jerome can't even see out of that eye in question. He can blink it, though, I understand, and he can't open or close the other one but a smidgen. And that's why they have to keep pouring the eye drops in there to keep it lubricated up. Yeah, I know all that. But suppose it's just a reflex, some kind of automatic nerve signal that blind eye's been given, and Jerome has got no more idea that it's time to blink or the blink is coming or it's done been blinked than I can decide to get up out of this wheel chair and do a double back flip.

Then what? Suppose the damn turkey has just at that exact time decided to keep its head still for a second or two, and that's when the automatic outlaw nerve impulse kicks in to make that bad eye of Jerome's quiver, and the spinal-cord therapist takes that for a duly thought out direction, squeezes off the round, and the bird's head disappears in a red rainbow. Are you telling me all the rest of us ought to holler at that and carry on and give Jerome credit for putting the turkey's lights out? Is that what you're saying?

She's looking at me right now, cutting her eyes over here like she's reading my mind and is thinking of a way to persuade me out of what I know is likely to happen. She probably thinks she can read my mind just by looking at the way my head's cocked to one side. All of them come to believe that in time, I'm convinced, that they can predict just what one of us is thinking and fixing to try to say. It's the arrogance of the TABs we're talking about now. The temporarily able bodied, the TABs, the ones who can do what they want to do by just doing it without having to waste an ounce of energy telling some part of the meat machine we live in to do something.

They just do it. Walk, spit, stretch, scratch an itch, drop trou and do their business, you name it, and never have to think to do any of it. It makes for a posture of confidence in themselves and what they believe they'll be able to do forever that just frosts me at times. I don't say what I know out loud to them, of course. That sort of announcement from one of us makes them think we're being difficult, and that's one label you can't afford to have slapped on you, especially when you're in the finals of the High Ridge Elks Lodge Disabled Veterans Old Fashioned Meat Shoot of Southern Illinois, 2008.

"Hello, Bill," she's saying now, Mary the spinal-cord therapist is, coming toward me on her own two feet, not watching a one of them and feeling in her nerves every time one of them hits the ground, but not noticing that because it's business as usual, same old, some old, what's new, ho hum. "Hello, Bill, are you ready to compete? Got your gun all loaded and your game face on?"

"Lock and load," I say. "Rock and roll." She acts like she understands what I mean by that, but I know she doesn't. I could be reciting the Gettysburg Address for all she can tell, her not being able to speak brain injury, much less in-country.

"Jerome's ready," she says. "You've got some real competition here in the finals." Then, realizing she's on the edge of talking to me like the meat shoot really amounts to something, she changes things a little. "Of course, it's all in fun, isn't it, Bill? No matter who hits the turkey, everybody gets to eat it when it's cooked, right?"

Everything the spinal-cord therapist lady says always ends with a question, like she's asking permission to be saying something to a sack of blood and guts that just sits there drooling at her. God knows what's in your crazy head, she's saying, but let's pretend for a minute or two there is something up there registering. I will not give it away, that questioning tone is saying. I will act like we are two folks conversing, not having to focus on a thing to make stuff work.

They are always more polite to a man who's not a man any more than they are to one who still is. Or thinks he is, and believes he's always going to be.

I'm giving her a smile, or at least I think I am, but who's to say what's really happening to my face. I can't feel the sucker, and I'm sure not going to be able to find a way to look at it to see what might be going on below eye level.

Jerome is ready, the spinal-cord therapist says, ready to compete. What does she mean by ready? How does she know? How can she tell? Trying to figure out if Jerome Miller is ready is like asking an egg tumbling around in boiling water if it's done yet. If the egg could talk back, it still wouldn't be able to tell you anything. Its yellow has done got too hard to run. Everything inside has cooked into a seize-up.

But the white of that egg has still got some run to it, still squirting back and forth as it tumbles in that hot bath that's making all of us curdle into a clump, and we've got to take what little advantage is left to us. Seize the movement, whatever's left of it.

So I smile at her or try to make myself think I'm smiling at her, no matter if it looks to her like I might be bearing down to effect a sphincter function. She'll smile back at me whether I break into song or break wind like a Shetland pony. One or the other, same or opposite, it don't matter to the spinal cord therapist lady. That's the thing about the line of work she's in. Her profession will not allow for making distinctions. When the body won't listen to what the mind says, picking and choosing goes down the tubes, and you got to take whatever gets throwed at you.

She has the piece of shiny metal in one hand, the device looking like a long-handled spoon for mixing pancake dough, and in the other hand she's carrying a wad of rubber bands she'll use to fasten the thing to my right arm, my flapper I call it. I can't tell where that arm's going or when or what it's going to do, but that baby will still flop around. That's a comfort to me.

Strap it on, I tell the spinal cord therapist lady, and get me ready to kill something. I say I tell her that, but to be honest, I think that's what I want to tell her and my mouth does open and my jaw works, and sounds tumble out. But I'm speaking in a language never heard before on this earth and never to be heard again. What I say is not reproducible. What matters in this world, I have learned through experience, is being able to do something more than once. Make it happen twice. If it can't happen again, it might as well never happen at all.

But here we are at the Old Fashioned DAV Meat Shoot of Southern Illinois, and I'm in the finals.

She acts like she understands me, though, laughing and nodding like a trooper as she works the rubber bands around the piece of aluminum and up my arm one by one to fasten the tool down tight. So I tell her some stuff out loud as I watch her work, something about what I'd like to be able to do with her after consuming a bottle of red wine and a hunk of bloody beef in a little bistro in

St. Louis, but to her it sounds no different than if I was saying the Lord's prayer or asking to borrow a tire pressure gauge. She is not offended, but I like to pretend I still got the power to insult and piss off.

Once you give up the notion that you can still act like an asshole and have people resent it, you might as well find a way to bite through the breathing tube, turn blue, and keel over. If you can't make somebody not like what you're saying and not take offense, you ain't here no more. Being able to torment your fellow man is the last true sign of life.

But here we are at the DAV Meat Shoot of Southern Illinois, and it's the finals, which I have made for the first time ever, and it's only me and Jerome left, and I know there's one person I can still torment by doing something. And I'm praying to all the saints and the gods above, domestic and heathen, to let me do just that. If I can bust a cap in that turkey's ass before Jerome does, I will surely make Jerome Miller suffer. It would be sweet, sweet, sweet. Let me do it, Lord, whatever your name is. Jehovah or Buddha or Allah or Unmoved Mover. Put that power into me.

It has come down to this, at last, and it would be a small triumph, I got to admit, to win this one. But I got to take what opportunity is still available, be it wasting a whole village of the able-bodied, or what remains of one member of the First Cav, drooling and blinking as he gets ready to have the spinal cord therapy lady touch off that .22 caliber round for him. She is fixing to judge him of a mind to pull trigger, I expect, the same way you know an infant needs its diaper changed. Not the mind, nor the mouth, but the body gives off a sign, and that sign is unmistakable.

One of the worst things about coming down to using this flapper of mine is the accompanying reduction in caliber I have to endure now. There was a time back in the Nam when I was master of a lot more firepower than a single-shot .22, I'd flat tell anybody. That is if I could get my speaking apparatus to do what it was designed to, rather than what it's come to.

I could always forage stuff that other people just left laying around, either through carelessness or sorriness or just suffering from a terminal lack of imagination. I'm talking about materiel now. Things you can drink and things you can blow stuff up with. That time I run up on a wing-mounted .75 caliber cannon that the F 16 fighter pilots got to shoot comes to mind. That plane was shot down, but it had landed so that one whole wing was in fine shape, looking like it had just come out of the box, that cannon as shiny as a kid's bicycle at Christmas back in Mascoutah, Illinois. I didn't know what had happened to the pilot and didn't care. He either parachuted out and got picked up by a Huey or he was currently humping his way down a trail north with a bunch of little bitty guys driving him along with sharp sticks. But I was on that wing-mounted cannon like white on rice, and before a half hour had passed, I had it detached, I had every shell still fireable put up out of sight, and me and a big old blood from South Chicago was bolting that thing to the front mount of our halftrack, getting it ready to fire.

Captain Phil Eddins, he didn't give a shit what we were doing with our customizing, long as he didn't have to think about it. He just stood back and smiled crooked at it like he did at everything, not saying a word.

"This here is going to improve our fire power, Captain," I said. "Me and Short Arm has about got it fixed up enough to try her out."

"How securely is that thing attached to the vehicle?" Captain Eddins said. "Will it fall off as soon as you shoot it? Not being standard, will it harm any equipment?"

"Only thing it gonna harm," I remember Short Arm saying, "is some slopes if we can scare some up."

"I am not seeing you doing this," the captain said. "I've been on the radio all afternoon. I am not here. Any shit comes down, it's going to roll right past me."

"Just like always," Short Arm said to me so the officer couldn't hear him, not that he would've cared if he had. "Captain be a shit-dodging mothergrabber."

"He learned that in college in the ROTC, Short Arm," I said. "That's where you and me missed out. All I know to do is how to catch, not dodge."

"Is it tight on that flange, Billy?" Short Arm said. "It ain't going to work loose, is it?"

"Listen, I have reared back on this wrench so hard, it'd take a company of marines and Jesus Christ himself to loosen these nuts."

"Jesus ain't worrying about loosening things up," Short Arm said. "All's on his mind is securing the perimeter."

"Praise him," I said and leaned back full-strength one more time on the wrench. It was up tight and out of sight. Time I got up in the gunner's seat, Short Arm was already rooting around in the ammo box where I had put the belt full of shells for the F 16 cannon, and we were ready to roll. Short Arm was beginning to sing one of the little ditties he was always making up for himself to describe what was going on around him at any given moment, and we were moving on down the line, looking for something to try out our new weapon on.

"Don't you just know when you trying to find a slope," Short Arm sang to a bluesy rhythm and beat, "you might as well be looking for a bunch of free dope."

"He ain't around," I put into Short Arm's song, "look up in the air or all over the ground."

"That ain't bad, Billy," Short Arm in his regular non-singing voice. "I believe I can make something out of that lyric."

We went on for a while, the halftrack's engine roaring and Short Arm singing, me trying to think of something else to add to the song, Captain Eddins slumped back in his seat toward the back of the compartment, his head not showing above the edge of the armor plate, like always. Far as he was concerned, we could have been crossing the Poplar Street bridge over the Mississippi about to enfilade. St. Louis, instead of where we were in the Quang Tri province, crawling along locked and loaded with the most firepower ever before in history hooked up to a T 3112.

"Looky here, looky here," Short Arm said all of a sudden, stopping his song and speaking in his regular South Chicago voice. "What do I see over yonder in that rice paddy?"

"Is it a squad of NVA?" I said, knowing full well it wasn't. Was, and we'd have been backing up and Captain Eddins would have been on the radio calling in an air strike, just jabbering about how many of them it was.

"It ain't but the one," Short Arm said, "and he's all dressed up like a farmer. He's what you call disguised."

"Not only that," I said, "he has positioned some camouflage over that field piece so it looks like a ox pulling a plow."

At that, Captain Eddins roused up and peeped over the edge of the armor plate to see what we were talking about. "Where?" he said, and then, "oh shit. Don't you silly bastards start shooting at that rice farmer. Don't you know we're trying to win the hearts and minds of these people?"

"This ain't no time to be making jokes, Captain," I said. "We have made visual contact with the enemy and we must engage him."

"Preach it on out, Billy," Short Arm said. "Hoo rah."

"Goddamn it," Captain Eddins said, "if you cut down on that farmer, I'll break you in rank and have you court-martialed and thrown in the brig."

"Sir, do you mean you ain't gonna let us run around in the woods here no more?" Short Arm said. "You gonna take away our combat status? Make us go back to town and be locked up tight in a room with walls and a roof over it?"

"Oh, Lord," I said, "don't say you about to do that, Sir. You get me so nervous I won't be able to draw a fine bead on that camou-flaged slope."

"Oh, bullshit," Captain Eddins said. "Shoot out into that field if you want to, but don't hit that man. You heard me, Pawlow."

"Onliest way Billy going to hit that slope is if he tries to miss him, the way he shoots a piece," Short Arm said.

"Bullshit, Short Arm," I said. "You ain't on the South Side now, banging away with a handgun in every direction. You talking to a man raised in Southern Illinois that knows how to shoot the nuts off a flying squirrel at fifty yards. Watch this. I'll show you close I can come with this cannon and still miss that dink."

I've got to admit it was a pretty picture, the farmer out in his paddy wearing his funny hat and walking up to his knees in water, his ox plodding along in front hooked up to the plow, switching its tail to discourage flies from landing on its back and a range of middling sized hills behind the whole scene almost purple under the sun and just about to begin that slow slide toward the horizon.

"Lord, Short Arm," I said. "Kiss my ass if that ain't a postcard fit for a calendar."

"Umm, umm," Short Arm answered. "I hate to see that evening sun go down."

The cannon having come off an F 16 wing, there was no proper sight like there would have been on a .50 caliber, so I was having to eyeball over the muzzle, using a wing nut on the edge of the mounting flange as a bead and moving my head up and down to try to line things up. "Check this out, Short Arm," I said. "I'm going to put a couple of rounds way ahead of the ox and then play it back closer when I get a feel of this ordnance."

"You ain't going to have to allow for no windage, I do believe," Short Arm said, but I didn't hear what he said next, because about then I pulled trigger and everything sounded like a house coming down on you during a tornado on a Southern Illinois prairie. House roofs lifting, trees jumping out of the ground like they had somehow learned how to hop straight up in the air on their own, and everything in the yard suddenly deciding to evacuate the premises with a rattle and a bang.

"Whoa," Short Arm said. "Look at that crater ahead of where the ox used to be. Ever bit of water jumped out of the hole the shells made and then flopped back in like it was trying to hide."

"You crazy bastard," Captain Eddins was saying, rising up with his eyes popped and his hands up to his ears, way too late to save them from the sound of the muzzle blast. "I told you not to waste that slope."

"Didn't waste the man," I said, hollering so I could hear myself talk over the dead feeling in my head. "He's taking off the other direction."

"What's that bouncing behind him?" Captain Eddins said. "What's he dragging at the end of that rope?"

"He pulling what's left of that ox's head," Short Arm said. "It appears to me like he's got one whole horn left and part of a nose."

"Where is the damn ox?" Captain Eddins said. "I don't see him."

"Some of him's in the paddy underneath the water, I imagine," I said. "I think this new style ordnance has turned the rest of him into ox tail soup."

"Several servings of soup," Short Arm said. "Look what color the rice paddy has turned."

The Captain made us take the cannon off the halftrack, and that took awhile, though he did let me shoot it off one more time, a long burst this time aimed at the horizon that set up such a torque it twisted the halftrack a yard or two clockwise. That did it for the Captain, and he gave me and Short Arm a direct order to throw the .75 cannon and the rest of the shells into the rice paddy.

After we got that done, Captain Eddins calmed down and laid back down in the rear of the compartment while me and Short Arm got the halftrack fired up and headed back to where we had started out that morning. Short Arm said he guessed the slope who'd been farming was still running, that ox horn and nose just bouncing behind him, but I said no he probably was trying to make himself remember if he had gone to work that morning or not and was maybe still sleeping and when he woke up things would be the way they were supposed to be.

"Bill," the spinal cord therapy lady is speaking distinctly into my line of sight, "I sure am glad to see you looking so happy and smiling so much. Are you ready to watch Jerome take his shots at the turkey?"

I gobble something at her, and I hope she's telling me the truth about the way she says I'm smiling. I feel like that inside my head, but damned if I know what I'm showing on my face. I might be smiling like she says, as I think about me and Short Arm and the F 16 cannon and that residue of memory could be showing on my face, but I sure didn't put it there on purpose. Of course, when you're truly smiling, you're not really pasting it on by thinking about doing it. Some things just happen, and the body follows along, a step or two behind where the conscious mind is thinking to go. That's what they mean by spontaneous. And a smile that ain't spontaneous is not a smile at all, if your meat machine is functioning in the normal range.

If you make yourself smile, and can do that, that expression is not a true smile. If the machine has lost all its connections, though, you might be smiling in the judgment of the TABs outside looking in, but inside your own poor old crazy head, you could be crying your heart out.

Just like that dink back in '68 running through the jungle with part of the head of his ox bouncing along behind him on a string. I never got a look at that farmer's face, but I do expect it wasn't showing any evidence of happy times rattling around inside the old corral of his cerebral cortex. He was spontaneous, not intentional.

Jerome Miller is ready, though, says Mary the spinal cord therapist lady, locked and loaded and ready to give her the blink to pull trigger on that .22 and bust a cap on that turkey's head sticking up out of the box. Believing she knows that he's ready is truly an act of faith on Mary's part for certain, but I've believed a lot harder things to swallow than that before. Hell, I volunteered for the army and the tank corps and all those probing missions in the mud and the dark and the places where nobody ever said a word I could understand. I fastened that F 16 cannon off the wing of a fighter to the halftrack I was gunner on, and I touched it off just to hear it bang and watch stuff that was whole and in one piece one second fly up into the air in particles the next. I looked for ways to turn meat machines into halos of red mist.

I liked doing all that, because I believed what I was doing was worth doing. If you had asked me to spell out and write down just exactly in words what I believed, I couldn't have done that. But put me up to the sights of a functioning piece of ordnance and show me where to put my finger, and be prepared to step back and get out of the way. I believed something strong and deep enough to pull trigger, see what I'd done, and then go back to base and eat me a big steak, drink me some red whiskey, and talk about it to whoever would listen to me.

I'm hearing the pop now, so I know Jerome has blinked, Mary the spinal cord therapist lady has pulled trigger, and if all the planets are aligned in the right order, that turkey's head has blossomed into mist like a red rose opening up.

She's looking at me, the spinal cord therapist lady, and she's smiling, and I can tell it's a real one because the tips of her eyebrows are showing muscle movement. Jerome Miller, damn him, has busted a cap in that turkey's ass, and nobody's going to be willing to listen to me argue them down about whether a completely paralyzed man should get credit for just blinking and having some TAB take that as a signal to pull trigger. If I could argue, that is. If I could make words come out of my mouth, and if I could get this meat machine to do what it's supposed to do.

Nothing to do now but to watch the spinal cord therapist lady strap that spoon-looking flapper to my arm and shove the other end through the trigger guard and tape it to the mechanism for firing. I'll pull it when one of these random electrical impulses rips through the synapses and makes it all twitch. And if I'm lucky and my turkey's not, we'll see another red rose open up like glory here in a minute or two.

I may not win the Old Fashioned DAV Southern Illinois Meat Shoot this time, but we'll see what randomness can do. That dink back in the rice paddy got to see his ox turn into something completely unexpected. Short Arm up there in South Chicago had the same experience outside that liquor store in 1978 when that strung-out kid popped him in the back of the head and laid his machine down for good, his perimeter permanently secured. I myself found my thrill on a no-name hill, when everything I saw in front of me jumped in the air and barked like a pit bull as big as a halftrack.

Maybe that dink is still running with what's left of his ox bouncing along behind him, and maybe my meat machine will do it one more time, even if the goal is just a turkey with his head sticking up out of a box. Let me twitch it, spinal cord therapist lady. Look at my face. I might be smiling. Let her rip.

Decoration Day

Maude

I can see the deep green of the cedars among the oaks and gum trees ahead, there in the clearing of the Blue Water Chapel graveyard, and the cedars are not so tall as the other trees coming toward us, but they are more serious. A deeper green, thicker in leafage, more gathered into themselves, silent in a way oaks and gum and sycamores can never be. They are restless, those trees not cedar, moving and sighing in whatever wind blows, their leaves turning and dying and falling by season, putting forth new growth, tender and delicate and pale in the spring. They are never finished, never settled into themselves the way a cedar is in its beginning, its growth, its flourishing and its death when its time comes, the same always. The other trees move, the cedar is.

I would like to think people plant cedars in graveyards because they recognize statement and meaning in them, and they may do so partially, but I am not content to believe they see more than one word of the language a cedar speaks. And that one word they translate into human language is evergreen, and that satisfies them, in the way an infant is first satisfied and clings so long to the first connection it makes between sound and what it conjures, whenever it learns to say that word mama.

What the cedar says in a graveyard is more and is part of the balance, too, I have come to know and believe, and the psalmist understood that when he sang of two meanings that tree has, each true and each opposed, one gain and one loss. The psalmist declares his hope when he says that the righteous shall flourish like a palm tree, he shall grow like the cedars in Lebanon.

And there in that song is celebration and the knowledge of the deep green of the cedar, and there is the comfort a cedar announces in the silence of its place in the graveyard, and in the intent of its planting there by the living.

But the psalmist sees the balance, the loss attendant upon the gain, the emptiness that accompanies the full, when he sings the other notes of his song, the remainder of the language beneath language. That is what he proclaims when he says the voice of the Lord breaketh the cedars, he breaketh the cedars of Lebanon.

And this song makes up the rest of the balance I see in the world as testified by the cedars, and in the people who spend their lives in it, the end that comes to each beginning, the coins that must be spent to empty every purse.

Abigail is speaking to Richard, pointing ahead over his shoulder as she leans forward on the bench to hurry the wagon toward the destination she craves. "Look," she says, "there's where the old church building stood before it burned, there's Blue Water, there's the cedars. See how green they are."

Papa's stone draws her first, as it always does, and we walk directly to it, past the clump of Moye and Johnson and Snodgrass markers, Abigail leading the way with Richard close behind and me trailing, the mules still hitched to the wagon and snorting as they crop the weeds and grass outside the graveyard. I let my fingertips graze the top edges of each stone I come to, rough and heated by the sun, and I don't allow myself to look yet to the left side of the way we go, toward the smaller blue granite one set off to itself, some distance from the spot we are headed.

That belongs to Carolina Cameron Holt, my mother, and Abigail's mother and Lewis's mother and Estelle's mother, and the mother of all the rest of us, alive and dead, and I will wait on that one and view it last, since by then I will need the balance it represents.

Abigail is saying again what she always does when we come to Blue Water, telling whoever is with her, whether they listen or not, about the way Papa's stone has been moved. It's now by Nelda's marker, and of course it's not the original one put at the head of his grave only a few months after he died and paid for by what his and Mama's children got together among us to make sure anybody who chose to look would know Amos Holt was resting by the wife he brought to Texas, Carolina Cameron Holt.

That stone is gone now, and no one knows who took it nor how they disposed of it, as small as it was and as light, light enough for a strong man to carry unaided. We thought at first, it would be in the woods around Blue Water Chapel graveyard, thrown there somewhere in the underbrush, in a location in the vines and creepers and palmetto and saw-briars, close naturally to the graveyard itself, where a person of that character who would commit such a deed would toss it aside, too lazy and sorry to spend the effort to transport it further away from the site from which it was stolen.

But it is not there, where we suspected, buried somewhere beneath the green thorns of summer and the dead leaves which fall and rot each year in the fall and winter. We have not found it, though each of us has looked every visit that's made to Blue Water. Abigail will do it again this time, I know, poking about with a stick and kicking at this year's accumulation of decay and damp, hoping to turn up that flat stone with Papa's name and dates cut into it.

I stopped doing that years ago. Whoever took the marker away we underestimated, and I am satisfied to accept that fact and to recalculate the depth of his intent. But my mind has eased about it, and what came to comfort me began in a dream granted me about Papa's stone and where it was hidden.

I had looked that day in the woods around the graveyard, with Abigail and Calvin from midday until the dimming light of the sun's going down made it impossible to see what might be at my feet. I forget where my sister and brother and I spent that night, somebody's house in Sabine County, I know, but somewhere in the course of my sleep I found myself watching a figure dressed all in gray, carrying the marker from my father's grave clutched tight against its breast and moving steadily away from me.

The stone was smaller than in reality, little more than the size of a book, but it was exceedingly heavy and the man who carried it, his face hidden from my view, struggled to hold the marker as he moved ahead of me in a stumbling walk. Yet he persisted to move away and seemed to know where he intended to go. I followed him, as you will in a dream, my legs heavy and reluctant to move and every action of my body slower than I wanted it to be, and my feet seemed barely to touch the ground enough to give me purchase to carry on. But I did, at great cost, feeling tears course down my cheeks from the strain and effort it took.

Then, of a sudden, the man before me reached the edge of a pond circled with high grass and bending willows, and I was surprised enough in the dream to wonder at where we were, knowing there was no pond of any description near Blue Water Chapel, and I was aware that I was thinking too much, and I became afraid I would awaken from the dream before I saw what the man in gray would do with the book-sized marker from Papa's grave. I don't know how to explain the next part of what I dreamed except to say that to my mind all the world began falling into layers, and I could see everything about me and before me repeated over and over, one level on top of the other and each changed in small detail from the one beneath yet still part and parcel of what had gone before and was to follow one step above it.

And the figure held the stone cut with the name of my father and his dates of coming into and leaving this world out before it over the water of the pond, and then he let it drop. It entered the water without a splash and sank from sight, and though I couldn't see beneath the surface of the pond to verify what I knew to be true, yet I did know that the stone reached the bottom of the pond upright, fixing itself in a position to last all time and forever, and I was as relieved by that knowledge as though a cool breath of air had come up to move across my face on a hot, close day in Texas.

In the dream I closed my eyes to relish the full benefit of the cooling breeze, and when I opened them again the figure in gray was gone, vanished like a fog burned off by sunlight, and the surface of the pond glistened before me like pearl.

And the memory of that dream has sustained and satisfied me from that night to this day, and that comfort allows me to accept what Abigail cannot.

When my sister looks at the slab of gray granite reared up beside its twin, the stone engraved with the name of our stepmother Nelda Faye Holt and her dates and the words Beloved Wife of Amos beneath the other letters, she sees repudiation and bald announcement. She reads a claim made that Papa never loved our mother in the way he loved Nelda, that his true wife and soulmate lies beside the gravestone put there by the children he had with her, that the words carved beneath his name and dates are truth and deed and monument to that love. "In Paradise Together," the words run as a bottom line across the gray granite of Papa's marker larger than Nelda's beside it.

These words are gall and ashes to Abigail, each time she sees or recalls them, and they draw down her lips into a look of disgust and dry up her mouth like cotton.

They're nothing to me but chisel marks on a stone slab shaped by a machine operated by a man, I imagine, somewhere in a state far off, a man who has never set foot in Texas, much less Sabine County, and who never will. There is no heart in that rock, nor in the inscriptions upon it.

I know where Papa lies, and where he will for all time, and it is next to Carolina Cameron Holt, no matter what statement on what surface in what location at what amount of expense of dollars spent to achieve it. I am satisfied.

"I wish you would look at this," Abigail is saying to Richard, speaking to him because she knows from experience there is little chance to gain satisfaction from addressing me. I cannot give her what she wants and needs, to hear about Papa's stone, though she thinks it is a matter of will not rather than cannot where I am concerned. "I believe to my soul somebody has tried to plant a rose bush between these two gravestones and get it to grow."

Richard murmurs something to her I can't hear and turns to look back at me where I am standing by the blank spot Papa's first grave marker occupied, the place by Mama's small blue one. From a small boy, Richard has always been tender about the feelings of others, and he wants to be sure now he is not leaving me out while talking to his Aunt Abigail. I nod at him and smile, and he turns back to say something to her.

"By the way the ground's been dug up, that's how," Abigail says, making sure she's talking loud enough for me to hear every word. "And see that little broke-off root there? That's a cutting from a rose bush, and I bet it's a Victoria Pink."

Giving in, I walk on toward where my son and my sister are standing by Papa's stone and Nelda's grave, and I can tell that Abigail is glad to see me coming.

"Look," she says, pointing straight down at the spot between the stones where she is convinced she's discovered evidence of a rose bush planting, her finger held at a stiff angle as though she's telling somebody where not to step in order to avoid getting something nasty on clean footwear, "they are trying to force a rose bush to grow up between these gravestones."

"They are?" I say, neutral as I can make it, "who is?"

"Oh, some of that bottom bunch," Abigail says, "who can tell which one? Lurleen, maybe, or Frances Marie. It'd be just like that two to come up with the idea to coax a Victoria Pink rose bush to pop up between Nelda's and Papa's stones and twine all over them. Can you imagine how it would look? Pink roses just all over everywhere, just growing and blooming and smothering away."

Abigail sounds as though she's about to cry by now, so I say not a word back to her, neither to comfort nor conspire with her mood. Instead, I stand quiet near Richard and watch her pull at the rose cutting that speaks so contrary to her opinion of Papa and Nelda together, muttering beneath her breath and so eager to remove the offending Victoria Pink she has cut her hand on its thorns.

"Haven't you got a pocketknife?" Abigail says to Richard, not cross but rushed in her voice's delivery, "Can't you see I need a hand with this cursed flower bush?"

Richard says yes ma'am and bends to help Abigail prevent any chance of pink rose blossoms popping up between the gravestones of husband and wife dead together for the ages, and I lift my face toward a little breeze just sprung up, relieving to me in the bald sunlight of that part of Blue Water graveyard, out of the shade as we all are.

Papa's true gravestone is cool, too, I tell myself, where my dream tells me it stands in the bottom of its pond, fixed in position upright for all time and touched on each surface always by the hush of water. Quiet, dimmed, unseen.

"I've got it all pulled up," Abigail is saying, clutching a dirt-covered root before her in both hands, as though to prevent any possible movement by it toward escape, "There won't be any roses growing around here now.. "Good," I say to my sister. "Good for you."

Richard

They always talk to each other just like they're doing now, every time they come to Blue Water Chapel to look at the graveyard, Mama and Aunt Abigail do. When they get to going at each other this way, it puts me in mind of the time in school when Mr.

Chambliss gets out one of his old books he tells us he studied in the academy and starts reading out loud to us. It's Latin, he tells us, and what I get from listening to him read it in his high little voice never makes any real sense. He could be reading anything to us, and saying it wrong on purpose, or leaving things out or putting wrong words in. How am I to be able to know? It's Latin.

But some of it sounds enough like words I do know and have heard and have read in books to make me think that what he's saying is actually true words that mean. There is something about what's coming out of his mouth to make me think that sensible matters are being treated of, people and places and things are being talked about, something took place sometime that somebody took notice of and wrote down.

Sometimes I imagine if I listen hard enough and take in what is being said out loud quick enough, why then I'd understand what he was issuing forth in a foreign language to me. It's foreign all right, I say to myself, but it's real close to making sense. If I could strain hard enough to get it in my head and my understanding, that is. Or if I could make myself want to strain that hard, maybe I could get my mind around enough of it to pick up some meaning, understand what's behind the sound.

So it is with Mama and Aunt Abigail, here in the middle of the Blue Water graveyard, standing next to my grandpa's headstone and the one by it, Aunt Nelda's. That is the spot, the very location where on each visit they start talking like a teacher reading Latin out loud in a schoolhouse to a bunch of half-grown boys and girls in East Texas.

Let me say it straight. Aunt Abigail and Mama are talking in English, all right, but the words they're saying, if you saw them written down on a piece of paper in print or in longhand, wouldn't be carrying near the meaning they have on them as they're going back and forth in the air between the two women right now in this place where all these dead people are under the ground.

Roses, Aunt Abigail is going on about, roses, pulling so hard on a root full of thorns that she cuts a gash in her hand deep enough to make blood run clear down to her wrist. Yet she is so glad to get the thing pulled up out of the ground between the gravestones that she's smiling like somebody's just handed her a Christmas gift. I'm glad she didn't give me time to get my pocketknife out to let her use when she asked for it. She probably would have cut a finger off, the way she was going at that rose bush, and not even noticed she'd done it, happy as she was to be finished with the job.

But she did put a stop to Aunt Nelda getting a flower bush started up by her head stone, Aunt Abigail did, and it was done all on her own, too. The reason that is such a satisfaction to her I don't understand completely, but I do know it comes from the same source that caused Aunt Abigail and Mama and the rest of my aunts and uncles to teach me and my brothers and sisters and all my cousins to call Grandpa Holt's wife Aunt Nelda instead of Grandma.

They let all of us know as soon as we could understand what they were saying, one by one as we got old enough to listen, that Grandpa's wife was not our grandma, but just a woman he lived with we were all supposed to call Aunt Nelda. Our real grandma was dead and buried in Blue Water Chapel graveyard, but that didn't matter. She was still truly our grandma and the mother of our mothers and fathers and the real wife of Grandpa Amos Holt, not that lady in his house, the one who managed somehow to have had half-children.

That notion of half-children, or half brothers and sisters, spooked me for a while when I was a chap, and I remember looking real hard at the uncles and aunts I was told were only half ones, whenever I happened to be around them, seldom though that was. Until I got old enough to have better sense, I believed that if I kept close watch on one of these half-uncles or half-aunts – Felder, say, or Effie or Nokomis or anyone of them – that they might forget I was studying them and let me glimpse where the part was missing that would have made them a whole and not just a half uncle or aunt to me. But none of them ever slipped up and showed me that lack during those years I was young enough to believe they might.

They always looked and seemed the same, up one side and down the other.

Aunt Abigail is still knocking that rose bush root against the top of Aunt Nelda's headstone to get the dirt off it, careful not to let any trash fly across the space between it and Grandpa Holt's and maybe land on his stone, even though I know she doesn't like the one cut for him or approve of it since it's not real somehow in her mind, and in a minute or so she's got the root cleaned up enough to allow her to sling it away to one side with a big grunt. You would think the root weighed as much as a cotton sack picked full-up.

I let my eyes follow it to where it comes down three or four graves away, over among some other family's stones, the Moye's I guess them to be, and that's when I first see the woman standing close to the bole of one of the big cedars, almost all hidden in the shadow of its branches, darker green than any of the hardwoods around it and not so easy to see into.

What my gaze first settles on are the shoes she's wearing, picked out of the cedar shadow by a beam of sunlight – hightops they are, a man's workshoes, worn and busted out with the toes curled up as they will come to be from getting wet and drying out over and over. There are no strings in the grommets, and it comes to my mind that you'd have to be thinking all the time if you were wearing them how you would have to step so as not to come out of your shoes whenever you put a foot down.

The legs going into the workshoes are thin and black, like straight lines drawn in ink on paper, and the woman is wearing a mingled-colored flour sack dress that comes down past her knees to just above the tops of the shoes. She has her arms crossed over her breast with one hand on top of the other one, so if she was in the same position lying down she would look like a woman laid out to be buried. But then, of course, she'd have her eyes closed, and that she sure doesn't. She's looking straight at me out of them, and they're not covered by a cedar branch in front of her which is hiding most of her face, and her eyes are opened wide, looking whiter and bigger than they really are, the way eyes always do on a person whose skin is black.

"Mama," I say, nodding toward the woman looking straight at me with her eyes fixed and unblinking, so big and white in the shadow, "Aunt Abigail, there's a colored lady over yonder standing inside that cedar tree."

Abigail

The root of that Victoria Pink has finally come loose after all my pulling on it, my nephew just standing there watching me work away at cleaning things up, when he says what he does about a woman inside of a cedar tree and her colored. My first thought is not even to listen to what he is saying. All his life back to the time when he was first beginning to learn to talk and right on up to the present day, Richard has been a boy who imagines things and makes up stories, stories not to fool whoever he's telling them to, really, but because he's made himself believe them and just has to give somebody an account of what he's come to think is true.

I remember Maude telling about how he would come in the house at the end of day at supper time, back before he was even big enough to be a help around the place, and she would find all manner of trash in his pockets when she was putting him and the rest of the bunch to bed. It'd be little rocks, or pieces of string, or leaves or maybe a bent nail somebody had thrown away, all manner of stuff, that Richard had found, and when his mother would chastise him for filling his clothes up with such truck, he'd start explaining how whatever it was she'd pulled out of his pocket was a thing he felt obliged to pick up.

Why? Because it was lost off from the rest of the things like it, he'd say, and it was lonely and afraid, and he felt like he had to bring it home to save it from the situation it was in. I'm talking about rocks now. And nails. And twigs and sticks. Just plain junk.

And then he'd cry and carry on, and Maude would let him keep whatever was the current item of attention, and she'd indulge him in the story he told about it and listen to him like he was making sense and was onto something worth worrying about.

That behavior from a mother will ruin a child, naturally, and no one would ever find me making that mistake. But that was Maude, and her child, and none of mine, thank the Lord.

So when he says that thing there to us in Blue Water Chapel graveyard about a colored woman, I just think to myself, well, Richard's a little old to be seeing people growing out of trees or being part of one or whatever it is he means by that statement out of nowhere. I guess he's entertaining himself again, trying to pump a little interest into what's probably a boresome space of the day for him. So I take my time in looking up or giving any indication to my nephew that he's fooling me or diverting my attention away from what we're there in the Blue Water graveyard for, to honor Papa, and Mama, too, and to undo any foolishness of public display that bunch of Nelda's might be up to.

Maude, being all ears all the time to whatever Richard might volunteer to say, has shifted her position where she's standing, which I can tell by hearing her shoes crunch in that sandy Sabine County soil in the graveyard, and is looking just as hard as she can in the direction her boy has indicated. Sometimes I think if Richard was to tell her he'd spotted a whale in Double Pen Creek, she'd throw down whatever she was holding at the time, no matter what it was, and run down to the water's edge to see if she could harpoon it.

But then Maude speaks, and I know I'm obliged to look up from where I'm focused on getting Papa's headstone properly redded up, if I want to know what's going on.

"Why, hello," Maude says, "are you trying to stay out of this hot sun?"

I look up toward the cedar tree Richard has been facing, and still is, knowing that Maude will be looking at the exact same thing he is, and I'm thinking two things at once. One is that if you could draw two lines on a piece of paper to show how Maude's line of sight and Richard's would look side by side that you'd have to use a ruler to do it, they'd be that parallel. The other thing in my mind along with that notion is that by the way Maude is speaking, the tone in her voice and how she has cast her words, you wouldn't be able to tell if she was conversing with an imaginary colored woman in a cedar tree or Governor Branch Colquitt at a tea party in his mansion in the state capital. It is all the same to her, no matter who she's talking to.

But the colored woman is not imaginary, I see as soon as I straighten up to look where Maude and Richard are facing. My nephew didn't make her up for entertainment while his elders worked, after all, and she is stepping out from the shadow of a big cedar I hadn't even noticed the whole time we've been in the Blue Water Chapel graveyard, and she's fixing to say something back to the white lady that's just greeted her.

"Yes, ma'am," she says. "It is cooler in the shade, but I guess I wasn't thinking about that none."

The woman makes a good appearance, not mumbling her words and looking down at the ground so you can't understand her, as so many darkies will do when talking to a white person, and the dress she's wearing looks clean and fits her pretty well. Her gaze is toward Maude, as it ought to be, since that's the white lady who's spoken to her, but the woman's not looking directly at my sister, just a little off to one side, showing she's got manners and knows how to act.

That's a nice thing in a colored woman, or in a man, too, when they know how to do and let you see evidence of that fact, as soon as you start dealing with one of them. It doesn't take much of a sign to do that, to let you know the one before you is going to behave in a dutiful and civilized manner and that you don't have to be worrying the whole time that some kind of event between a white and a colored is fixing to take place.

What a colored man or woman giving such a signal to you does is simple enough, to run the risk of belaboring the point, and it's important, too. It greases the way to a clear communication. That's the way I see it. And, I swear, fully half the trouble that comes up between us as white folks and them as colored has got more to do with them not taking the time or effort to let the white person understand there's no reason for concern, nor harm is intended. But to do that, of course, requires the colored to think ahead and be mindful of appearances and the possibility of misunderstanding.

That is not the black man's long suit, thinking ahead. Nor the black woman's neither, though being a woman helps in all cases of understanding what somebody other than yourself might be thinking or meaning, no matter what color you are. Men are the ones who fly off the handle, not women, nine times out of ten, and men are the ones who go off half-cocked about situations.

But this woman now before me, talking politely to Maude like she's doing, and showing she knows how to address a white lady, I do feel good about right off, though I don't know who she is or what she's doing in Blue Water Chapel graveyard. She's dressed presentable, in addition to the way she's carrying herself in front of the white people she's faced with, she has got a nice head cloth tied close and flat around the front of her hair and hanging down loose in the back, showing she wants to control the way kinky hair can lump up on a colored person's head if they're not careful, and she's holding one hand in the other in a composed way, which testifies she's ready to pay due attention to what's going on and her part in it.

I can tell she is not fully calm, though. She is nervous, but holding it in. Her lips, which are not real thick ones, are tight pressed together, and there's a little tremor in her hands, clasped together so close as they appear to be. Some of that condition is understandable, and I would expect her to be on edge about what's going on, her being in a white graveyard by herself having to talk to white folks who belong where they're standing.

So when she says what she does to Maude about the difference between being in the shade and standing in the sun, I figure I ought to speak up, too, say something or other, not just let my sister set the tone of the conversation with this strange colored woman who's popped up in Blue Water graveyard unannounced, not withstanding that she seems to know how to act when dealing with a white lady who's just spoken to her.

"And what might that be?" I say in a clear voice, careful not to hurry my words, "This matter you're thinking about other than how hot it is today?"

"This is my sister," Maude says to the woman, as if she's just asked my name and Maude is compelled to answer, "Mrs. Abigail Mott, and I'm Maude Winston."

"She's married, too," I say to the colored woman who is still looking at Maude, despite the fact I'm the one speaking, "just like me. Winston is her husband's name, not her maiden name. We're Holts. Me and my sister, Mrs. Winston, both of us are. Holts."

"Yes, ma'am," the colored woman says, turning her attention finally to the woman who's been talking to her, me, I mean. "I done already know that, Miss Abigail."

"Mott," I hear myself say back at her quick, twice, "Mrs. Mott." I don't even have to think to do it; the words just come out when I hear her call me by my first name like that. The woman has moved further away from the cedar tree where she's been standing, a good deal closer to us and Richard a little way behind still, and Maude actually reaches out a hand toward her when she hears my first name come out of the woman's mouth, as if my sister is about to touch her on the arm.

"I know you," Maude says, "You're Joleen, Joleen Bobo."

"Yes, ma'am, Miss Maude," the colored woman says, now a step even closer to my sister, who's smiling at her like the sun coming up in the morning, "but I'm like y'all are now. Married, too. I'm Joleen Broussard now."

"Broussard," Maude says and then does reach out to grab hold of the colored woman's shoulders, using both hands to do it and moving to face her head on, "what a pretty name that is. It's French, isn't it, Joleen?"

"Yes, ma'am, Miss Maude," the woman says, "redbone French." She's smiling too now, not so much as Maude is - nobody's ever smiled as big as she does when she feels like it - but the two of them together, white and black in Blue Water Chapel graveyard, are fairly beaming at each other. But as soon as I can notice that to even remark on it to myself, the colored woman's smile turns down, and she just of a sudden bursts into tears, as the saying goes, just sobbing and moaning with her hands all drawn up to her cheeks as though she is trying to keep her face from splitting in two. Maude is embracing her, as if the woman is a child grieving over something lost and gone, and my sister is cooing like a turtle dove and saying the woman's name over and over.

"Joleen," Maude says, "Joleen, what's the matter, honey? What's wrong?"

"Maybe she's just overjoyed to see you again, Maude," I say, "All broke up over it." Neither one of them pays me or what I've said any mind, though, and I am not surprised one bit by that. They're just having a high old time, standing there hugging and crying over each other not over twenty feet from the graves of mine and Maude's mother and father, and I note to myself for future consideration that at least Maude is proving she's still capable of shedding a tear in Blue Water graveyard. By now she's proving that by joining Joleen in her weeping, and that's the first time I've seen my sister cry in the vicinity of Papa's grave in years. That breaks a drought.

I remember Joleen Bobo by now, and I did as soon as Maude said her name before all their waterworks got started up. Not having thought in years about her or any of the rest of that family of colored folks who sharecropped down in the Sabine River bottom close to our family's old place all that time ago, I couldn't have been expected to recognize Joleen all grown up at the age she is now, backed up into the shade of a cedar tree in Blue Water graveyard. Why should I have?

"I guess your mama and daddy are dead by now," I say to her, trying to get a little attention directed away from all the crying that's going on and toward some sensible communication between grown women. "I know our's are gone now, these many years, mine and my sister's, Mrs. Winston's." I point over toward Papa's real grave, the empty spot next to Mama's little old blue stone, but neither one of the two of them there, still locked up in an embrace, make a sign of looking where I'm directing them, still too wrapped up in commiseration.

"Papa's buried yonder, but you can't tell it if you don't know how to find his resting place. We could tell you a story about that, Joleen, that would make a stone cry, if we had time to do it, me and my sister. Couldn't we, Maude?"

My saying that seems to make some difference in the situation before me, and both women break their holds on each other and step back a little, though Maude keeps a hand on Joleen's shoulder, patting away at it as if she has been assigned the task of soothing the woman down and is determined to make her best effort at it. I look over at my nephew, and Richard is studying the ground at his feet as though he has found something fascinating to consider about sandy soil in East Texas. I feel like saying something reassuring to him, something like "Just hold on for a while longer, son, and your mama will be calmed down here directly enough to rejoin the human race," but I don't say that, of course.

"Yes, ma'am," Joleen says, "Miss Abigail. I know where your papa and mama are buried. I seen both of them put into the ground here at Blue Water them years ago."

"You did?" I say, not believing a word of it, but figuring she meant well by the statement. They will say whatever they think a white person would like to hear from them, about any matter. I have never held that against colored people, though, like some people will do when they're arguing that you can't believe a word a darky says to you. Black folks do mean well, most of the time, when they're telling you stuff like Joleen is saying, and they're like children that way. As long as you understand that and can separate out the truth from the fiction they give you, you can know how much to depend on their stories and statements. It just takes patience and experience, and a whole lot of forebearance.

"How did you happen to do that?" I say, pushing Joleen just a little to see how much truth I could get out of what she had just said, conscious or not. "I didn't see you here, and I do believe I would've noticed you. I saw everybody that came to Papa's and

Mama's funerals both."

"No, ma'am, Miss Abigail, you wouldn't have seen us, over where we was standing in the woods yonder."

Joleen points across the graveyard toward a stand of pine and youpon and palmetto where the ground slopes down toward the spring that bubbles up at the base of the hill. I never spent any time over there even when I was a young'un at the graveyard workings. It's too snaky for me and for anybody else who's got sense enough to be careful where they put their feet in the woods.

"We?" I say to Joleen, who at least by now has stopped all that crying and carrying on and is speaking clear enough to be well understood. "You said we. Was somebody else with you?"

"My sister," she says, "she and me always liked your Mama and the way she treated us when we used to play with Miss Maude back in behind y'all's place them years ago."

"I think many times about those day," Maude speaks up to say, and I'm afraid if she gets started into recalling childhood memories with this colored woman we might be in for another session of crying and carrying on, so I rush on to ask another question, which I already know the answer to.

"What is her name, your sister? Isn't she a twin to you?"

"Yes, ma'am. She was. Boleen her name was, and she's been gone now for over two years."

Oh, Lord, I think to myself, this will get her all fired up again, her twin being dead, and we'll never get to the bottom of why they were sneaking around Blue Water graveyard, watching white folks bury their kin. What's going to be next?

"Boleen's with Jesus, now," she says, teetering on breaking down, but she doesn't as she keeps on talking, thank the Lord for small favors. "That keeps my mind satisfied, knowing that Boleen's done in Gloryland before us and that I'll see her up yonder again and we'll be together for eternity."

"So y'all watched Mrs. Amos Holt's burial," I hurry on to say, keeping things moving as well as I can manage it, "and Reverend Holt's, too."

"We did," Joleen says. "Yes, ma'am."

"I'm so glad to hear that," my sister pipes up. "That was so good of you and Boleen to do that. I wish I had known that before."

"Reverend Holt did many a good deed for my daddy and mama," says Joleen, "and I done told you ladies I thought the world of your mama, Mrs. Holt. So did Boleen. We just wanted to come see their funerals at Blue Water Chapel and think about their souls going on to be with the Lord."

"Thank you, Joleen, thank you," Maude says, her voice all low and choked up, so I see I've got to plunge in again to provide some direction to things so I'll be able to find out why in the world this colored woman has showed up from the past here at Blue Water on the very day Maude and Richard and I arrive from fifty-two miles and a county away.

So I ask her in the form of a direct and pointed question, and after just a little hemming and hawing she gets some explanation out for us to consider. She says she knew we were coming, though I don't see how that's possible, and when I press her to prove the truth of what she's claiming, she relates that some colored man got word to her about the progress we were making in the wagon from Double Pen Creek, and the way he knew came from another colored man that had connections with Mr. Fate Waldrup on whose place we had spent the night before.

She doesn't say how all that communication got to her and how she got to Blue Water Chapel before we did, Joleen doesn't, and I think to myself it must have been by African tom tom, but I don't say that out loud, though I do think it's a funny thought, one Joleen wouldn't understand and Maude for sure wouldn't appreciate or ever forget I'd said, if I said it out loud.

Colored folks have ways of getting news around, that's all I know, and it doesn't depend on government mail service or telegraph wires or telephones, even if there happened to be that kind of machinery in Sabine County that they could get at and use. When they need to know something or want to know it, they will and do find it out and then spread the news everywhere.

All this about how Joleen happened to be standing in the shade of that big cedar tree waiting on us when we got to Blue Water Chapel takes me a while to learn, what with Maude's interruptions of Joleen's discourse and her encouraging words to the woman as she parcels out the story. I shouldn't leave out how its progress also has to wait for Maude to remember out loud the happy times together as girls running through the woods she and Joleen and Boleen had enjoyed, catching turtles, picking blackberries, tying June bugs on strings, and getting into I don't know what all.

I know one thing that comes to my mind during Maude's reminiscences. If my sister and those colored twins had done half of what she claims and had Mama found out about it, Maude would've been a child well-acquainted with a hickory switch across her legs.

I don't quarrel with anything she says, not wanting to prolong the performance, but I am well satisfied with the amount of childhood memories Maude trots out long before she runs out of her supply of them.

So when she slows down at the conclusion of one of her anecdotes, something about her and Joleen and Boleen finding a baby squirrel in the woods and trying to raise it on cow's milk – an event I have no recollection of, and I am a woman known by all for remembering – I see a chance to jump into the conversation.

"Did you just want to say how-do-you-do to me and Mrs. Winston then?" I say to Joleen. "That's why you came to Blue Water when whoever this man was told you we were on our way up here?"

"I am glad to see you, Miss Abigail, you and Miss Maude, I certainly am, but that's not why I come out here to wait for y'all to get here in your wagon. Nome, it's not just that."

Maude is giving me one of her looks, her head turned a little to one side and her eyes cut over at an angle, like she is just daring me to say something that she knows is coming and despises to hear. As always, I can't predict just what that terrible thing is that she dreads so to hear me say, and I don't know any method of figuring it out. So I just speak up.

"If you're looking to borrow some money, Joleen, I can't help you, and I don't calculate that Mrs. Winston can, neither."

In answer to that, my sister says my name to me like it is something that hurts her mouth to spit out, her voice almost like a growl, and then she adds on to that a curse word, not even under her breath, but loud enough for Joleen to hear perfectly plain and her standing there a colored woman.

"The Lord's name in vain," I snap right back at Maude, and I'm proud to say that I'm not even feeling like I'm in danger to cry yet, "you just took His name in vain right in the presence of Papa's grave, right here at Blue Water Chapel."

"I can say Jesus all I want to," Maude says back to me in that same tone of voice, "Jesus, Jesus, Abigail, Jesus, Jesus, Jesus."

I am speechless, of course, on hearing that kind of use of the name of our Lord and Savior coming from my sister in such a location, but Joleen begins to talk, answering the question I had posed to her, acting and sounding like she has not even heard the exchange between me and Maude. Maybe she's not understanding what just took place, I think, and believes that there's only one way to say the name of Jesus and that it can't be misused so as to sound like a curse word. Such a simple faith and a simple mind must be a blessing and a consolation to those so constructed, but that's not me. No, I know better, and I understand what's going on between people, almost all the time, and that's the burden I have been given and have to endure. But I wouldn't trade that talent for anything, nor hide it under a bushel.

"No, ma'am, Miss Abigail," Joleen is saying while I look deliberately directly at her as she speaks, though I can feel, like a heavy presence, a pressure, on the side of my face, Maude aiming that look and the expression of her eyes at me. The skin of my left cheek feels hot and drawn from the weight of that gaze.

"That's not why I decided to come here to Blue Water just as soon as I found out from Sully Boatwright that y'all was on your way in the wagon. I hadn't planned to ask nobody for no money. I don't need that. I need y'all to help me."

"Help you?" I say. "How in the world can we help you, Joleen?"

"I need y'all to help me save him. You the only ones I could think of, and when Sully told me you was coming to Blue Water, I knowed the Lord was figuring a way to answer my prayers. He's sending Miss Maude. And you, too, Miss Abigail."

"Save who?" Maude say, "Who are you meaning, Joleen?"

Maude's voice when she says that is different as night from day from the way it sounded when she was speaking to me not a minute before, and I literally can feel the pressure ease on the side of my face where my sister has been laying her look of utter meanness on me. Thank goodness she's aiming her attention in some other direction, I am thinking, even if her doing that is evidence she cares more about a colored woman's feelings than her own sister's, and that colored woman somebody she hasn't seen since they were girls running through the woods together like wild Comanches.

"Eldridge," Joleen says, and I can tell she's on the verge of another spell of tears, "my husband Eldridge Broussard, that who and that's all."

"Save your husband?" I say. "Is it drink or gambling? Won't he work, Joleen, to earn y'all a living? Maybe the one to help you is your preacher, if you believe your husband needs saving from some weakness of character."

"No, ma'am. It ain't nothing like that. Eldridge done gave his heart to the Lord a long time ago. He's a churchgoing Christian man and been that way long as I known him."

"What's wrong, then?" Maude says in that same soft voice she seems to use with most everybody in the world but you know who. "What is your trouble, Joleen, you and your husband?"

"The worst kind it is, Miss Maude," Joleen says, "the very worst kind a colored man can have."

I start listing in my mind what kinds of trouble that a colored man might think was the worst that could happen to him, or at least what a colored woman would think was the worst predicament a colored man could get himself into, and I haven't got past wondering if there was a possible way Saturday night could be outlawed, just removed from the calendar somehow, when Joleen goes on to tell us what the cause of her being in Blue Water Chapel graveyard today is.

"They claiming Eldridge did something to a white lady, but it ain't true what they saying, and if they catch him they going to hang my husband to a tree."

A loud buzz comes into my ears and head, so strong I can't hear anything of what Maude is saying to Joleen, though I can see her lips moving and know that she's talking to the woman who has by now collapsed onto her knees next to somebody's grave, mounded up to show that the family of the dead person buried there still takes good care of what's left of them in this world. Maude drops down beside Joleen and is holding her again all clutched up to her breast, and Joleen's mouth is twisted and her eyes shut tight as though she is a woman who's been in a dark cave and has been snatched out all of a sudden into bright sunshine and cannot bear the burning light.

Somebody is not there, somebody who was, and I look around to see who it might be, like a person will do trying to see something they actually know is not present but can't stop themselves from looking for. I see my nephew Richard who's moved off to do something with the mules still hitched to the wagon, and when I glimpse him I feel a relief that maybe he is the one I've missed, and that feeling lets me start to hear something again other than the deep buzzing sound in my head.

I can tell Maude is talking to Joleen now by hearing her, though I can't make out what she's saying yet, her words just a murmur on a level beneath the rise and fall of the whirring inside me.

"Richard," I call out loud, thinking if he hears me and looks my direction that will mean he is the one I thought was missing and things will begin to come together again in the graveyard and we'll all be back where we were before Joleen said what she did.

But he doesn't look up from whatever he's doing to the mule harness, and that tells me he's not the one I thought gone missing. Richard is there, I can count him and Maude and me and Joleen on four fingers. But there's still one not there that I cannot find to number, no matter where I look.

Maude

Somewhere in the thicket of pines and palmetto and yaupon that comes all the way up to the last row of graves at Blue Water a mockingbird is calling like a mourning dove and is doing a good job of it, the sequence and number of notes it copies convincing enough to persuade anybody listening. But the tone is not right, too deep for a bird the size of a mocker to reproduce, and not resonant in the way a dove makes it when its song carries that dark sound of loss and solitude.

Thinking of that distinction between a good performance by the mockingbird with no living investment of feeling and that dark song of the mourning dove which can call forth a true absence in the listener's heart helps me as I kneel there in the graveyard, my arms around Joleen. I keep my mind on that difference, even after the mockingbird has hushed its attempt to deliver the dove's song, and has gone on to a bird's song easier to copy.

In a little while, Joleen will tell us more and maybe we'll be able to understand then what she means and think of a way to comfort if not aid her, but in the meantime she has to weep and mourn and there's nothing to be done to lengthen or hurry that. What she expresses she must express, and that is no copy trotted out for display.

I look up at Abigail who's standing with both arms extended as though she is balancing on a log thrown across a stream for a bridge and is afraid to move forward or back. Wobbling a little from side to side, she moves her head in a semi-circle as she appears to be looking for something and then she calls out my son's name.

"Richard," she says, twice, her voice gathering strength the second time she speaks. "Richard."

He pretends not to hear, fixing his attention even more firmly on whatever he's found to do at the wagon. My son doesn't want to be where he is, as he has not for most of his life, the thing he dreads most are people disagreeing and yelling at each other, particularly the women folk in his family, and especially his Aunt Abigail seeking to enlist him in some exchange between her and me.

Abigail seems to have found some better purchase on the sandy ground of Blue Water graveyard and has let her arms drop to her side, having crossed that treacherous log to the other side of the stream, I figure, and now she is touching her forefinger on one hand to the tips of the ones on the other, over and over.

"Abby," I say, "Abby, are you feeling all right? Are you faint?"

Joleen is withdrawing to herself now, beginning to wipe her eyes with the sleeve of her dress, and I expect we'll begin to learn more from her soon. Richard has loosened the mules' harnesses, and they are cropping at weeds and grass, and I sit back and begin dusting away at the sand on the front of my dress.

"Who is it, Maude?" Abigail asks me. "Who is it? I can't get them counted up right, no matter how many times I go over it. See, look at this. One, two, three, four."

"We'll figure it out later, Abby," I say. "Go over to the wagon, please, and bring me that jug of water. Joleen is completely parched, and so am I."

As Abigail trots toward the wagon at a good clip, looking relieved to be told what to do, I think back to the first time I met Joleen and remember we were both thirsty then and looking for a drink of water.

Behind our first dwelling place in Sabine County was a little spring at the foot of a hill at least a quarter of a mile from the log house Papa had built for us. We used it for our supply of water for the first couple of years we lived there, but carrying buckets that far was a burden to all of us, especially during the daylight hours when Papa was clearing land and planting and chopping cotton and bringing in crops and all the rest of the work that goes into farming. So as he could find time and get other folks to help him, he got the property close to the house witched by Mr. Jesse McNeill who had the diviner's gift, and he dug a well where the willow fork indicated the sweet vein of water underground would be.

It was a good well, and the water was clear and always abundant, but it bothered me always that it was quiet and dead and unmoving. When the sun was at the right angle in the sky, I could look over the edge of the plank enclosure built around the well and see the surface below as blank and fixed as a mirror, showing my face staring back at me smaller than it really was, of course, and so dark I couldn't make out my features.

I never liked what looking into that still water said to me about the existence beneath the surface of the earth – the silent, the fixed, the unchanging, the inexhaustible nature below what we all walked around on. It said to me that all our movement to and fro, the freedom we assumed was ours to go where we wanted, the way we talked and made plans and laughed and ate and drank – all that was a lie. Nothing ever really moved. And we were fools.

To save myself from dwelling on the truth revealed to me in the still water of our well, I made it my habit back then to drink only from the old spring, our first source for water for our life in Texas. The water in the spring bubbled up in constant supply, it moved and rushed and sang and flowed, and it was alive. When I dropped pebbles or leaves or flower blossoms into the bowl it had scooped out for itself, the spring pushed these things aside, tumbled them over and over, carried them away in the stream it made as it worked away day and night, in light and shade and darkness.

But when I dropped a pebble into the well near the house where we Holts all lived, it made a plunking sound and a ring of ripples disturbed the image of my face in the water, but that movement slowed always to a stop, and the mirror of water was still and fixed and dead again.

The day I met Joleen I had gone down to the spring to drink and watch the water bubble and flow in the manner I had come to count on, and I remember I had gotten hot on the way, coming across the field of cotton, almost waist high to me that time of year. It was cooler by the spring, as always, and I was kneeling beside it, my face wet from plunging my head into the water over and over, to cool off and to drink from it. I always kept my eyes open when I did that, thinking that someday I'd be able to see the exact spot from which the water came from the darkness of the earth into the light of day in the life above ground. I never could see the exact source, naturally, that hole into the earth beneath, but I always sought it.

I had just lifted my face from the surface again for a breath of air, my eyes too full of water to see anything but a blur when someone spoke.

"I always look for little fish when I do that," the voice said. "But I never did see one, not nary a time I have looked."

That was Joleen speaking, a colored girl I had seen only at a distance before then, with her sisters and brothers and now and then a grown person or two in the yard place of the little cabin across Hickory Creek which marked the boundary of our property. I didn't know her name, nor that she had a twin or anything about her or her people, except that they were colored and lived in the quarters.

I don't remember what I said back to her then at the spring or anything else about the time we met on that hot day, but it proved to be the beginning of a phase where we saw each other almost everyday for what must have lasted for over two years.

Then that phase stopped on a single day, one I didn't mark at the time and never thought about since, and Joleen left my consciousness of her as though a door closed to a room I had been in once and was never to enter again. Why that time ended, I don't know, except to think that grownups were a part of it. That, and Valery Blackstock, who was to become my husband. When I think of that time now, what comes to mind is the spring where I first met Joleen.

The water bubbling then in that spring pushed on as steady as ever, and what it touched moved with it, and it still does, it still does, it still does.

"See what my sister has brought us," I say to Joleen, calmer now beside me in the graveyard, "a jug of water that's been sitting in the shade. Don't you want a drink from it? It's still a little cool."

Joleen

I do not feel sorry for myself, never a time, no matter what is happening to me or my own. I was taught that from when I was a child, and my daddy was the one who brought it home to me, that way of doing and looking at life in this world and getting through it the best way you can.

It took him a while to do that, with me and my twin sister and the other sisters and my brothers, too. It's a lesson you have to get in your mind over and over, he would say to me, and you have to learn it by heart. You don't get that lesson by hearing me tell you to get it, neither, he would say, the way you understand what a bird's name is when somebody tells you and you remember you supposed to call that name each time you see that same bird or hear it holler in the woods.

That is a connection that can be told you, and it is a easy thing to get right the first time you hear it and then carry with you the rest of your days without having to worry about whether you got it right. You ain't got to check it for the truth every time you see a blue jay. That bird is always a blue jay, and if you got normal human understanding, you got that right and you got it learned the first time through.

But there's another way of getting a thing set in your head and in your heart, and it is never just a simple connection another person can tell you once and be done with it.

"It goes like and is like this, but it comes to your understanding a little at the time, bit by bit, and it is engraved upon your heart, the mind behind your mind, in the same way I can take a pocketknife and carve you a doll out of a piece of soft pine that wasn't nothing but a lump of wood before I got to work on it. You understand what I'm telling you, child?"

"No," I said, "I don't, Daddy."

"Child," he said, "Joleen, pay attention, you and your sister."

He's telling us this while we're sitting by the fireplace. It's cold outside, but the fire is built up and the whole house is warm, and I can see the shadows of the flames on the hard clay wall of the chimney behind where the fire's burning. They're making all that they touch move up and down, not the same way each time, but it's still the same fire burning and the same fireplace and the same house and my daddy the same man talking to us. I like that, and I can tell Boleen does, too, though she never talks as much as I do or asks as many questions.

It's good when it's cold outside, but warm inside, and I shiver a little bit because I want to, not because something's making me do it. Shivering makes it better.

"Yes, Daddy," I say. "Tell us some more, but not about the blue jay, the other thing. I understand already about the blue jay's name and the way I know how to call it."

"When you're hungry," Daddy says, talking to us, but looking at the fire burning and the shadows it makes on the clay wall of the fireplace, "when you're hungry, how do you know that? Does somebody have to tell you? Does your mama have to say she believes you want something or another to eat?"

"No sir," says Boleen, the first thing she has said that night. "I just know it all by myself."

"That's right," Daddy says and looks at her and nods his head. "And the way you know it is because you tell yourself what it is your feeling means. It's inside you, the thing you know and have learned, and it don't depend on nobody else letting you know what it means."

"How did you learn it in the first place, then?" I say, "if nobody told you what it was and the right word to call it?"

"Bit by bit," my daddy says, "Bit by bit, from the inside out. You learned it as you went along, and it all come to you that way because you was made to know it, and that's the way you got that lesson. It becomes your own because you got it by heart, from all the things you go through in your life, day by day, staying in the world and making it through by noticing and bearing down by yourself, just like you got to do."

He stopped talking for a minute and looked back at the fire and the shadows moving up and down, never the same but coming from the same place always, no matter how the shapes it's making might change from one thing to the other.

"Depend," my daddy says to me and Boleen, "on yourself. Get it by heart."

So I did learn that by heart, and I never do feel sorry for myself, no matter what troubles come to me in this world. And I still keep what I learned by heart inside me, without worrying about it anymore than the flames of a fire care anything about the shape of the shadows they cast, and how the shapes can change, big and little, clear and cloudy. They got no choice and are not able to find their own way, and neither am I or anybody else that's got knowledge locked inside them, learned by heart.

I take my troubles and sorrows one by one as they come to me, and I think about the shadows on the wall and where they come from, and I get through the living I got to do in this world, by putting my mind in that location.

So did my twin sister Boleen, I know and feel in my heart, and so could anyone else of my brothers and sisters that paid mind to what our daddy said about lessons and the way they're learned. Not everybody can give full attention to what is offered them, though, and even if you do, there come shaky times when nothing is solid and you forget the true names of what makes up the world and this life in it.

What difference does it make, I have done asked myself when times have come hard on me, what word is stuck to what? What does bird mean, or cotton, or water, or work, or living itself, when nothing seems to have any weight you can appreciate or put a hand to?

But when I have found myself thinking that way, when I have tried to put too much faith in what somebody else has told me is true and real and matters most, I think of that firelight rising and falling as it casts its shadows, not caring what the shapes might mean or if they even do mean. Then there comes what comforts and soothes me, and that's the things I have got by heart.

Boleen, my twin, is dead now, and that's all right. And Eldridge Broussard, my husband, is hiding in a canebrake by the white folks' graveyard at Blue Water Chapel, no more home left for him and me together than if he was the last bear in Sabine County, Texas, one jump ahead of a pack of baying dogs.

But I'm thinking of the shadows thrown by fire on a clay wall, and I am depending on what I got by heart and on myself.

I am through crying about it now for a while, and looking at Maude Holt, I can tell by her eyes that she is about through just remembering me and her as children playing together them long years ago and is beginning to study on my predicament. She is coming to terms with what's real now here on this hot day in a graveyard, not just what used to be, and that makes my heart lift.

I can feel it in my breast, beginning to rise up, as I see Maude turn her mind in the direction of where we be now, with everything dislocated and shook apart.

"You want some more water, Joleen?" she says. "Where is he right now?"

"He's just yonder," I say. "In the middle of the canebrake just the other side of the spring where we used to go, you and me."

Maude's big sister hears me tell that location, and she begins to sway back and forth again like she was before Maude sent her for the water jug. She's not knocking her fingers together over and over this time, though, like she was before. But she's bad restless.

"Lord," Abigail says, sounding like she's fixing to start moaning, "Lord, what did your husband do to that poor white woman, Joleen? What did he do?"

"Abigail," Maude says before I can begin to think what to say back, her voice as hard as I ever heard it, "he didn't do anything. You heard what Joleen said. Mr. Broussard didn't do anything to anybody."

"Mr. Broussard? " Abigail says. "Mr. Broussard? Who?"

"His name is Eldridge," I say. "That's his given name."

"All right, then," Maude says, "Eldridge. Eldridge Broussard is the name of Joleen's husband, Abigail, and we'll be meeting him here in a little while, I expect. Until then, I want you to go talk to Richard about the mules and the shape they're in this morning after that fifty miles they pulled the wagon from Double Pen Creek in the last couple of days."

"Fifty-two miles," Abigail says, sounding a little like a schoolteacher. "It's a good fifty-two miles."

"You're right, Abby," Maude says. "I never have had your head for figures."

She stops talking and looks off toward the treeline and the shadows the sun is casting, and so do I. It's a little before one o'clock.

"By about two this afternoon," Maude says, "we ought to be able to start back toward home, don't y'all think?"

"I thought we were going to see if we could find some crepe myrtle somewhere for cuttings," Abigail says, "and bring some back here and plant them by Papa's grave, his real one. Now you're telling me we can't?"

"We can do all that, too," Maude says. "I expect Joleen knows right where to go to get some crepe myrtle. Don't you, Joleen?"

"Y'all want pink, or y'all want purple, I know exactly where we can get the prettiest in Sabine County. Drova Jessup has got a yard full of both kinds at her house. Even got some crossbred, pink and purple on the same bush."

"You don't mean it," Maude says. "I never saw that done before."

"I have read about it," Abigail says. She's looking like she's standing more flatfooted on the ground now, and she's swigging away at the water jug like she is full thirsty. "It was in a book Ferguson got from somewhere. I already knew about that subject, how that will happen in nature."

Abigail looks over at me now to let me know something. "Ferguson is my husband. Ferguson Mott, that's who I'm referring to when I say that name."

"Yes, ma'am," I say.

"My sister keeps up with current developments," Maude says. "She always has, since the time we were children together here in this part of the country on the old place."

"Well," Abigail says, "I have always liked to read up on things and keep current."

"You always had a book in your hand, Miss Abigail," I say, "I remember that like it was yesterday."

"Let's go get us something to eat," Maude says, reaching out to touch Abigail on the arm and get her started up to moving. "Mrs. Waldrup packed us some biscuits and ham slices, wasn't it, Abigail?"

"Pork shoulder," Abigail says, "some call that ham. I don't, because shoulder's not ham."

It seems like the air in the graveyard has lightened up somehow, like it will after a rain has finally come after threatening for a long time, and I can feel myself being able to get my breath better. We all go to where the young man they been calling Richard has got the wagon and the mules under the shade of a sycamore, and Abigail pulls some food out of a tow sack in the wagon bed, pokes it at me, and then starts eating away like she is plumb hungry.

I can't stand to look at what she's eating, but I drink me some more water and ask Maude if I can put aside a little of what they got for Eldridge to eat when I go back to where he's lying down hid in among all that cane. She has already thought about that, naturally, as she would, and shows me what she has put together for me to give him.

"Am I allowed to ask Joleen now what's been going on with her husband and that white lady, Maude?" Abigail says, then she tells Richard to go down to the spring and fill up the water jug. "I don't want him listening to what Joleen may have to say," she explains to me and Maude, but neither one of us says anything right back to her.

"Joleen may tell us whatever else she sees fit to," Maude says, as we all watch the young man follow the path out of the graveyard down the hill toward the spring. You can't see him for the under-brush after he takes the first two steps out of the clearing. "If she wants to speak about her and her husband's trouble, we'll listen. But if she doesn't, that won't influence what we do."

So I start telling them what has happened, and as I begin to do it, I feel like I did a minute ago when the air seemed to lighten up and let me breathe better. It seems to help the way I feel when I start to talk and to let go a little bit of what I been holding back inside me.

We are standing in the shade of one of the big sycamores at Blue Water, the mules and Abigail making eating sounds as I begin to talk, and here is what I start to tell the Holt sisters. As I talk and lay things out, it begins to help me in my own mind to get what happened set out straight.

"Eldridge and me been cropping twelve acres of cottonland for Mr. Lee Lester for a long time. I don't know how many years it's been now, but it goes back a good long while it seems like."

"I know Lee and that whole bunch of Lesters," Abigail says as she's finishing up her last bit of that pork shoulder and biscuit. "Him and the Sexton girl he married, Edith her name is."

"Not no more," I say, "Mrs. Edith Lester done dead, and that's part of the story, but that comes later." When I say that, Maude holds up her hand to Abigail like she is stopping a child from busting into the grown people's conversation, and Abigail hushes up, looking a little pouty again, but I'm glad Maude does that. Abigail won't be putting in her share, like she always has liked to do, so I'm going to be able to keep things straight and move along the way I need to do to get what I'm remembering told right.

"I say Eldridge and me been sharing that crop, but I mean we done it along with our children, too. Of course, a boy or girl bound to leave home when they get old enough, and so everything changes bit by bit, but me and Eldridge stay the same.

"Everything go along all right for a long time with Mr. Lee Lester, it go along, go along, go along. Sometime the cotton come in good, sometime it don't, sometime it rain when you need it, sometime it don't. Y'all know all about farming. I don't need to tell you the ups and downs, and the droughts and the floods and the boll weevils."

"Not hardly," Abigail says, but that's all she feel she have to add, and I ask for it when I say y'all. I remind myself not to do that again. We got things to do here, and Maude has got to have time to figure out what they going to be, so I get back quick into putting people and what they done into the right way for making sense of a situation.

"When the trouble started up between Mr. Lee Lester and my husband, it come after Mrs. Edith Lester died and Mr. Lee Lester married him a new wife.

"It was some kind of a sickness in her breast killed Miss Edith," I say fast to cut Abigail off from asking about that and getting me all sidetracked again. "It come up quick, and it killed her quick. She was walking around one day, pert as could be, and they was burying her less than two months later, right here i. this graveyard. I could show you her marker if we had the time, but we don't."

"In her breathing, or in the heart itself?" Abigail says, but I act like I don't hear her because I'm thinking what to say next. I go on talking.

"Mr. Lee Lester didn't stay single long after his wife died, but he went after getting married again quick, like a man will do lots of times. They are used to having a wife, even if they don't know it during the time they got one. So he married a widow lady from up around Teneha, and showed up one day on his place with her and her child, the only one she ever had, from her husband that died. The lady's name is Corinne, and her little girl was Alice Jeanne.

"She was the one that caused it all, that little girl Alice Jeanne, but it wasn't no fault of her's. What happened to Eldridge and me come out of her being in the world, that poor child, like things will. When one rock starts sliding down a hill, it make another one start moving, too. But it didn't mean nothing to begin with, that one rock when it slipped loose, nothing you could see coming.

"She was the same age as our granddaughter, the one who live with me and Eldridge because her mama can't take care of her no more. I say can't, not won't. My grand and Alice Jeanne remind me of how me and Miss Maude used to play together all the time back when we was little here in Sabine County, them years ago."

"What's her name?" Maude says. "Your granddaughter?"

"Opal," I tell her. "Opal and Alice Jeanne just two little girls together, playing all around the place whenever they could, and that was most days, since Mrs. Lee Lester, the new wife to him, she liked for her girl to have the company. She told me that, Miss Corinne did, many a time.

"That went on for over a year, and them little girls was never cross with each other, and they knew how to act, and they purely enjoyed themselves. And Mr. Lee Lester, he never took no notice, nor exception, and neither did anybody else.

"And then, oh Lord, it happened, and sometime it seem like it was a long time ago and sometime it feel to me like it was just yesterday on that morning when my grand come running up from the creek bottom screaming and covered with mud and her eyes just wild."

"What was it?" somebody says, and this time it's not Abigail, but Richard who's speaking, standing at the far side of the wagon from where I am, holding a jug of water, back from the spring.

"That baby had got snakebit," I say, "not Opal, it was Alice Jeanne, and I had always told them girls not to play down there where it's water moccasins all over the place."

"We always used to," Maude says, "you and me."

"Yes, ma'am, we did," I say, "and it's times these few days when I wished it had been me bit by a water moccasin back then when I was a girl. And then none of this misery would've ever come on us all."

"Don't question the working out of providence," says Abigail, looking not at me but at her sister. "That's the business of the Lord."

"I question it night and day," Maude says. "Let Joleen talk, Abigail."

"The poor little girl ended up dying from that snakebite," I say.

"Eldridge run on down there where Opal told him she was, and he toted her back up to Mr. Lee Lester's place. And her mama was there, of course, and they tried to bleed her where the snake had bit. But it had got her twice, and the place where the fangs had hit was on Alice Jeanne's throat. You can't cut into that spot and have nobody live after you done it.

"That poison worked fast, and she was gone before they could get to nary a doctor, even if a doctor could have helped her."

"Lord in heaven," Abigail say, "just the one child was all the one that woman had."

"Yes, ma'am," I say.

"How did that lead to any trouble between Lee Lester and your husband?. Maude says. "Surely Lee nor his wife didn't blame any of y'all for what a snakebite did, did they?"

"No, Miss Maude," I say. "That wasn't what made all this trouble come on us. It wasn't no blame ever laid on us by nobody for what caused Alice Jeanne to die. Not by Lee Lester, and sure not by Miss Corinne. Everybody seem to understand that to be a terrible thing that wasn't nobody's fault but little girls being where they shouldn't a been, after they been warned off from doing it.

"The next thing that happened didn't come directly from Mr. Lee Lester. It was Miss Corinne. Her mind got wrong. She couldn't get over thinking about it, and mourning and grieving about her girl being gone. She just roamed through Mr. Lee Lester's house all night, from what I could tell, not able to sleep nor rest, and she walked over the farm everyday, every part of it, wandering down through the creek bottom where that moccasin fang put the poison in her little girl, and talking, talking, talking to everybody she see on the place.

"And the main one she wanted to talk to was Eldridge because she had it in her head he was the last one to be with Alice Jeanne when she was still able to speak and know who she was and who people was around her.

"She would come up to him at all hours of the day whenever she saw him, out in the field plowing or grubbing at weeds with a hoe, or carrying water up from the spring, or tending to the vegetable garden, anything he might be doing. And she would make him tell the whole story of what he saw when he got down to the place where Alice Jeanne was after the snake bit her, and what she looked like, and did she say anything, and could he remember this time something he had forgot the last time she talked to him. All like of that, over and over, again and again.

"She was what you could call crazed with grief," Abigail says, looking around at all three of us to be sure we appreciate what she's figured out. "That poor woman was."

"Yes, ma'am," I say. "And that was the way my husband understood it and what it was that was making Miss Corinne the way she was, and that was the way he treated it. He would put down whatever he was doing every time that lady would come up to him, asking him to tell her what she needed to hear, and he would do just that. Talk about it each time, as full as he could, trying his best to call up all he could about that morning and put it in words for the mother of that little girl again."

"How did that affect Eldridge?" Maude says, "I know it must have been a strain on him."

"It was that, but he never showed that to Mr. Lee Lester's wife. Never made a sign, and he never cut nothing short in going over every bit of what he could remember. Just as patient the twentieth time as he was the first.

"I asked him about that, said to him maybe he could kind of keep an eye out for her and when he was able to do it without her noticing, just kind of get out of her way, you understand. Plan what he was going to work on so as to let him stay out of her sight whenever he could manage it."

"Did he start to sneaking off, then, after you told him how to do?" says Abigail.

"No, ma'am," I say. "Eldridge ain't that kind of a man. Told me he figured it was a comfort to Miss Corinne to hear him tell all he could about the last little while of that child's life in this world. Said he wouldn't try to hide from her in no way and that she would finally wear out listening to what he had to say, and little by little get over it and not need to hear it told to her again, again, again."

"Did your husband ever make things up to tell that lady?" Richard asks. "I think I would have been tempted to, myself."

"Richard," Abigail says. "What an opinion to express."

"I told Eldridge that very thing, Mr. Richard," I say. "I said to him that after I had told the same thing so many times I would've tried to put stuff in to try to satisfy whatever it was Miss Corinne needed to hear, and then maybe after she heard that she would leave me alone about it."

"I would have put in new parts to the story just to entertain myself," Maude says, "for the sake of variety."

"But no, Eldridge wouldn't do that, and he just looked at me funny when I said what I might want to do in the situation he was in. So I never mentioned it to him again.

"But Eldridge was wrong about thinking Miss Corinne would get her fill and slack off. It seemed the more patient he was in talking to her and answering every little new question she had thought up to ask since the last time he had told her about what caused her to lose her only child, the more she wanted to look for him to talk to. And that's what it was finally led to it, finally caused what got Mr. Lee Lester to get bad in his mind toward my husband."

"Was it one thing in particular?" says Richard, "That made it get worse, I mean."

"It was, yes oh Lord, and it happened just two nights ago, but it seem to me like it's been two years done passed since then," I say back to him. He had done left off fooling with the water jug on the other side of the wagon and has walked around to stand by his mama. Maude acts like she hasn't noticed Richard doing that, but I can tell she has. She moves a little to give him room to stand.

"It was way past sundown, full dark, and I had done put supper on the table for Eldridge and Opal and me, and I was just putting away the last of the dishes and the cook pot I'd just finished cleaning up. Opal, she had gone on off to bed but wasn't asleep yet, I don't think. Eldridge was sitting at the table close to the kerosene lamp trying to put something together that was broke. I never noticed what it was, nor paid no attention to what he was messing with there, thinking about something else and turning it over in my mind, I reckon.

"Since then, though, these last two days I have wished time and time again I had looked at what Eldridge was trying to fix that night, sitting there in the lamp light, and everything quiet in the house, and the same as it always was at the end of a day before we'd lie down to rest before the next sunup come to get the next day started. Because that then was the last usual and expected time we ever going to have together, me and my husband, where life if going on like it's supposed to be. The same, you know what's coming, and it's waiting there ordinary as that dishpan I had before me, full of water and soap to make a dirty thing clean.

"In these last couple of days it seem to me if I could just know what it was Eldridge was working on before that knock come on our door that it'd be a comfort to me somehow. It'd be a thing I could hold in my mind and know what it was for sure and for true, and it would be a marker I could call up whenever I needed it and behold it as the final end of something."

"What knock on your door?" Abigail says. "Was it that crazy woman Corinne Lester?"

"No, ma'am," I say. "It was the girl been working for her, one of the Jefferson bunch, her name LaVelle, and she was sent to fetch Eldridge. You got to come up to Mr. Lee Lester's house, she start saying, almost yelling at us, as soon as Eldridge he opens that door to see who's banging on it. Oh, you got to come up to the house. Miss Corinne say come get you, come get you now."

"I would not have gone up there," Abigail says, shaking her head back and forth like a mule or horse will do when it's refusing the bit. "I would have kept on sitting in that chair, working on whatever I was working on, like my feet was nailed to the floor."

"Oh, yes, you would," Maude say. "Anybody would have gone, with things being the way they were. Being the way they still are."

"My husband didn't hesitate," I say. "Eldridge just turned back to look at me and said he would be back home as soon as he could, and he followed that Jefferson girl on out of the house, and that was the last time I seen him his normal self and things the way they ought to be. Me, I felt the same way you would have, Miss Abigail. I felt like I was paralyzed, like I couldn't move my legs or arms, like the strength just all give out of me. I knowed something bad was going to happen. I knowed it in my bones, and they had done turned to water."

"Was Mr. Lee Lester up there at the house, too, with his wife?" Richard says.

"No," I say. "No, no. Not at the first. And that's what make everything come to grief. It was just Miss Corinne waiting when Eldridge and LaVelle Jefferson got up there, and she had done got into one of them bottles of whiskey Mr. Lee Lester keeps to sip toddies out of, and she had done started that, started drinking it, because she was feeling so bad about that little girl being dead and gone, and she was crying and hollering and carrying on and calling for Eldridge to talk some more to her about that day down in the creek bottom when that poison from the snake first got set.

"That little Jefferson girl, LaVelle, as soon as she see Eldridge go in the backdoor to the house where Miss Corinne told her to bring him, she just run on off back to the cabin where her folks stay."

"And mighty glad to do it, she was, I expect," Abigail says. "She was quit from the whole thing then."

"Yes, ma'am," I say, "I expect that's what LaVelle was thinking, if she was thinking anything at all. With her done and gone, that just left Eldridge there with Mr. Lee Lester's wife in the house, and she start in like always wanting him to tell what all he seen happen when he run down to the creek bottom to do what he could about Alice Jeanne being snakebit. He never complained, but he start in again saying all he could, remembering every little bit he have in his mind about it, trying to answer every question Miss Corinne come up with to ask him, all like of that, on and on."

"Was she asking anything new that time?" Abigail says, her

hand held up to her forehead like she is trying to imagine what else Miss Corinne might be able to come up with and want to know. Abigail is looking way off with her eyes half-closed like a person will, concentrating hard on something. "Had she already asked your husband if he actually saw the water moccasin that bit her little girl, or had it already crawled off and hid somewhere, maybe back in the creek or under some bushes or something?"

"For God's sake," Maude says, "Abigail, will you let Joleen talk?" That hushes Maude's sister up, and Abigail stands up real straight now and folds her arms across her breast with the look on her face of a person not much interested any longer in what is going on around her. I expect she's not likely to ask me nothing else here for a while, so I pick up where I left off.

"I don't know what all Mrs. Lee Lester ask him, Miss Abigail," I say, to give her something, which I can tell she appreciates me doing, "Eldridge never told me. But he do what he can to satisfy the questions she did ask him, and then Miss Corinne she offer my husband some of that whiskey she been drinking as he stand there in the kitchen of her house. Hold out a water glass toward him and fix to pour from the bottle into it.

"He say thank you, ma'am, but no, I don't want none of that. See, besides him not having a drink of liquor nor beer nor nothing else like that since he take Jesus Christ as his personal savior years ago, Eldridge knew it wouldn't be proper for him to be drinking no whiskey in the company of a white lady. Miss Corinne pour some anyway into that water glass and hold it to him and say something like come on and take a sip of whiskey with me, Eldridge, just for social sake. That probably wasn't the actual words she use, but that's the meaning, and Eldridge say no again, as polite and nice as he could make it. He take the glass out of her hand where she has put it right up in his face close enough t. where he could smell the fume rising up, and then he put it down as soon as he touch it, right there on the table in the kitchen.

"That's when he heard somebody stepping up behind him, and he look around, and it's Lee Lester coming through the doorway from the room at the front of the house. He never even heard the man come into the building until then, and neither had Miss Corinne, Eldridge said, because she looked real surprised and said well look who's here for a change.

"My husband greeted the man, said something like howdy, Mr. Lester, how you this evening, and then Lee Lester start in hollering at Eldridge. What you doing in my kitchen, nigger, he said, drinking my whiskey, making my wife get drunk with you? What you fixing to do to her, look like I got here just in time to stop you from doing something else, too, don't it? Have you put your damn black hand on her yet? He turn so red in his face, Eldridge say, until he thought Lee Lester was going to fall out on the floor in a full fit.

"Eldridge start in to say no sir, I ain't done nothing of that kind, I'm just here up at your house 'cause Miss Corinne send somebody to my place to get me to come talk to her again about y'all's little girl being killed by the snakebite.

"Miss Corinne start to say something to her husband, but he tell her to keep her damn drunk mouth shut, he knows what's going on, and he will be found in Hell with his back broke before he will let a nigger molest his wife in his own kitchen. And Eldridge try to say something again about why he's there in the house talking to Miss Corinne, and Lee Lester said goddamn you, don't call my wife by her first name. And then he hit Eldridge full in the face with his fist all balled up, and Eldridge turned to leave out the backdoor, and Lee Lester picks up that glass of whiskey from where Eldridge had set it down on the table after Miss Corinne push it up at him. He throw that glass to hit Eldridge, I expect, but it miss my husband and hit Miss Corinne on her forehead and broke.

"By then, Eldridge is going out the backdoor to run through the dark toward where we stay, and he can hear Mr. Lee Lester cussing and screaming at Miss Corinne and her crying and hollering, and that sound follow him like the Devil himself is stepping in every footprint Eldridge makes on his way home.

"And now look where we be. Me standing here in the graveyard, my grandchild Opal yonder staying with Claudine Ramey and her bunch, and my husband hiding in that canebrake with white folks wanting to put a rope around his neck and hang up to a tree."

"Maude and me will just talk to Lee Lester," Abigail says, "and see if we can't straighten this whole thing out. We'll take care of it, Joleen. Don't you worry."

"I appreciate you saying that, Miss Abigail," I tell her, "but things've done gone too far for y'all to make no headway talking to nobody. That road done been took."

"Joleen is right," Maude says, "but bless you, Abby, for helping us think. You put your finger on it, though, the problem we've got to deal with now. Everything has gone beyond reason, I'm afraid, and we can't afford to put any faith in trying to deal with Lee Lester."

Maude gets quiet for a spell, then, all of us do, not speaking, and we stand there in the shade of the sycamore, while Maude looks way off like she is trying to see into the woods beyond the graveyard to find out if she can tell where a noise she has heard is coming from. I notice she is patting her son on the shoulder. Richard has moved up a little closer to her, and he looks in his face as though some pain has kicked up somewhere in his stomach and he is waiting to see which direction it will take. Will it pass on off in a minute, or will it just get worse?

"What is going on back in Sabinetown, Joleen?" Maude says. "What have you heard?"

"We didn't wait around none after Eldridge come busting into the house and told me what happened at Mr. Lee Lester's place," I say. "He started throwing some things into a tow sack, some cold biscuits left from supper, and his other shirt and what all, and I rousted Opal up from bed and walked her over to Claudine Ramey's to leave her there. Time I got back to the house, Eldridge was done outside waiting in that little whitepine thicket behind the hog pen. I didn't know where he was until he whistled low to call my attention."

"What did Lee Lester do after Eldridge ran out of his house?

Could you figure that out?"

"I don't know exactly what he done, Miss Maude, there in his house with his wife, but by sun-up, I'd done had two people from the quarters come to tell me what Mr. Lee Lester did after he left his place in the middle of the night."

"He spread his story, did he?"

"He did that. Told all that bunch of white folks around Sabinetown that Eldridge tried to molest Miss Corinne and he had caught my husband in the act of trying it. Said he chased him out of the house, but not before Eldridge had fought real bad with him and put scratch marks and bruises all on his face and neck."

"At least she did that to him," Richard says. "Give her credit for that."

"Didn't Corinne say anything to people to tell what really happened?" Maude says, then answers her own question. "No, she didn't. Nothing they'd listen to."

"Miss Corinne, they say she's out of her head," I say. "Supposed not to be making any sense in anything she says, after what Eldridge tried to do to her there in the kitchen of her house."

"I wish Papa could get ahold of Lee Lester," Abigail says, pointing over real direct toward a graveplace, holding her arm straight out and steady as she talks. "He'd teach that booster a lesson."

"We're on our own, sister," Maude says, "Papa's gone, but that's nice to imagine, I do grant you."

"Joleen," she says, looking at me with her eyes all settled like she has come to where she wants to in her thinking, "how long have they been looking for Eldridge? And are they using dogs?"

"Since about the middle of the morning yesterday, and they wasn't using no dogs at first, but they got them now. Sent over to Hemphill to get old man Buck Tolliver and that pack of redbone hounds he runs.

"First thing they did was to come to our place, a bunch of men together to ask me stuff and look under and in everything they could put their hands on. Turned the house upside down like they might find my husband hiding under the floorboards or up in the rafters. They even looked in the hog pen, like they might find him hid somewhere in there."

"I expect Lee Lester is right there now with old Buck Tolliver and his pack of hounds," Abigail says, "looking to cause as much mischief and confusion as he can."

"Far as I know," I tell her, "Mr. Lee Lester ain't able to leave Miss Corinne there by herself in his house yet. Claim he got to stay there to tend to her, keep her kindly quieted down, he say, till her nerves get better and she stop having all them troubles in her head."

"That lady keeps saying things her husband doesn't want to hear," Richard says. "I bet that's the trouble with her."

"I expect we've talked as much as we need to," Maude says, "here today in the graveyard. We have to start doing something practical other than trying to figure out Lee Lester and the everlasting trouble he's made for himself."

"That man has got plenty to worry about, all right," I say. "Here in this world where he's been stirring up misery for everybody, and in the next one, too, where Jesus be waiting, just restless to get at him."

"We need," Maude says, looking sharp around her, toward first Richard, then Abigail and me, "we need to get those crepe myrtle cuttings first. Who did you say had all those bushes growing in her yard, Joleen? And how far is her place from here?"

"Drova Jessup, she the lady with the crepe myrtle. Pink and purple both, and like I said, even got some bushes with pink and purple blossoms side by side."

"Crossbred," Abigail says, "Y'all remember I said that before."

"Yes, you did," Maude says, "Now where is her place, Joleen?"

"Not over a mile, mile and half down the Damascus Road," I say, and point in the general direction I know it to be. "This end of the quarter is where Drova got all that crepe myrtle growing."

"Now, Maude," Abigail says. "I know I said we had decided before we left Double Pen Creek to come up here to Blue Water Chapel that we needed to get some crepe myrtle cuttings to plant by Papa's grave, his real one. But do you think we have time to be driving the wagon all over the country hunting for flowering bushes when we got Joleen's husband to worry about? I mean, Lord, sister, we got a pack of hounds trailing in these woods. Do you think Buck Tolliver's going to wait around for us to get crepe myrtle cut and put in the bed of that wagon before he shows up here with his dogs?"

"No, I don't think that," Maude says, "but we have to have the crepe myrtle cut and loaded before we put Mr. Broussard in the wagon, down under it, covered up."

"Down under it?" Abigail says, looking at Maude as though her sister has just remarked that cows can fly, if they just put their minds to it.

"If it was dark," Maude says, "we could take the chance of having him lie down in the bottom of the wagonbed and probably nobody would see him while we were going to Drova Jessup's to cut and load the crepe myrtle. But we can't take the gamble, middle of the day like this, and bright and clear as it is."

"Oh," Abigail says, "I guess I'd thought of that myself in a little while." Her face dropped when she was saying that, but then it brightens up a little when another idea hits her. "But what if the dogs track him down while we're gone?"

"Did Eldridge come straight to that canebrake from your place, Joleen?" Maude asks me.

Eldridge hadn't, and I tell them how Eldridge had walked in the creek north first, then got out on one side, and got back into the water again, and come downstream and then turned back again, and finally down creek until he reached the mud flats where the bottom gets wide, circling around until he ended up in the canebrake in behind Blue Water Chapel graveyard.

"That'll work for a good little while, to confuse the dogs," Maude says. "Go tell your husband what we're doing and for him to be ready by about four o'clock for us to come fetch him to come up to the wagon."

"Is Joleen going with us?" Abigail says. "Won't it look funny to anybody seeing her?"

"Yes," Maude says, "you're right. Give her your bonnet, Abby, and you have to ride in the bed of the wagon going over there to Drova Jessup's, while Joleen sits by me."

"Coming back, too?"

"It'll be easier on the way back here," Maude says. "You'll be sitting on all that crepe myrtle."

After I took Eldridge the biscuits and pork shoulder meat and told him what Maude done had us doing to get him out of Sabine County and away from all the lies Mr. Lee Lester been spreading to get him killed, we all four of us get in the wagon and Richard hums up the mules to get us going to Drova Jessup's place. I'm wearing Abigail's bonnet, a big one with a long top and sides and extra material cut into it to hang down over the back of the neck.

Abigail tells me three times she made it herself, big like it is to keep the sun off her face and neck as much as could be since her pale skin burns always in the sun like it does. Her bonnet gets the job done all right, it shades, I got to allow Abigail that, and when we pass the one wagon we come to on our way to Drova Jessup's, can't nobody see nary sign of my face or who I am when I keep my head dropped like I am dozing off as I ride, like people will do. I keep my hands stuck up under the material o. my dress front, and with the long sleeves of Abigail's dress I'm wearing, can't nobody even tell what color I am, much less who I am.

Maude made Abigail and me switch dresses, too, after she gets a look at me with Abigail's big old bonnet on. "It needs more," she says to me and Abigail, "y'all step off into the woods and swap garments."

I think about how my husband looked, backed up into that stand of cane in the mud, as we get close to Drova Jessup's house in the wagon. Eldridge is a cleanly man, always careful to dress himself particular and neatened, and there he sat on the ground covered with that old black creek bottom mud, clothes all nasty and torn and scratches on his face and arms from running through briars in the woods and along the streambed. Nowhere of his own to lay his head no more.

I'm not going to dwell on that sight of him now, though, and let myself get to crying again about what all's happened. I'll look at all the pink and purple crepe myrtle, instead, coming toward us as we come into view of Drova Jessup's yard, and I'll make myself find some of the different color ones mixed up together on the same branches of a single bush. There is one, standing out, just at the corner of the yard where the road goes right by it, some bigger in size and fuller than the rest, and I point it out to Abigail, speaking low to her as I do.

"It's one of them crossbreed crepe myrtles, Miss Abigail," I say, "looky yonder at it, all by itself."

"Well," she says, leaning forward from where she's riding in the bed of the wagon, feeling the bumps from every rock and every hole in the road we're traveling. "I have read about this freak of nature, and now I've seen it." Abigail sounds satisfied, nodding her head up and down hard while she looks.

Drova is home with some of her children, and they help us cut the limbs off the crepe myrtle bushes and stack them in the wagonbed, not stopping until the pile reaches plumb over the level of the sideboards. By the time we get enough cut and stacked to the standard Maude has set in her mind and has put us to work to get to, the bushes in Drova Jessup's yard look like a small storm has come through, snapping off limbs right and left.

"Naw, naw," Drova says when Maude start saying she's sorry we took so much off her crepe myrtle bushes, "them things grow back like a weed will do. It tickle me anyhow to watch how Miss Abigail go after them mixed color bushes with her knife. She act like she got plumb mad at them boosters. Just stacking them up."

Everybody laughs, and I join in to be social with people, but inside I'm feeling like I want to jump back in the wagon and whip up the mules into a gallop and get gone from here. Maude speaks up to say the very thing I'm thinking, when she declares it's getting on in the afternoon and we got to get on the road with our crepe myrtle cuttings.

I'm leaning forward in the seat as we start back down the Damascus Road, as though I could hurry us on by straining myself toward the front of the wagon. All my muscles feel hard in legs, any my neck is stiff from leaning ahead.

"Hum up, Jack," Richard says to the mules, "hum up, Shirley," and then he pops them a smart lick with the reins, and we get going back toward Blue Water Chapel graveyard, back where my husband in laying down in the mud hiding from dogs.

Abigail

I have never in my life seen purple and pink blossoms on the same crepe myrtle bush, and here I am riding in a wagonbed just full up with them. Talk about your freaks of nature.

Maude

Every nerve, every fiber, every ligament in her being is stretched to its limit. I try not to look directly at her while we ride along together side by side on the wagon bench, since I know she always feels obliged to acknowledge every glance, every notice, every sign of attention directed toward her. She has lived all her life, at least the part of it around white people, on a hair-trigger, constantly on edge and ready to respond to any acknowledgment of her existence, knowing she can't ever afford to appear unprepared to furnish whatever one of us may be wanting from her. A bowl to be handed to us, say, or an outcry from one of our children to be dealt with and solved, a needle to be threaded, a nod, a smile, a reassurance to be served up to us on demand.

Riding along beside her now, though I keep my gaze fastened straight ahead for the most part, looking at the back of Richard's head as he drives the wagon or glancing off to the roadside as though I'm interested in whatever presents itself, I can tell from the corner of my vision that Joleen's mind and body and soul are bound together as tightly as hard knots in a strand of yarn. The ligaments and arteries in her throat stand out like wires running just beneath the skin, her eyes opened as widely as a blind woman hungry for a flash of light, her lips parted in anticipation as though she was starving for water in a desert and she believes she hears a trickle somewhere ahead and unseen.

Why isn't she mad? Why isn't any last mustard seed of her reason scattered and vanished and lost? Why doesn't she tear at her own flesh, throw back her head and howl at the empty sky like a wolf with its foot half-chewed off by a steel trap?

When we were young girls together in Sabine County, there in that brief phase when Joleen was the first thought in my mind each morning and the one I sought out to see everyday as soon as Mama would release me from chores and the house and her and my sisters and brothers to run down the path which led to the spring and the colored quarters beyond it, Joleen was the same as she is now. Alert, attentive, composed, ready in mind and spirit to meet whatever the day brought.

That morning when for the first time I knew I was not simply my mother's daughter, not just one of the girl children of Carolina Cameron Holt's, I came to that knowledge because of Joleen Bobo. It was nothing Joleen said nor did that led me there, put my mind up against the knowledge no child desires ever, but cannot push aside nor forget when it comes. But it will come, and the child who struggles with success not to receive it will always remain a child, no matter how many days and years march across the calendar to disappear into the dust.

And that day is a sad day and a long one not to be measured by the sun's rise and its setting and the moon's coming up. The prophet's truth is written then in the mind and blood and spirit of each person alone, not just in the words put into God's book, saying that knowledge is sorrow.

I had risen that morning earlier that usual, up even before my mother and father, to sit quietly in the dark and wait for the light of the new day to come and shine on a clear cut-glass vase, the only beautiful thing my mother ever had and the only thing brought b. her from Louisiana into Texas that had lasted, she kept always high on the top of a sideboard, out of the reach of me and my brothers and sisters. I was in the habit, when alone, of standing on a chair, taking the vase down to touch and press against my face to feel its coolness and pattern on my skin, and then returning it to its resting place, undetected.

That day it came to me that if I were to put the vase in the middle of the table where we took our meals, setting it there in the dark before I could even tell by sight what I had in my hands, that I could keep my gaze fastened on it as sunlight came to announce the day, and thus be able to appreciate the ending of the darkness of one day and the growing of the light of another.

I didn't put thought to myself in those words, child as I was at the time, but I acted on the impulse and was able to observe the vase coming into itself and defining its existence against the smooth wood of the table as the light grew around, in, and through the cut glass. First I could see a difference develop between the vase and all that was around it, then the shape begin to announce itself more and more clearly as the light opened up the world of the cabin in which I lived, and the county of Sabine, and the state of Texas, and finally as fuller day came, the vase stood alone and separate and not anything but itself.

I beheld the vase, I watched its light, and I saw it become itself.

At the sound of movement from someone other than me in the house, I replaced the vase on the top of the sideboard, and no one could know what I had been able to see come into the place where I lived with the people who thought I was simply part of them, a girl child named Maude Holt, awake and needing to eat and drink and breathe early one morning.

As my mother tended to what she had to do, and my father worked outside with the animals before he would come back inside to breakfast on what his wife prepared for him and his children, I carried out the duties of helping my mother as she directed. But I held in a secret part of myself the experience of the vase growing into itself in the light, and I planned what I would say to Joleen about what I had done and what I had seen take place. Something had happened, and only I had seen it. It was mine.

Breakfast eaten by my brothers and sisters and me, the table cleared and food put away in the safe, my father gone outside to his work – I then asked my mother for permission to leave our place and find Joleen.

"Why do you want to do that so early this morning?" she said, not looking at me as she spoke, busy with something I can't remember. "You played with those twins yesterday, and the day before, too. I think you ought to help Abby red up the house this morning."

"All right, Mama," I said. "I'll help Abby right now, and then after we're done, can I go see Joleen? And it's just her I want to see, not her twin sister."

"Is there a real difference between those two little colored girls, Maude?" my mother said. "They look just alike to me, Joleen and Boleen Bobo, no difference between them at all."

"They aren't the same at all, Mama," I said, "and they don't really look just like each other, either, if you know them. I like Boleen, too, just fine. But I love Joleen."

I remember it was then that my mother first really looked at me that morning, turning from whatever it was she was doing, and putting that thing aside. Her eyes as they fixed on mine had a look in them I had never seen before, one that made me think my mother had forgotten who she was talking to, that she had thought she was speaking to one person and had discovered a stranger before her, instead.

"Mama, " I said to reassure her, convinced by the way she was looking at me that she had made a mistake in her thinking as she sometimes did when her mind was burdened with one thing and someone asked her about a completely different one. "I'm Maude, Mama," I said, that being what seemed logical for me to say at the moment.

"What did you say?" she said.

"I'm Maude."

"No, not that. Before you said that, you said something else. That's what I want to be sure I heard you say."

"I said that Boleen and Joleen don't really look just alike," I said, looking away from my mother's eyes and searching about the room for something else to fasten on, something that might appear to me the same it always had been. That was the cut-glass vase, and I stared at it, but the light I had seen it take into itself earlier in the morning was now gone, and the vase seemed flat against the wall behind it, like a picture of a vase, not the thing itself at all.

"If you know them," I said, "and who they are, they aren't the same at all."

"What else did you say?"

"I said that I liked Boleen," I answered. "I said I liked her, and I said that I love Joleen."

"You like them both, Maude," my mother said. "You like the little colored Bobo twins, Boleen and Joleen. You like to play with them."

"Yes, I do," I said. "I do like them both, but I like Joleen more. I love Joleen."

"You do not love Joleen," she said, coming closer to me and lifting her voice to cause me to look at her again, and I did. There was no comfort to be had now in the cut-glass vase, flat against the wall and empty of light, no different in that from the cups on the table. "You do not love Joleen. You cannot love a colored girl from the quarters. And you may never say that again, you must never say that again, to me or to anybody else, particularly."

"All right, Mama," I said and put my eyes on hers and tried to look into them deep enough to get behind the knowledge that I was not really seeing my mother's eyes, but an eye that might belong to anybody, a sister or a brother or a stranger I had never met before. But I could not believe it was her eyes, stare though I did. The eye that looked back and fixed me in its stare was as flat and indifferent to me as the cut-glass vase brought from Louisiana to

Texas across the Sabine River by Carolina Holt had become. It was not my mother, the way she always had appeared to me, looking at me now.

"I won't say that to anybody ever again," I said. "I won't tell people that I love Joleen."

That promise I kept, and it was on that day I learned I was not truly a part of anything or anybody but myself, and I never lifted my mother's cut-glass vase again from its due and proper location on the top of a sideboard where it was kept, not subject to direct light from the sun, ever.

We are moving at a good pace, the mules leaning into the harness and Abigail rustling around behind me and Joleen in the wagonbed full of crepe myrtle branches as she tries to find a way to sit that will crush as few blossoms as possible, paying particular attention to the limbs covered with the mixture of pink and purple flowers, the ones she's so taken with. The angle at which Richard is sitting as he handles the reins matches almost exactly the way Joleen is leaning forward to strain at the distance between her and her husband.

Her position reminds me of the way I always felt when I was apart from Valery Blackstock in the years when I was with him and he with me in this world – at attention, poised to move at an instant toward him as soon as I caught sight of him waiting somewhere for me. And he always was, each time we were away from each other, no matter if it was a half-day with him at work in the field or it was overnight for some reason or someone from my family or his with a matter to be attended that had drawn us apart. He waited to see me, and I waited to see him, and that was always.

Thinking of those times, I reach over to pat Joleen on her arm and she turns her head to look at me out of the stovepipe bonnet borrowed from my sister, her eyes dark and deep as I have always known them. She tries to offer me a smile, and that smile is now different, remindful though it is of something familiar and almost known to me, in the way a passing thought will be when it barely touches your mind and vanishes not to be had again no matter how you strain to recover it. You know what came before and what came after, but there's nothing but a blankness in between. And you are not satisfied.

"We're on our way, Joleen," I say, "and we've made a good start. You'll have him with you again in just a little while now. You just wait and see."

"Yes, Miss Maude," she answers, "please, Jesus." And she lifts her hands from beneath the material of the dress where she's been holding them, and she shows me her fingers crossed one over the other, all four on each hand.

"Double," I say.

"Double doubled," she says back to me, and we laugh together again, the first time in forty years we've done that and traded those words between us.

When we arrive back at Blue Water Chapel graveyard, meeting no one on the way this time, Richard drives the wagon around the margin of the cleared ground all the way back to the far line of trees where the woods begin, without being told to do so. We all climb down to the ground, Richard walking around to the front to the mules and Abigail the last to alight, fighting her way out of the wagonload of crepe myrtle and groaning a little with the effort.

"It's a bit after four o'clock," I say, looking at the length of the shadows of the headstones the sun is casting. "We need to leave here as soon as we can to get to Jasper County before dark."

"You want me to go fetch Eldridge, Miss Maude?" Joleen says. "Bring him up here from out of the canebrake?"

"Yes, but don't y'all step out into the clearing just yet, when you get back. We need to take a good look around first and see what we're doing."

"No," Jolee. says, "we won't," and she heads for the yaupon and pine thicket at a fast clip, out of view in no time.

"What am I supposed to be doing?" Abigail says to nobody in particular, sweeping her gaze from one side of the graveyard to the other as though checking to make certain no one has slipped in and rearranged something in our absence.

"What would look nice," I say, "I think, would be some cuttings of those mixed pink and purple crepe myrtle planted in between Papa's and Mama's graves. Don't you believe that would suit all right, Abby?"

"Yes," she says, lengthening out the word so it sounds like she's planning a campaign as she speaks it. "I'm going to need some water waiting on me after I get the hole dug. Where's my shovel I brought with me from home?"

"Here it is, Aunt Abigail," Richard says. "I'll go down to the spring and bring back a bucket of water."

"Help me start getting all this crepe myrtle moved around, Maude," Abigail says. "We got to do that anyway to fix a place for Joleen's husband."

"Yes, sister," I say and move toward the wagon, glad to speak up and give her that acknowledgment of family rank. Abigail appreciates it.

It is not until we've crossed the Jasper County line and gone maybe a mile beyond it that we see them up ahead. There are several silhouettes, and it's not easy to get them all counted in the fading light of day, particularly since a good number of them are moving around, busying themselves with one thing and another. They've built a fire, of course, like a bunch of men waiting together somewhere always will do, summer or winter, needing to cook or not, and some of them are throwing chunks of fallen timber onto a pile to make ready for the night to come.

I can see an ax go up and come down, and it's on the way up again before I hear the sound of the completed blow from the first lick. The sound is dull, as though it's coming through a thick curtain. Six, maybe, or five visible to me, I count, men at the end of a day of deer hunting you might think, if you didn't know better. They'll all be acting the same way deer or bear hunters do, anyway, finding something to eat, looking into the fire which is built up well beyond what's needful, telling stories of famous hunts they claim to have been part of, and passing around whiskey some-body's brought in good supply. They'll talk, and they'll laugh, and they'll do that as long as anyone will listen to them do it.

"Oh, Lord," Joleen says, sitting beside me, her voice which had calmed considerably back at Blue Water Chapel as soon as El-dridge was in the wagonbed, now crawling higher in her throat. "Sweet Jesus, hold my hand."

"It'll be all right," I say. "Just sit where you are and don't make a sign. We'll say all that needs to be said, Abigail and I will."

Before we left Blue Water, when Joleen came up from the creek bottom and the canebrake with her husband beside her, she had already begun to settle in her person and behavior, even though all three of us had stopped whatever we were doing to watch them take each step of the way from the edge of the thicket across the graveyard toward the mules and wagon. None of us could resist do-ing that, even Abigail as she put the last touches to the two-colored crepe myrtle she was planting between Papa's and Mama's graves. She set the bucket of water down, not yet painstakingly emptied at the new location for her flower bush for Papa, and turned to watch, her muddy hands held out in front of her so as not to soil her dress.

The first thought that came to me was that Eldridge Broussard was much older than Joleen, his hair gray and age lining his face, and I wondered at that until I looked at Joleen beside him. Taken together and viewed as husband and wife, they were indeed of an age, and it struck me that I had been seeing all day not really the woman but only what was left of the girl in Joleen, my companion from that time in childhood when we saw ourselves in the other's face and time was of no consequence to us.

"This is my husband," Joleen told us in a strong voice, "El-dridge Broussard." He stood beside her covered in mud, but his stance erect and his gaze directed toward us.

"We are pleased to meet you," Abigail said, taking the lead as I stood there speechless, "Get into the wagonbed, Eldridge, if you will, and start covering yourself up with all this crepe myrtle."

"They see us coming, Mama," Richard is saying to me, pulling back on the mules' reins, "What am I to do?"

"Tip your hat to the gentlemen, son," I say, "as you're supposed to do, and stop the wagon when we get there so we can see what they may want to say to us."

Well before we near the spot where they're gathered, one of the men lifts a hand to hail us and begins walking up the road toward our wagon. His hat, a light colored one, is squared up on his head in contrast to those of most of the other ones, I notice, and I figure from that that he's in charge of the bunch and is ready for business. He is dressed neatly, as well, his boots appearing to be brand new, and he is carrying something in his left hand, gloves I think, which he is tapping against his pants leg as he walks our direction.

I start to tell Richard to slow the mules as we approach, but he's already doing that, and our progress stops with the man still several yards away. All four of us watch him near us in silence, the only sound that of the mules groaning and blowing their breaths now that they've stopped and the rhythmic flick of the gloves against the man's pants leg.

"Good evening," he says, "ladies," and then nodding toward Richard, "young man."

We greet him, Abigail's voice some louder than mine and Richard's, Joleen saying nothing.

"You've got a nice brace of mules to pull you, I see," he says and puts out his hand to make a patting motion at the head of the mule nearest him, but he doesn't actually touch the animal.

"My husband's proud of them," I say. "Thank you."

"And who is your husband, Ma'am, if I may inquire?"

"Ezra Winston," I say, "of the Double Pen Creek community in Coushatta County. We farm a few acres there."

"I know what you mean by saying a few," the man answers, "it never seems to be enough, does it, to grow enough cotton to get ahead these days, no matter how much you put in."

"Yes, indeed," Abigail says, her voice falling into the lighter tone she habitually uses with men, particularly those she doesn't know. "But my sister's husband does tolerably well. We all do, so far in Coushatta County, the ones willing to work hard at it. My husband is Ferguson Mott, and he's pursuing the same livelihood as my sister's."

"Well, yes," the man answers, no longer flicking his gloves as he stands near the head of the team of mules, but bouncing them up and down in his hand as he looks from one to the other of us there in the stopped wagon. "I've heard there's some productive land in Coushatta County, all right. But me, I'm a Sabine County man, and I guess I'll never leave these old gumbo bottoms, no matter how hard they are to work."

"We're from Sabine County ourselves," Abigail says, "to start with. Raised over there close to Blue Water Chapel. Our father's buried there. Amos Holt. Maybe you know the name."

"My goodness, yes," the man says. "Now I'm too young myself to be able to claim it, but I remember my daddy saying he had heard Amos Holt preach. Even went to school to him for a while."

"What is your family name?" Abigail says.

"Slater, I'm J. T. Slater, and my daddy was Truman Slater."

"Y'all's place was north of Bear Creek," Abigail says. "Your daddy's brother was Jesse Neal Slater, and I can't call up the name of a sister in the Slater family, but there were several ladies, as I remember."

"That's the way this part of Texas is," the man who identified himself as J.T. Slater says, "if you talk long enough to people, you're bound to find out you know somebody in their family. Might even be kin to them, if you're unlucky."

We all laugh at that, of course, in obligation, Abigail louder than Richard and I, and I can tell my sister is warming to the occasion and would be prepared to converse with J.T. Slater until full dark, given the opportunity. I take a deep breath, and the sleeve of Joleen's dress is touching my arm now, so that I can feel a steady tremor transferring through it.

"Yes, yes," J.T. Slater says, smiling as he looks around at all of us again, his gaze on Joleen's face a beat longer than it is on the rest of us.

"But let me tell you folks why we're all here this time of day on the road, these other men and me, rather than home eating supper and getting ready to go to bed and get some rest before tomorrow gets here. I expect you're wondering."

With that, he turns his head a little to one side as though he's about to look over his shoulder toward the clot of men a good distance behind him, but he doesn't. Instead he flicks his gloves in their direction and takes a couple of steps closer to the wagon.

"It's not a thing I like to talk directly to ladies about, but I must let you know what's happened. I'm obliged to, you understand. Maybe you've already heard about it if you've been up in Sabine County, but it bears repeating, just to be on the safe side."

"My goodness," Abigail says. "What is it?"

I figure it's time for me to speak up, so I chime in. I can't just sit here mute. "What do you mean by mentioning the word safe, Mr. Slater?" I ask, casting my voice a tone lower than Abigail's. "Has someone seen a panther or a bear somewhere in the county. I remember when they used to sometimes take pigs right out of the pens at night when we were children in Sabine County."

"No, ma'am," J.T. Slater says. "I wish it was that, to tell you the truth, but it's a whole lot worse than a bear or a stray panther looking to make a meal out of somebody's livestock. That'd be easy to handle compared to what we're facing."

J.T. Slater is pushing up his hat brim now as he looks in my direction and twisting his body a little to one side as though he's about to deliver news to us that may physically knock us as a group off the wagon benches where we're sitting. The tremor coming from the sleeve of Joleen's dress ceases suddenly as though she has willed every muscle not to move, and I tell myself to keep the expression on my face what it now is until the man before us reveals all he thinks we can stand to hear. He has shifted his eyes a little to look directly at Joleen now.

"We've got the worst thing you can have happen, right here in

Sabine County, ladies, and I would not unduly alarm you. But it's my bounden duty as county constable and as a Christian man to give you warning."

"My Lord," Abigail says. "What could it be?"

"We've had a nigger man go crazy and molest a white lady, and we're looking for him everywhere we can think to."

"Did he kill her?" Abigail says, her voice crawling higher in her throat as she speaks, that letting me know she's almost convinced herself she's learning a truth for the first time, brand new to her, and horrible. "Is she dead?"

"No, ma'am," J.T. Slater says in a tone calculated to be reassuring to this wagonload of white ladies and their colored woman and their boy. "He didn't get to do that. Her husband fought him off, thank the Lord, but he's loose now still, and we're after him fulltilt and foursquare."

"Was he able to," Abigail says, still caught up in her conviction she's hearing an account of a disaster and a violation for the first time, completely unknown to her. "You know, finish what he was trying to do, the nigger man?"

For once, I am gratified by my sister's ability to work her imagination so fully into an expression of complete shock and belief. It serves well now in the current circumstance, if it never has before. I could hug her.

"No, praise God," J.T. Slater says, slapping his gloves briskly into the palm of his hand. "She's unstained, though marked up pretty bad."

"Who is the man?" I ask, knowing it's time for me to add something to the conversation if I want to appear to be a normal woman in East Texas hearing news of such abomination. "Do y'all know?"

"We do, Mrs. Winston," he says, "and it's a puzzling thing, but it really shouldn't be any surprise, if you know the race and the breed. He's a cropper name of Broussard, never been in no trouble before that anybody knows of, a middle-aged nigger man, a hard worker, but you know how it will happen with any one of them. He just went crazy, like they are liable to do at anytime. And it's not predictable, and it's always the case after something like this happens. You know how people will say they never would've expected it of him."

"You are right, Mr. Slater," Abigail says, "I've heard it said just in that way time and time again when one of them goes out of his mind. 'Well, I never,' people will say, 'never would have predicted that of Tom or John or Ben or whoever the nigger happened to be.' Everybody is just flabbergasted by it."

"Yes, ma'am, but they will go plumb African on you, and you've always got to keep watching close and tight."

"Broussard," Richard says, speaking for the first time, and I feel something inside my body give way as though I'm about to be sick when I hear my son's voice. "That was the name you said, sir?"

"Broussard," repeats J.T. Slater, "Eldridge Broussard, that's the man we're looking for. I should say that's the man we're going to find. Rest assured of that, folks."

"I wonder which direction he's running?" Abigail says, "This Broussard? I hope and pray it's not south toward Coushatta County where we're headed."

J.T. Slater begins to answer Abigail's question, but he's looking at Richard as he speaks. "Well, ma'am," he say, "we can't tell where he's headed just yet, but we know where he's doing his best to get away from, and that's Sabine County. That's why we're covering the roads leading out of here."

"That's a comfort," Abigail says, "But wouldn't this Broussard fellow run through the woods and stay off the roads where people travel? Wouldn't he know he'd be easy to spot out in the open where wagons and the odd automobile go back and forth all the time?"

"We sure hope he'll think that way," J.T. Slater says in a pleased tone, "If he sticks to the woods he won't last long. We've got the best pack of tracking hounds in this part of the country on his trail right now. They may take a while to pick up his track, but once they do it'll be all over before he knows it. They may be a little slow at first, but this pack of dogs is sure as death."

"Praise the Lord," Abigail says, "I sure hope so. That'll ease my mind and everybody else's, too, once y'all catch him."

"Son," Slater says, tapping his gloves against his leg again and addressing his words toward Richard, "You asked about this nigger's name a little while ago. You don't happen to know him, do you, by any chance?"

"No, sir," Richard says, his voice and tone as polite and reserved as it always is, an aspect of his behavior I've always treasured in my son, but the sound of which now causes me to want to scream at him to keep his mouth shut and to sit quiet as he usually does. Why is he volunteering to speak to this man before us as we sit stopped here in the road?

"I don't know the man at all, but the family name is one I've heard before. It belongs to a family of colored folks up in Shelby County that my Papa trades seed with. You remember, Mama," Richard says, looking at me in his guileless, earnest way, "that fellow Papa gets the cotton seed from, that seed for the higher-growing variety?"

"Oh, yes," I say, fixing my eyes on a spot on Richard's forehead just below the brim of his hat, "I do know who you're talking about. Certainly. Broussard."

"Shelby County?" Slater says, "all that way away from Coushatta County where you folks are from, huh? A higher cotton plant, you say?"

"Papa claims it's easier to pick from," Richard says, "and the yield's as good as what the lower-down plant will give you. I reckon that's why he's traded with this Shelby County man name of Broussard."

"Well, thank you, young man," J.T. Slater says, "I'll mention that to my people, that there's a family of Broussard niggers north of here in Shelby County. Might not be no connection to the man we're fixing to round up and catch, but maybe it's a direction to look. Who knows? One thing I do understand about a man on the run, white or colored, he will run to cover where he's known. He will go to ground where it's others kin to him located. Seems almost like a natural instinct."

"I don't know a thing about chasing men who've committed a criminal act," Abigail announces, "but I have learned something about niggers in my time. And one thing I learned is when they get in trouble they'll run to their kinfolks looking for help."

"That is the truth, Mrs. Mott," J.T. Slater says with energy, "with both hands stuck out in front of them waiting to be filled up."

The wagon creaks as the mules lean against the harness and the reins, trying to stretch their necks to reach a patch of weeds beside the road, and J.T. Slater steps back to avoid being touched by anything outside himself.

"You ladies have sure got yourselves a nice load of flower bushes," he says, turning his head a little to look at the crepe myrtle in the wagonbed, pointing with his chin in that direction as though his hands are too occupied to lift them.

"I would say that it appears y'all are going into gardening in a big way," he goes on, looking at the wagonload of branches as though he's trying to guess their volume and weight, "but I see all those limbs have been cut off. They're all going to turn brown and die, ain't they?"

Through the sleeve touching my arm, I can tell that Joleen has begun to tremble again, and I want to touch her hand, but I can't do that. I lift my gaze from J.T. Slater's face, and I can see over the top of his hat that the men behind him have built their fire even higher, its flames dancing orange and red and great clouds of sparks flying up as someone of its tenders tosses another chunk of wood on the pile. Abigail is answering Slater's question about the dying crepe myrtle, and I make myself listen to what she's saying.

"If we intended to plant any of these cuttings, you'd be right," she says. "They wouldn't do us any good at all by the time we get back to Double Pen Creek. It'd be exactly like sticking a walking cane in the ground and expecting it to take root and put out blossoms. What we're doing, though, is getting these crepe myrtle cuttings together to decorate the church building down at the Double Pen Creek community. See, our graveyard working is this coming

Sunday, and that's what me and my sister and her boy have volunteered to do. Get the decorations up, and make it pretty for folks that're coming."

"I know you ladies always like your flowers," J.T. Slater says. "You mean to tell me there is no crepe myrtle in Coushatta County? Had to come all the way to Sabine County to find something growing pretty enough to use, did you?"

Abigail laughs at that, throwing her head back to let a real chortle escape her throat. I feel a chill come over me, as though a north wind had come up out of nowhere to cut across the wagon bench where I'm sitting. It's April, I tell myself, don't shiver like you're dying to get near a fire.

"Sabine County does have the prettiest flowers in this part of Texas, as far as I'm concerned, all right," Abigail says in a tone that sounds like she's experiencing genuine enjoyment, "but we have combined reasons for coming back to Sabine County, like we always do. You know our Papa's buried at Blue Water Chapel, don't you, Mr. Slater? And Mama, too, and so we get a chance to visit their graves and fetch back crepe myrtles all in one trip. This here's a big expedition for us."

"I reckon it must be," Slater says, "and that's why you brought your colored woman with you, I guess, all the way up here."

He's looking again at Joleen, as he speaks, and I force myself to turn toward her, as well, reaching over to pat her on the hand. It feels as cool as marble. Joleen is suffering from the chill of that north wind out of nowhere, just like me.

"We don't go anywhere without her if the trip involves work," I say. "I must confess and own up to that. Isn't that right, Annie?"

"Yes, ma'am," Joleen says in a voice I've never heard her use before, her words blurred and mumbled like those of an eighty-year-old mammy who speaks to white folks only when she visits a commissary store to buy a little sugar or a can of snuff.

"We depend on Annie," Abigail chimes in, "that's the truth my sister's speaking. We don't know what we'd do without her."

"You know, ladies," J.T. Slater says, stepping back from his position near the front of the wagon, "that's the way it's supposed to be, and I appreciate what you're saying about our colored friends. When things're going like they ought to, that's the way it is between us and the colored population. All of us just helping each other and trying to get through this world together and make do as we go along."

"That's what we all count on," Abigail says, "don't we, sister? Don't we, Annie?"

Joleen and I speak together in one voice, "That's right, that's right," nodding our heads like twin dolls lined up on the wagon bench.

"Now, son," J.T. Slater says to Richard, fixing him with a gaze that communicates the relationship of one man to another seeking to address a shared problem facing men together, "you just drive your mules and wagon straight on. Don't stop until you get to where y'all are staying the night, and you'll be all right. Just tend to your business, take care of these ladies, and things will be fine."

"Yes sir," Richard says, beginning to fiddle with the reins. "I will, thank you."

J.T. Slater reaches up, pats Richard on the knee, and turns to address me and Abigail. His hat is on straight again, in perfect alignment with his eyebrows, and he points toward us with the gloves in his left hand, shaking them in a deliberate rhythm as he speaks.

"Ladies," he says, "put your minds at ease. That nigger will not be anywhere around y'all as you journey your way home. And if there's a length of rope left in this part of Texas, come morning, he won't be around to interfere with another white woman ever again."

"Praise Jesus," Abigail says, and the mules lean into the harness, the wagon groaning in sympathy as its load begins to move forward. "I thank God for you men of Texas who protect us women so well."

J.T. Slater lifts his right hand slowly, extending his arm at full length as he watches us move by, holding that stance much longer than a farewell ordinarily will require. As we reach the place where the fire is burning beside the road, the men who've built it nod at us sternly, a couple of them tipping their hats as we pass by. I look in their direction, but I don't focus my gaze on anyone in particular, concentrating instead on my sense that the cold north wind from nowhere that has been cutting me into a shiver seems to have abated.

Up ahead the road bends to the right to avoid some obstacle long vanished that it was laid out at its beginning to bypass, and I feel like urging Richard to whip up the mules to get around that bend as soon as we can. But I don't say anything of the sort, and I strain my body forward a little on the wagon bench in place of speaking, instead. Move, I am thinking, move, move.

Beside me, Joleen says something which I don't hear well enough to understand, and I ask her to repeat it.

"Annie," Joleen says, "all I said was Annie. The name Annie. My, my."

I turn back to look over my shoulder at Abigail, sitting a little sideways near the front of the load of crepe myrtle branches, under which Eldridge Broussard rides more than two feet beneath, near the rear of the wagonbed. Abigail is holding a branch of crepe myrtle, the two color variety, pink and purple, frowning intently at a cluster of blossoms. I can't see her feet for the flowers.

"They sure are fading fast," she says, "and I wish we did have the chance to decorate the Double Pen Creek church building with them all fresh and pretty for the graveyard working."

"Someday we will," I tell her. "We'll plan for that to happen some graveyard working, and we'll do it. We'll carry out that idea that you came up with. It's a perfect one."

"We won't have the ones with pink and purple together on the same branch, though, when we do. Never again."

"No," I agree. "We won't. We'll just have to make do, like always."

We've rounded the bend in the road now, and there's no sign behind us of the roaring fire and the men who built it. Richard asks a little more out of the mules, and we're moving more quickly now away from Sabine County. Joleen has twisted back to look toward the rear of the wagonload of crepe myrtle hiding her husband, and she calls Eldridge's name.

"All right," comes his voice from beneath the flowers, low and distinct, "I'm all right. Just rolling on, thank you."

Joleen's hand is warmer now when I touch it, telling me that north wind from out of nowhere has died down for her, too.

"Abigail," I say, "big sister, you did so well for us back there. I'm so proud of you for that."

"Maybe that cutting I planted by Papa's grave was fresh enough to take root," she says. "If Sabine County gets some rain in the next couple of days, it just might take hold and make it."

"I predict it will. We'll be able to see it the next time we visit Blue Water graveyard. Just you wait and see."

"That's right," Abigail says. "We will. Now let's get on back home and get Mr. and Mrs. Broussard situated right."

I think of my mother's cut-glass vase, sitting high on the safe where she kept it those years ago, gathering the light of the growing day as it announced itself alone and separate, safe and secret in my mind. The mules lean into the harness, and we move on down the road to get to where Joleen and Eldridge will be situated right, just the way my sister says we should do. And as I behold the vase, I will let her have what she wants.

I grant her the last word.